TROUBLE
in *Paradise*

Terrye Robins

TATE PUBLISHING & Enterprises

TATE PUBLISHING
& Enterprises

Published in the United States of America

ISBN: 1-5988657-1-4
06.06.29

Trouble in Paradise is dedicated to my husband Dan, with love.

ACKNOWLEDGEMENTS

I would like to thank the following individuals for their help in editing this book: Nita Chartier, Freda Riggs, Jackie Green, Pam Robins, Joan Walker and Linda Reutlinger.

I would also like to thank the following people from the Polynesian Cultural Center for their input: Susan Naihe; Alfred Grace, Vice President of Sales & Marketing; and Ray Magalei, Marketing Director.

I appreciate the guidance and help I received from all the kind folks at Tate Publishing, LLC. Thank you all for your hard work and encouragement!

spring break? We'll be finishing a unit on birds by then. I'd be glad to speak with your dad and your teacher, Mrs. Miller, about it."

"That would be terrific, Allie, could I?" She was bouncing up and down in her chair. "I'll talk Daddy into it! I can bring some of their toys and show the class some of the tricks they've learned. I might even tell the kids about the birds' breeding habits."

"I'll make the arrangements, but let's not spring the breeding part on them, okay? I know they would enjoy seeing the birds do some tricks and petting them." I looked at my watch. "It's almost 4:35, so I'd better be going."

They all rose from the table and walked with me toward the entryway.

"Are you coming to your grandpa's place to watch the game tonight, Allie?" Grandad asked. "That OU team is really heating up. If they continue at the rate they're going, they're bound to make it to the Final Four."

"Since I saw the game last Sunday, I don't think I'll come out tonight. After I check on Aunt Edith, I'm heading home. I've got some progress reports to redo and I haven't talked with Traci in a couple of weeks, so I may give her a call. But please tell everyone I said hello."

"How are Traci and her husband doing?" Gramma asked. "Is she still playing the piano at that little church?"

Traci Morris and I have been best friends since we were five years old, and Gramma gave her piano lessons for several years. She married her high school sweetheart, Tommy Morris, just two months following our graduation. Soon after, he joined the marines and was sent to the Kaneohe Military Base on the island of Oahu.

"Yes, she's still playing for some of the services as well as teaching second grade at a private elementary school." I told her. "In the last email I got from her, she said that Tommy had been promoted to captain. They are very excited about the pay raise he received with the promotion because she just found out they're going to have a baby."

"Oh, that's wonderful news. I'm so happy for them," Gramma said. "Traci is such a sweet girl. When you speak with her, please give her my love."

"I will. You guys have a nice evening." I said, then headed out the door to my car.

CHAPTER 1

I could hear the intermittent ringing of bells and struggled to push myself through the fog that engulfed me. Plodding through the heavy mist, it seemed I was getting closer to my destination because the ringing was louder. As I pushed myself forward, the sound was disrupted by an annoying buzz that had entered the mix.

Suddenly, the fog vanished, and I awoke with a start. I sat up and realized the ringing was coming from the phone beside my bed. As I reached for the receiver, I knocked off the buzzing alarm clock and sent it clanging to the floor.

"Hello," I said, trying to get some slack in the cord. I gave it a jerk and the phone tumbled off the nightstand.

"Good morning, sunshine," a male voice said. "Having a little trouble getting your day started?"

My mind cleared and I recognized the caller as my cousin Michael Winters. He sometimes calls me an endearing name, while the rest of the family calls me Allie. I'm Allison Kane—single, blue-eyed and twenty-five years old.

"Sorry about that, Michael. I was up past midnight getting progress reports done for my class, and my alarm clock wasn't getting its job done." I teach third grade at Elliott Kane Elementary, which is one of three elementary schools we have in our town of Paradise, Oklahoma. I looked over the edge of the bed at the clock on the floor. "Shouldn't you be on the road by now?"

"Just pulling in front of the building," he said. Michael is the controller for the oil and natural gas company my Grandpa Kane started over forty years ago. "Would you mind giving Riley a lift to Gramma's after school today? Aunt Debra has to have three wisdom teeth cut out this afternoon. She insists she can keep Riley as usual, but I told her she needs to get some rest." Riley is Michael's six-year-old daughter of whom he has had sole custody for the last four years.

"Sure, I'll be glad to do it. I haven't been to Gramma's for a few days, so that will give me an excuse to visit. I heard she is starting her chili today for the Senior Citizen's Center cook-off. Riley and I can be her taste-testers. Too bad you'll miss out."

Gramma has won many blue ribbons at fairs over the years for her tasty dishes. It's always a treat to eat anything she cooks, but I know that her chili is one of Michael's favorites. I couldn't help rubbing it in that we might get some and he wouldn't.

"Thanks, Allie, you're a peach. I know Riley will be in good hands. And by the way, Gramma made a test batch of her chili last night and invited Riley and me over for supper," he said. "See you later." Without giving me a chance to respond, I heard him chuckling as he hung up the phone.

Rushed for time, I hurried into the shower. Standing under the spray, I smiled as I replayed my conversation with Michael. He's the oldest cousin on the Winters' side of the family, and he often has the last laugh, but I don't begrudge him that.

When he was twelve years old, his mom and dad were killed while driving home from a business trip during an ice storm. An eighteen-wheeler jack-knifed, taking their car over an embankment with it. Michael had stayed with Gramma and Grandad Winters, as he sometimes did when his folks traveled, and it had no doubt saved his life. Following the tragedy, his father's twin brother Jake and his wife, Debra, invited Michael to move in with them and their two sons.

After showering, I blow-dried my shoulder-length blonde hair and put on a dab of makeup. I had decided on a coral pantsuit the night before, so I was dressed and heading to the kitchen for my orange juice in no time.

I grabbed my purse and canvas tote bag and stepped out the front door into the beautiful February morning. As the sunshine hit my face, I couldn't help but smile. The weatherman was forecasting a sixty-degree day, and it would be a welcome change after the dreary rain and frigid temperatures we had had everyday for a week.

Stepping off the porch, I could hear a robin singing on a branch in one of my Bradford pear trees. He seemed to be beckoning to spring. Walking toward my car, I couldn't yet see any signs of the daffodils that I had planted last fall along the sidewalk. My mother and Nana Kane each possess green thumbs, and I was anxious to see if I had inherited any of their gardening talent.

A screen door slammed, and I looked across the yard and saw my neighbor, Mrs. Googan, standing on her porch.

"Good morning, Allison," she said. "Isn't it a splendid day?"

"It's gorgeous, Mrs. Googan. How are you and Ginger doing?" I asked, watching her Pomeranian chase a squirrel across the wet grass.

"Just fine. Ginger saw you from the window and insisted on coming out to see you."

I had my doubts that Ginger's desire to get outside had anything to do with me. Her attention was focused on the squirrel barking at her from a low branch in the oak tree.

Across the street, I noticed Davy Scaletta heading toward his mother's minivan. He tended to be quiet and a bit gawky, but was always friendly. Seeing us, he raised his arm, and I returned the wave while Mrs. Googan hollered, "Good morning, Davy. Driving your mother's minivan today?"

His shoulders slumped a bit when he said, "I'm afraid so."

Remembering back to when I was a senior in high school, I suspected that the minivan wasn't the type of vehicle he would like to be driving. It just wasn't cool enough for a teenage boy.

"See you later, Mrs. Googan," I said as I unlocked my red Mustang. "You and Ginger enjoy the nice day."

I had been parking in the driveway for most of the week because I was using the garage to refinish some furniture for my spare bedroom. *At least there's no ice to scrape today*, I thought as I fastened my seatbelt. I started the car and turned on the wipers to remove the thin veil of moisture from the windshield. After shifting into reverse, I backed down the driveway.

I've lived in a duplex owned by my Grandad Winters since graduating from college. One of my cousins, Doug Blessing, lives in the unit on the other side. He's studying to become a pediatrician and dates a lot, so our paths don't often cross. Even so, my parents feel that I'm safer with Doug living close by.

I stepped on the accelerator and started harmonizing with the song about lost love playing on the radio. Sighing, I knew that something couldn't be lost until you possessed it, and Mr. Right hadn't yet come into my life.

Glancing in my rearview mirror, I saw Davy following me, then a blur of burnt-orange by my right fender caught my attention. The squirrel that had been in the oak tree darted off the curb in front of me, with Ginger hot on his heels. Slamming on the brakes, I heard the screech of tires behind me and braced myself for the impact of the minivan. When it didn't come, I turned around and saw that it had stopped mere inches from my back bumper.

I jumped out of the car and ran back to check on Davy. "I'm sorry I stopped so quickly," I said. "Ginger ran out into the street and I was trying not to hit her. Are you okay?"

"Yeah, I'm fine. Thank goodness I didn't hit you. My dad would have had my hide if I had messed up Mom's car."

From the yard, I could hear Mrs. Googan calling for Ginger and saw that the dog and squirrel were still zigzagging in the street.

"Don't worry, Mrs. Googan. I'll get her for you," I shouted as I started after them.

"I'll help you," Davy hollered.

While Mrs. Googan stood wringing her hands, Davy and I chased Ginger through the overgrown yard next door. I caught her once near the birdbath, but she got away when my feet slipped in the mud and I went sprawling to the ground. She led Davy on a chase around the yard before he cornered her in the flowerbed. Sniffing at the ground, she started digging in a hole that had been washed out by the rain.

Brushing away the leaves and debris from my clothes, I walked over to Davy. I saw that Ginger had uncovered a man's sneaker from the mud. I bent down and scooped up the dog, then pulled the shoe from the mire.

"Well, Ginger, I'd say we've had our exercise today, wouldn't you?" I asked, looking at her.

The dog struggled to get out of my arms. It was difficult for me to hang onto her and also to keep the dripping shoe away from my clothing. Shifting the sneaker to my other hand, I noticed a syrupy, rust-colored stain on the inside of it.

The front door of the rundown house opened, and a scruffy-looking man wearing a torn T-shirt stood glaring at us. He looked like he hadn't seen a barber in months, and stubble covered his face.

"What do you think you're doing out here?" he yelled, slamming the screen door against the house as he stomped onto the porch.

"Sorry if we bothered you," I said. "We were trying to get Mrs. Googan's dog for her." Passing Ginger to Davy, I walked toward the porch. Still holding the soggy shoe in my left hand, I extended my right hand to the man. "I'm Allison Kane and this is Davy Scalletta. We're some of your neighbors."

For several seconds he stared at me, then strode down the steps toward me. He was so close when he stopped, I could smell his fetid breath. Ignoring my outstretched hand, he looked down at the shoe and said, "What have you got there? That doesn't belong to you." He yanked it from my grasp, then tossed it under the swing on the porch.

"I wasn't trying to take anything from you," I said, surprised by his rudeness. "Ginger dug up the sneaker from the flowerbed."

His demeanor changed as his eyes left my face and roamed the length of my body, coming back to rest in the chest area. The look made me squirm, and I wanted to get away from him. He took a step toward me, then put his hand on my arm. "Sorry about my manners, little lady. I'm Luke Davis. How about coming in for a cup of coffee, you know, to be neighborly?"

Cringing at his tone, I shrugged off his hand. "No thanks. We've got to get to school. Come on Davy." I turned and hurried from the yard, with Davy following close behind. The man's soft laughter sent shivers up my back.

When we got back into Mrs. Googan's yard, Davy said, "That guy was creepy."

"Bold and offensive also comes to mind," I said. "He sure was mad about that old shoe."

"He and his father moved in a couple of weeks ago," Mrs. Googan said. "The landlord is a friend of mine, and she told me he repossesses cars. I hear his wrecker pulling in and out all hours of the night."

I glanced at my watch. "You'd better get going, Davy. I've got to change out of these muddy clothes, then get on the road myself."

Waving goodbye to my neighbors, I hurried to my house to get cleaned up. After stripping off the dirty pantsuit, I washed the grime from my hands and arms, giving extra attention to the area that Luke Davis had touched.

While I put on a pair of red slacks and a matching cashmere sweater, I thought about his reaction to the shoe. The red ooze inside looked like dried blood. Whoever it belonged to must have had quite an accident.

Before heading out the door, I pulled some one-dollar bills out of my cookie jar on the kitchen cabinet to use at the car wash after school. It would be nice to drive a clean car for a change.

Driving to school, I went over my plan for the day and put the incident with the new neighbor behind me. We had concluded a unit on reptiles and amphibians, and the owner of the local pet store was bringing some animals to show. Several of my students were also bringing their pets to share. Since it promised to be a warm day, I decided we would take show-and-tell outdoors.

When I reached the school, I signed in at the office, then headed to my classroom. Sometimes I stop and visit with other teachers, but this morning I needed to clear off the activity table so the students would have someplace to put their pets.

Just as I finished, the children began coming into the room. Backpacks were put into lockers, and I helped the ones who had brought pets get their cages arranged on the table. With the excitement over the animals, it was hard to get everyone settled down.

After the pledge to the flag, I told them the plan for the morning. "Boys and girls, we're all tired of the rain and inside recess days, so we're taking show-and-tell outside." I waited until the cheers died down before continuing. "As I told you yesterday, Mr. Barnett from Paradise Pets will be here about 10:00. As soon as the spelling lesson is finished, we'll head outdoors."

Anxious to get it out of the way, the students pulled out their books and paper and started the lesson. After taking a bathroom break, they put on their jackets, and we gathered up chairs to take outside with us. The students with pets led the way to the blacktop on the playground.

Heather Sharp had brought her iguana, Barney, and she had some interesting facts to tell us about him. Sammy Jacobs brought his two frogs that he had raised from tadpoles and Jeremy Smart brought a turtle that he and his grandfather had found at a pond. The last student to show his pet was Rufus Pennington. He had brought an eighteen-inch long black snake.

Unlatching the cage, he pulled out the snake and held him up for us to see. "My grandpa and I found Elmer in the hen house last fall," Rufus said. "He was sucking an egg from the shell. They like to eat mice, birds and small rabbits, too."

After the "poor bunnies" and "ooh, gross" remarks died down, I asked him to continue.

"Black snakes aren't poisonous, but I have to hold Elmer behind his head, or he tries to bite my hand. Grandpa said he was just a few weeks old when we found him, so he's half grown now. They're important on a farm to help keep down the mice and rat population."

Several students asked questions and wanted to touch it. Some of the girls weren't interested, but the boys clambered to be the first to pet it. I was surprised to find that the skin wasn't slimy. Before putting Elmer back into his cage, Rufus made it a point to shove him in Heather's face as he walked by her.

"Get that thing away from me, Rufus Pennington!" she yelled. "And you be sure his cage isn't next to Barney's when we take them back inside."

I was helping Rufus secure the loose latch on Elmer's cage when Mr. Barnett and his helper came walking down the sidewalk pulling a cart loaded with animals. "Okay, children," I said. "Put the pets under your chairs and give your attention to Mr. Barnett."

The pet store owner had no trouble holding our attention as he showed a variety of frogs, snakes, lizards and turtles. To top off the presentation, he let the students touch a baby alligator while he held the mouth shut.

After a round of applause for the pet show, chairs and pets were gathered up and carried back to the classroom. Once the cages were back on the table, I checked to be sure that all of them were locked. The flimsy latch on the snake's cage kept coming undone, so I pushed the door of it against the wall, then had the students line up for lunch.

After recess, I read aloud a chapter from *A Dog Called Kitty*, by Bill Wallace, before bathroom breaks. When I had finished reading and the students were lining up, I reminded them not to bother the pets on the table during the afternoon.

When we reached the restrooms, I noticed a couple of boys missing. I walked back to the room, and when I stepped in the door, I saw them messing with the cages on the table. "Rufus, you and Sammy must have forgotten what I said about the animals. We're down the hall taking breaks. Let's go."

"Sorry, Miss Kane, but we were checking on Elmer. He looked lonesome," Rufus said as I followed them down the hall.

"He'll be fine until time to go home," I said. "Now, you two hurry. The rest of the class is already lined up to come back to the classroom."

In the afternoon, I taught the math and penmanship lessons. While I walked around the room assisting different students, Heather came up behind me.

Pulling on my hand, she said, "Miss Kane, I was at the table checking on Barney and I saw that the snake isn't in his cage."

Turning my attention to the pets on the table, I walked back to investigate. Elmer's cage had been pulled away from the wall and the door was ajar. I looked around at all the other cages on the table, then knelt down and searched the floor beneath it. There wasn't a sign of him anywhere.

Not wanting to start a panic, I whispered to Heather to go to the office and ask the secretary to page Mr. Logan, the school custodian, and have him come to my classroom. I continued looking for Elmer while the students finished their work, but I wasn't having any luck finding him.

"Boys and girls, we have a little problem," I said. "Elmer has decided to go exploring and I need your help to find him." Some of the girls squealed and got up on their desks, but most of the other students were anxious to help. "If you find the snake, don't touch him. Mr. Logan will be here soon and either he or Rufus will pick him up. Let's check inside the lockers, behind boxes and in the bookcase. Also, since snakes can climb, look inside your desks, too." Though that comment started another round of squealing, I knew it was a possibility that needed to be checked out.

Mr. Logan came in, and after I explained what had happened, he joined in the search. While he hunted through all the cabinets, I looked through my desk. Elmer was nowhere to be found.

"Maybe he crawled down the hall into another classroom," I said to the custodian. *Wouldn't I be the popular one if another teacher found the snake,* I thought.

"It's almost 3:00," Mr. Logan said. "As soon as the kids are gone, I'll start checking the rooms in this wing. He's bound to turn up somewhere."

14

After the custodian left, I had the students put things back into their desks and start gathering up what they needed to take home.

With a sad expression on his face, Rufus walked up to my desk. "I'm sorry, Miss Kane. Sammy and I shouldn't have been messing with the cages. If I hadn't scooted Elmer away from the wall, he wouldn't have gotten out. It's all my fault."

"I know you're feeling bad, Rufus, but Mr. Logan and I will keep looking after school for him. Now, go get your things together. The bell is about to ring."

As I watched him walk to his locker, there was a knock on the door. A former student of mine, who is a fifth-grader now, was delivering a box of Girl Scout cookies that I had ordered. Motioning her inside, I walked to my desk to get some money from my purse.

All I had in my wallet was a twenty-dollar bill. I hated to write a check for three dollars, so I looked through my desk, hoping to find enough spare change. There was only sixty-two cents there, and then I remembered the one-dollar bills for the car wash.

I reached for my totebag that was leaning against the leg of my desk. The cloth handles were crisscrossed holding the top closed, except for a small gap on one end. As I opened the bag, I gasped when I saw the snake curled up on the progress reports that I had forgotten to remove that morning.

Laying the bag down on my desk, I said, "Rufus, please bring Elmer's cage up here."

The noise and confusion that occurred as the students prepared to go home subsided as Rufus headed up front with the cage. Pointing to my bag, I said, "I found Elmer."

Picking it up and looking inside, Rufus shouted, "Yahoo! He's in there taking a nap, Miss Kane!"

"That's one place I didn't think to look," I said.

"Come here, Elmer," Rufus said, pulling him out. "It's time to go home."

While he was putting the snake in the cage, Mr. Logan stuck his head in the door. "Did the snake turn up, yet?" he asked. "There's a toilet that is clogged in the boys' bathroom. Could be the snake crawled in there."

With a big grin on his face, Rufus held up the cage. "Elmer is right here, Mr. Logan. Something else must have clogged the stool."

"I'm glad you found him, Rufus," the man said. "Be sure he gets home safe and sound, okay?"

"You bet I will. Miss Kane is going to help me lock him in good and tight."

With a smile and a wave, Mr. Logan headed down the hall.

While a few remaining students watched, I weaved a large paperclip through the latch, then twisted it around the wire cage. I felt confident it would stay secured for the bus ride home. I didn't think the driver would appreciate a runaway snake on her bus.

As Rufus hurried out of the room, my cousin Riley walked in.

"Hi, sweetie. How was school today?" I asked, walking back to meet her. She is the mirror image of Michael with her soft brown eyes and angelic smile.

"It was good. We've started studying birds, and I drew a picture of Flip and Fluff. Do you want to see it?"

"Sure I do."

Setting her backpack on one of the desks, she pulled out a large sheet of white paper. The birds on the page looked almost identical to her two pets.

"It's beautiful, Riley," I said. "I love the bright colors you used."

A few months ago, Michael took a trip to one of the Kane Energy offices in Peru. While there, he heard that a conservation compound had rescued some macaws after a logging company destroyed their habitat. He was able to obtain two Camelot hatchlings, for a small donation, and gave them to Riley for her sixth birthday.

"I'm taking it home to show Daddy," she said. "He'll probably put it up on the refrigerator."

"I'm sure he'll love it. Now, I'm going to start getting things in order, so we can get out of here."

"I'll straighten the bookcase for you."

"Thanks. That will speed things up."

We talked about her birds while we worked. I wasn't surprised when she told me that she had been doing research on the Internet about them. In kindergarten, Riley had been tested for the school's gifted program. Michael had told me that the testing results had placed her I.Q. at 138, far above the national average.

"Flip and Fluff are only ten months old and I've already taught them to say 'hello,' 'pretty girl' and 'terrific,'" she said.

"That's quite an accomplishment," I said, looking around the room. "I think we're done here. Let's get our bags and go. I want to wash my car before I take you to Gramma's."

I picked up my tote bag and dumped the soiled progress reports into the trash can. I hadn't wanted to send them home after the snake had been sliding around on them. After getting some new blank copies from the cabinet, I grabbed my grade book and put everything inside my bag.

"Have you been assigned to a T-ball team yet?" I asked as we walked down the hallway. I knew the signup period had ended a week ago. She and Joey, my cousin Kristin's son, had been practicing on nice days all winter.

"Yes, I heard from my new coach last night. Joey and I are both on the Champions' team. Grandad has been practicing a lot with us, but I'm anxious to start working with our team next week. I'm going to hit a lot of home runs this year, and I don't have to have a *winky* to do it."

Her back was to me, so she didn't see my eyes widen, or the grin appear on my face. The Winters' boys had always referred to their "manly part" as a "winky." They loved shocking their female cousins, so when the adults weren't around, we were exposed to their colorful vocabulary. Evidently, Riley had overheard the term and figured out that some boys think they are better than girls are when it comes to sports.

As we stepped outside the building, Riley started skipping across the parking lot toward my car.

"I'm sure you'll hit a lot of home runs," I said. "Now let's go give the Mustang a bath."

you don't understand! Do you remember when your cousin Michael was in the student exchange program in high school?"

Now she had really thrown me for a loop. First summer school and now back to my childhood.

"Yes, he stayed with a family in Hawaii for a few weeks," I said. "Then the boy from that family came here and stayed with Michael. His name was Richard. I was only eleven, but when a handsome guy from across the ocean pays attention to you, you don't forget."

"Well, I recently found out that Miss Kahala, Richard's aunt," Traci said. "When I told her that I had a good friend back home that is an excellent third-grade teacher and happens to be Michael Winters' cousin, she asked me if you might consider coming for an interview for one of the positions."

I sat there speechless, trying to take in what she had just said.

"Well, say something! Wouldn't you love to come to Hawaii for the whole month of June? Even though you'd be conducting classes for four hours each morning, you'd have the rest of the day off to see the sites, go to the beach and hang out with me. In other words, live it up."

A month in Hawaii sounded like a dream, but I didn't think Traci had considered everything. Where would I live, and how would I pay for the plane tickets? Lots of expenses figured into a trip like that.

"Traci, I appreciate the fact that you talked to your principal about me, but it would cost a lot of money for me to come. A teacher in Oklahoma isn't paid as well as teachers in Hawaii."

"That's the good part, Alice," she said. "A grant has been awarded to Prince Kuhio Elementary for the purpose of helping mainland teachers become more culturally aware of the Polynesian students' study habits. What better way to do that than to have mainland teachers observe and interact with the students right here in Hawaii?"

She went on to say that the grant pays for travel expenses of prospective candidates for the interviewing process, as well as travel to and from the island for the June session. A local stipend of seven hundred dollars would be given to each person hired, and the school system had vehicles available for their use.

"Okay, I agree, it sounds fabulous, but where am I supposed to stay? The food, travel and transportation are provided, but would I have to pay for a hotel? That could run well over a hundred dollars a night."

CHAPTER 2

We pulled into one of the stalls at Wash 'N Go, and I walked to the change machine next to the office to trade in my one-dollar bills for some quarters. In cold weather, I go through the automatic washing bay, but since it had warmed up, I decided to tackle the job myself.

The change machine kept spitting out one of the bills, so I knocked on the office door and was surprised when Johnny Ramsey opened it.

"Hey, Allie, what's going on?" he asked. "I was just talking to your brother on the phone. We're supposed to go bowling when I get off work." Johnny and my younger brother Jeff have been friends since junior high.

"This thing is refusing to take my dollar," I said. "Maybe you would have more luck."

"It gets picky sometimes. Give the bill to me, and I'll get the quarters from in here."

When he handed the coins to me, I said, "Thanks for your help. Riley's in the car, so I'd better get back over there. Tell Jeff I said 'hi.'"

I walked back to the stall and set the quarters on top of the coin box. I dropped in the first four, then soaped the car, but the cycle ended before it was clean. After putting in more coins, I concentrated on the tires, then bent down and started rubbing the front bumper with my hand. When the second soap cycle was finished, I stood up to go start the rinse cycle and bumped into someone standing behind me.

"Excuse me," I said, turning to see who was there. My heart skipped a beat when I saw Luke Davis.

"Need some help, neighbor?" he asked.

I stepped away from him and held the wand between us. "No, I can handle it," I said, backing toward the coinbox. "Thanks anyway."

As if he hadn't heard me, he sauntered toward my car and leaned on the hood. "Yeah, I was driving by and saw you alone in here. A lady shouldn't have to wash her own car, you know."

I didn't reply as I pressed the rinse button and water started shooting from the wand. I began rinsing the hood of the car first, hoping Luke would take the hint and leave. He jumped back, but not before his boots and pant legs got wet. He watched me during the entire cycle, and I was more aggravated than afraid by the time I finished. Putting the wand back in the holder, I walked around the car to get inside.

"Looks nice," he said, standing between the door and me. "Real nice. Red is a good color for you."

I didn't know if he was referring to the car or my clothing, but I really didn't care one way or the other. Looking eye to eye with him, I said, "My cousin and I have somewhere to go. Would you please move so I can get into my car?"

Instead of moving aside, he took a step toward me. I felt droplets of water from his pant legs fall on my feet. "Well, sure, Miss Kane. We can get together some other time." Leaning closer to my ear, he whispered, "You can count on it."

"Is everything alright in here, Allie?" I turned my head and saw Johnny standing there.

Luke looked at him, then back at me and said, "My neighbor and I were just shooting the breeze, young man. But I need to be going. See you around, *Allie*."

As soon as he moved away, I assured Johnny that I was fine. I climbed into the car and locked the door.

Riley had been reading the entire time we had been there, but as I fastened my seatbelt, she looked up from her book. "Are you okay, Allie? Was that guy a friend of yours?"

"Not a friend, but a neighbor," I said. "Everything's fine. I'm ready to go see our grandparents. How about you?"

As I pulled out of the stall and onto the street, I saw Luke standing next to his wrecker watching us. *This isn't over yet,* I thought. Just the end of round one.

Driving out of town toward my grandparents' place, Riley and I chatted about the evening ahead. She was looking forward to spending time with

Gramma and Grandad. Aside from dropping off Riley and rewriting the progress reports, I had no plans.

A small group of family members, including my dad and older brother Jamie, were planning to spend the evening at Grandpa A.J. and Nana Kane's ranch. They were going to watch the Oklahoma University men's basketball game on television. Their place had been chosen this time because Grandpa had just purchased a new forty-two-inch plasma television set.

A lot of my family members are dedicated OU sports fans. There's always a standing invitation open to any of us who want to join the group to watch the games, regardless of the gathering place. The season for the Sooners was going well, and I enjoy watching, but I really wasn't in the mood for it tonight.

I pondered other options and decided I would continue working on my furniture-refinishing project. Just then, my phone started playing Beethoven's *Moonlight Sonata*, one of my favorite pieces. When I answered it, I heard my mother's voice on the other end.

"Hello, sweetheart," she said. "How was your day?"

"Hi, Mom. It was good, though a bit unusual." I told her about the snake taking refuge in my bag. Rufus's grandparents have been customers of my mother's flower shop for years, so she has seen him in action since he was a toddler. "What's going on?"

I heard her sigh. "I have six more arrangements to oversee for the Wilson funeral service tomorrow morning. Cynthia is still receiving orders for it, so I won't be leaving here for several more hours."

My mother is talented in floral design, and she owns a thriving flower shop and plant nursery called Paradise Petals. There are three other shops in town, but my mother's store is the busiest. Her two sisters, Cynthia and Emily, help her on a part-time basis, and she has three full time employees as well. I know she has confidence in her assistants, but she is a perfectionist and wants to be sure everything is just right before an item leaves the shop.

"Would you like me to come in and help you?" I asked. "I have Riley with me, and I'm going to drop her off at Gramma's, but then I could come by." Mom has owned the shop for over ten years and trained me to take orders and do some simple flower arranging. I have often pitched in and worked during summer breaks and after school during busy times.

"I appreciate your offer, and you can help, but not here in the shop. Earlier I was talking with Gramma over the phone and she mentioned that Aunt Edith is still battling her bad cold. Gramma took over some food yesterday, but every time she has tried to call Aunt Edith today, the line has been busy. Would you please go by and check on her?"

"I'll be glad to," I said. "After I leave Gramma's, I'll drive over and make sure everything is alright. If she needs anything, I'll take care of it." Aunt Edith is Gramma's older sister and a bit unconventional. She adds spice to our family and I love her to death. "Would you like me to bring some food to you?"

"No, thanks, hon, but I appreciate the offer. Grandad is bringing a big pot of Gramma's chili and some crackers to us in a couple of hours. By then, we'll be ready to take a break and relax for a few minutes."

"Don't overwork yourself. We're just turning into Gramma's driveway, so I'll talk with you later."

"Please tell Riley I said 'hello,'" she replied, "and you have a nice evening. Love you."

"I'll tell her, and I love you, too," I said before ending the call.

As I drove up the long driveway toward my grandparents' spacious, two-story house, I looked over at Riley. "Your Aunt Maggie told me to tell you 'hello.' I'm sorry we didn't get to talk more during our ride."

"Oh, that's okay," she said. "I hope Aunt Edith is all right. She's so neat."

"Don't worry. I'm sure she's fine."

I pulled my car in behind Gramma's Caprice that was sitting under the carport. After we got out, we started up the long sidewalk leading from the driveway to the front door of the elegant, Victorian-styled house. At night, the large front windows remind me of a lighthouse welcoming a lost ship home. My grandparents are loving and kind, but also strict in upholding good morals and values.

As we reached the front porch, we both turned our heads toward the sound of a shrill whistle coming from the side of the yard. Grandad was waving at us from his garden a short distance away. He was wearing his old, sweat-stained gardening hat that had been around as long as I could remember.

Riley and I both waved back, and she yelled, "Hi, Grandad! I've come to visit you for a while."

Grandad nodded and slowly started walking our way.

"I'm going to go meet him, Allie. I'll see you in the house in a few minutes," she said, running toward the garden.

"See you inside," I hollered as I watched her race across the yard to the gate.

Riley adores her great-grandfather, and I know the feeling is mutual. She has stayed with them a lot in the last few years, and they are very protective of her. Michael and his wife, Sandra, had been married for five years before Riley was born. After she came along, Sandra was unwilling to put motherhood before her law career. They toughed it out for two years, then Sandra decided that Riley was better off with Michael and left.

I stepped up to the double front doors and lifted the sculpted door-knocker that had belonged to Gramma's grandparents many years before. Using it, I knocked twice, paused and knocked three more times. For safety's sake, our family had devised the simple code to alert the older folks that the visitor was a family member.

I could hear Gramma's swift footsteps coming toward the door. As she opened it, I was met with her bright smile. "Come in Allie, it's good to see you. I thought I heard your car."

As I stepped inside the lighted entryway, our arms encircled each other, and I could smell the soft hint of roses from the cologne she wears. After releasing me from the hug, she asked, "Allison, are you losing weight? I think you need to come out here and eat with your Grandad and me more often. I can put some meat on your bones."

I had been an early bloomer and had had to monitor my weight while growing up, but had never had to diet. I've been a size eight since graduating from high school, but I do feel tightness in my jeans after family dinners featuring Gramma's and Nana Kane's delicious cooking.

"No, Gramma, I'm not losing weight," I assured her. "But I don't want to gain any more, either. Our Sunday dinners are a challenge as it is. If I start eating yours and Nana's cooking more often than that, I'll have to start shopping for a larger-sized wardrobe."

My paternal grandmother, Susanna Kane, and Gramma have been best friends since starting school together almost seventy years ago. Everyone who knows them agrees that they are the foundation of the Winters and Kane clans. They helped raise each other's children and now help with each other's grandchildren, as well.

When we have our regular family dinners every second and fourth Sunday of the month, everyone from both families is invited. We all contribute something to the meal, so the menu may be a bit of a surprise, but it's always tasty and fun.

Gramma took my hand, and we walked together toward the kitchen. "You need to have a big bowl of my latest batch of chili," she said. "I've added a new secret ingredient that is sure to produce another blue ribbon at this year's contest."

Drawn by the luscious smell of cayenne pepper, onion, garlic and other spices, I wandered to the stove and lifted the lid from the Dutch oven. Fragrant steam from the bubbling mixture swirled up, causing my stomach to start growling.

"If this tastes half as good as it smells, you've got a winner for sure," I said.

I could hear Grandad and Riley singing as they came into the mudroom. I recognized the strains of an old song about "heading home after having a little drink" that Grandad had taught to my cousins and I when we were kids.

Gramma reached into the cabinet for two bowls, then walked to the stove. "That man! I don't know what I'm going to do with him!" she said. "He taught that drinking song to all you grandchildren and he's at it again with the great-grandkids, too!"

As stern as she pretended to be, I knew she wouldn't admonish Grandad. They fit together like a hand in a glove, and arguments are rare. She knows Grandad would never do anything to harm anyone, or lead them astray, but I know he does delight in aggravating her with his antics.

"You know, Allie, he's been in that garden all afternoon, biding his time until that youngster got here," she confided. "And I have to admit, I enjoy her company, too. She sure livens things up around here."

Heavy thuds sounded from the mudroom as their shoes and boots were removed. The door burst open with an excited Riley crooning the last of the song.

I started clapping, and she took a bow, relishing the attention of her audience.

Gramma bent down and said, "Come over here and give me a hug, Miss Riley."

In her stocking feet, Riley rushed over to Gramma and put her arms around her neck. As she gazed over Riley's shoulder, I saw Gramma frown at Grandad. In return, he gave her an ornery grin.

As Gramma rose from Riley's embrace, he walked past her and gently swatted her ample behind. He never missed a step as he continued toward me and said, "How about a hug from you, young lady?"

Startled and blushing, Gramma whirled around and watched him move away. Then, acting as if nothing between them had occurred, she walked toward the stove.

"Allie, you and Riley sit down, and I'll have some food for you in a jiffy."

"Sounds good," I said as I followed Riley to the large dining table that filled the center of the room. "But just a small bowl for me, please. Mom is tied up at the shop, and I told her I'd run by Aunt Edith's on my way home to check on her."

"Oh, I appreciate that," Gramma said. "The cold that Edith's been fighting has been hard on her. She must have taken the receiver off the hook, because I've tried calling her four times today and kept getting a busy signal."

As Gramma began ladling chili into our bowls, she asked Grandad, "Since you're going to eat and watch the basketball game at A.J.'s later, do you want anything now?" Her back was to him and couldn't see what he was doing. "I made fresh coffee and there are some blueberry muffins leftover from breakfast in the breadbox, if you need something to tide you over."

With a cup of coffee in one hand, Grandad had already opened the breadbox before she had finished her first sentence. Watching them, I hoped I would find a mate someday that could discern what I was about to say, even before I said it.

We all sat at the table for a few moments in companionable silence while Riley and I ate. After a while, she began telling us about a new towering perch that her daddy had bought for Flip and Fluff. He had also bought a couple of new toys for them.

While listening to her talk about her pets, an idea occurred to me. Carrying our dirty dishes to the sink, I asked, "Riley, does your class still have show-and-tell on Fridays?"

"Yes, but sometimes the things the kids bring aren't very interesting."

"Would you like to bring Flip and Fluff to my class the Friday before spring break? We'll be finishing a unit on birds by then. I'd be glad to speak with your dad and your teacher, Mrs. Miller, about it."

"That would be terrific, Allie, could I?" She was bouncing up and down in her chair. "I'll talk Daddy into it. I can bring some of their toys and show the class some of the tricks they've learned. I might even tell the kids about the birds' breeding habits."

"I'll make the arrangements, but let's not spring the breeding part on them, okay? I know they would enjoy seeing the birds do some tricks and petting them." I looked at my watch. "It's almost 4:30, so I'd better be going."

They all rose from the table and walked with me toward the entryway.

"Are you coming to your grandpa's place to watch the game tonight, Allie?" Grandad asked. "That OU team is really heating up. If they continue at the rate they're going, they're bound to make it to the Final Four."

"Since I saw the game last Sunday, I don't think I'll come out tonight. After I check on Aunt Edith, I'm heading home. I've got some progress reports to redo and I haven't talked with Traci in a couple of weeks, so I may give her a call. But please tell everyone I said 'hello.'"

"How are Traci and her husband doing?" Gramma asked. "Is she still playing the piano at that little church?"

Traci Morris and I have been best friends since we were five years old, and Gramma gave her piano lessons for several years. She married her high school sweetheart, Tommy Morris, just two months following our graduation. Soon after, he joined the marines and was sent to the Kaneohe Military Base on the island of Oahu.

"Yes, she's still playing for some of the services as well as teaching second grade at a private elementary school," I told her. "In the last e-mail I got from her, she said that Tommy had been promoted to captain. They are very excited about the pay raise he received with the promotion because she just found out they're going to have a baby."

"Oh, that's wonderful news. I'm so happy for them," Gramma said. "Traci is such a sweet girl. When you speak with her, please give her my love."

"I will. You guys have a nice evening," I said, then headed out the door to my car.

CHAPTER 3

My great-aunt, Edith Patterson, lives less than a mile from my duplex. Since I'm not married and have no dependents, my family tends to rely on me to help keep an eye on her, which I'm glad to do.

Prior to her husband, Ben, passing away about eight years ago, they often rode their Harley motorcycles together. Even now at seventy-eight years old, donned in black leather and wearing her fire-streaked helmet, Aunt Edith is still active with the Screaming Eagles, an over-fifties motorcycle club they had joined. Our family has breathed a sigh of relief every year that she hasn't insisted on attending the annual Harley convention in Sturgis, South Dakota. The event is held in late summer, and anytime she mentions going up there with her club, someone comes up with a special dinner, a need for a babysitter, or some other reason why she should stay here.

Last year, it worked out perfectly that my cousin Randy and his wife, Julie, had just had their first child, Jakie, a few weeks before the convention was to take place. The baby's dedication at church just happened to be scheduled on the Sunday that Aunt Edith would have been gone to Sturgis.

I suspect that she caught on several years ago that the family *needs* her more than usual during that particular week. After Jakie's dedication, I heard her tell Mom and Dad, "This is the seventh year in a row that something has come up and the Eagles have traveled to South Dakota without me."

When I arrived at Aunt Edith's, I pulled into the driveway that ran along the side of her three-bedroom brick house. Before getting out of the car, I repeated the signal with the horn that I had used with the door-knocker at my grandparents' house.

I opened the wire gate, then walked up the steps onto the back porch. After knocking on the door, I stood waiting, then heard a *crash*! Afraid she had fallen, I opened the door and hurried inside calling, "Aunt Edith, are you alright?"

She was sitting in the middle of the floor with her head bent over. Dozens of clothing catalogs were scattered across the tile. A chair was lying on its side. Apparently, the books had been stacked on the chair and she must have brushed against it, causing it to topple over. If she was trying to catch the catalogs, she had missed.

I knelt beside her, and she lifted her head and looked at me. With a goofy smile on her face, she said, "Hello, Allison. It's so nice to see you!"

The strong odor coming from her mouth was unmistakable. She had been drinking something stronger than her regular lemonade. I helped her to the nearest kitchen chair, which wasn't an easy feat. Aunt Edith only weighs about a hundred pounds, but in her intoxicated condition, she was dead weight. Once she was settled at the table, I pushed the books against the wall so that neither of us would trip again. I picked up the chair and sat down next to her.

She started giggling, then cut loose laughing. "Oh, Allison, it was the funniest thing you ever saw!" she said, twirling her arms like a Ferris wheel. "The catalogs tumbled down and down and down." As she spoke, her whole body began moving in a downward spiral, and I knew that if I didn't grab her, she was going to go headfirst back onto the floor.

I reached over and put my hands against her shoulders. "Aunt Edith, Gramma has been trying to reach you all day. We were concerned that something might have happened to you, and I can see that *something* has. What have you been drinking?"

"Just lemonade and orange juice," she said.

"I smell alcohol on your breath. Have you been mixing something with the juice?"

"I've been trying to get rid of this cold, so Daisy gave me a bottle of her homemade herbal elixir," she said, slurring her words. "It's a recipe her daddy used, and she guaranteed it would fix me right up. I've been taking it like she told me to everyday since Monday, but I wasn't getting better fast enough."

"Did you start doing something different?"

"Last night, I started doubling the dose. I took two doses before bedtime, then several since then. And you know what? I sure feel a whole lot better now!"

I'll bet you do, I thought. "Okay, you sit here and rest a minute. I want to take a look at the elixir."

I spotted a large bottle sitting on the kitchen cabinet that was half full of a dark red liquid. There was a serving spoon resting next to it. Walking over to take a closer look, I assumed it was the *guaranteed* elixir her neighbor Daisy Johnson had given to her. Looking closer, there was a label on one side, and in handwritten letters, it said to take two teaspoons every four hours. The spoon lying next to the bottle was a tablespoon—triple the size of a teaspoon.

When I took out the cork and sniffed the contents inside, the fumes made my eyes start to water. Since I don't drink, I'm not an expert, but I'd say the bottle contained more liquor than anything else.

I held the bottle up so she could see it. "Is this what you've been taking for your cold, Aunt Edith?"

"That's it. The spoon I've been using is right there handy."

"The directions say you should take two teaspoons, but if you've been using a tablespoon and doubling the dosage, you've taken an awful lot of this stuff."

"Daisy said it's full of herbs and natural ingredients and it would be okay to take a little more than directed if I wanted to."

I put the bottle inside one of the cabinets so that it wasn't as accessible, then walked back over to the table. "I think you'll be okay, but I'm going to make some hot coffee and a snack for you."

"That's sweet of you, Allison. I think I'll just go into the den and rest a minute on the sofa while you do that."

As she started to rise from the chair, I put my hand under her arm and helped her to the den. She put her feet up on the couch, then I took an afghan from the back of it and placed it over her.

I turned to go back into the kitchen and heard a beeping sound coming from across the room. I followed the noise and saw that the receiver wasn't straight on the phone. It must have been off the hook all day. After fixing it, I turned around and heard Aunt Edith snoring.

Slipping through the kitchen onto the back porch, I took my cell phone from my purse and dialed my mother's number. After two rings, a male voice said, "Good afternoon, Paradise Petals."

I recognized the voice and said, "Hi, Dad. What are you doing answering the phone?"

"Hi, pretty girl. I left work a little early so that I could swing by here and see your mother before I go out to your grandparents' to watch the OU game. When I called her early this afternoon, I got the brush off because she said she was too busy to mess with me."

Since my dad is the President and CEO of Kane Energy, he can set his own hours, though it isn't uncommon for him to work over fifty hours a week.

In the background I could hear a muffled, "Oh, James, you know that's not true," coming from my mother.

"Well, she might not have put it in those words," he said, "but I knew she had a lot of orders to fill. I dropped by to make sure she wasn't cracking the whip too hard over her helpers." My dad loves to tease my mother and he attracted her attention again with this remark.

I could hear her laughing as she said, "James, you know I wouldn't ever work anyone too hard. Now please let me have the phone, so I can talk with Allie."

"Here's your mother," Dad said. "Take care of yourself." I could hear the smack from a kiss he gave her before relinquishing the phone.

"Sounds like you have some extra help tonight," I said when my mother got on the line.

"Yes, I think he just came by to check up on me. He wanted to make sure I'm really working and not out running around somewhere."

I knew Dad must still be within earshot and she was saying this for his benefit. Fun banter still continues between my parents, even after thirty years of marriage. He was probably giving her one of his sly winks.

"I wanted to report on Aunt Edith," I said.

I relayed what I had discovered regarding the "wonder drug" and the condition in which I had found our aunt. I assured my mother that I would stay until she woke up, then fix her something to eat before I went home.

"I appreciate you doing that for her, Allie. She may not be feeling very well when she wakes up, so some food may help."

"I know you're busy, so I'll talk with you later."

"Okay, I'll let Gramma know things are under control," Mom said before hanging up.

While I had been talking with my parents, Samson, Aunt Edith's tomcat, had shown up and was rubbing against my legs. I reached down and stroked his head a few times; then he decided he had had enough affection and meandered over to his food dish.

I got my tote bag from the car, then went back inside to check on Aunt Edith. She was still sound asleep, so I settled at the kitchen table to get some work done.

❀   ❀   ❀

As I finished the last progress report, I heard Aunt Edith stirring on the couch. I walked to the sink and filled a small glass with water, then grabbed the bottle of aspirin that I had found earlier in the medicine cabinet.

When I stepped into the den, she was holding her head with one hand and trying to push away the afghan with the other. I moved the cover out of her way so she could sit up.

Groaning, she said, "Whew, have I got a headache!"

I sat down on the couch next to her. "Would you like some aspirin? It might help you feel better."

"Thanks," she said, taking the pills and water from me. "I don't know why my head is pounding."

"Do you think the elixir that Miss Daisy gave you might have caused your headache?" I paused, giving her time to ponder my statement. "It might not be a good idea to take any more of it, unless you check with your doctor first."

Considering, she said, "Well, maybe you're right. But you know, I think that elixir did cure my cold. I haven't coughed all day and my congestion is gone. I think Daisy may really have something there. She might be able to sell her daddy's recipe to one of those big pharmaceutical companies and make a mint!"

"Hmmm, maybe," I said, then changed the subject. "Would you like me to fix you something to eat before I go?"

"No, but thanks for the offer. This is Thursday, you know, and *CSI:* night. Clarence and Daisy will be coming over soon to watch the show with me. Your grandmother brought over some chili yesterday, so we'll be eating high-on-the-hog while watching that hottie, Gil Grissom."

I had forgotten about the Thursday night gathering of the "three musketeers," as my granddad refers to them. They have been sharing dinner and watching *CSI:* on television together every week for three years now.

I smiled at the "hottie" comment, then said, "Oh, yes, *CSI:* night. The ratings sweeps are going on this month, so it should be a new episode for you to watch."

"Oh, that doesn't matter. We watch all the reruns, too," she said. "You know I'm the youngest one of our bunch, so we don't always catch all the clues the first time around. Besides, I enjoy watching Gil anytime. Clarence is big on Catherine Willows and Daisy moons over Clarence."

My great-uncle, Clarence Hayden, is Aunt Edith's and Gramma's eighty-year-old brother. He was the manager of the Paradise Feedmill for fifty years. Shortly after he retired to care for his ailing wife, Emma, she passed away. He's been a widower for almost ten years and is one of the most sought after bachelors at church. Besides Daisy Johnson, I know of four other widows that would like to catch him. He told me one time that he enjoys "playing the field" and doesn't intend to settle down again.

"It sounds like you'll have a fun evening," I said.

Aunt Edith stood up and slowly tilted her head to the left, then circled it back to the right. "I'm starting to feel a little better now. You know you're welcome to join us tonight, if you'd like to. There's plenty of food, and a little young blood around here would be a nice addition."

"I appreciate the invitation, but I ate earlier at Gramma's, and I have a furniture refinishing project to work on. How about a rain check?"

"You know you're welcome anytime."

We walked together toward the kitchen. As I reached for my bag, I asked, "Would you like a ride to the Senior Citizen's Center on Saturday? I know Gramma's expecting another blue ribbon this year."

"Oh, I wouldn't miss it for the world. Sarah would pout for days if I wasn't there to see her receive another prize for her cooking. Besides, I wouldn't want to miss a chance to see all my nieces and nephews, since I know a bunch of them will be there."

Many of the Kanes and Winters come to the annual event. It is an informal time where we can visit and enjoy good food together. For a set price, each person can sample all the entries. Gramma usually brings three crockpots full because many folks want second helpings of her chili. Plenty of crackers and cookies are provided to round out the meal, and various school choirs provide entertainment.

This year, two of the six judges were going to be Grandpa A.J. and my dad. Samples of the chili are put in identical bowls on a large table, so no one knows who made what kind. It's always entertaining to watch the judges' reactions. Some of the recipes are very spicy, while others are bland. Sometimes the judges have a hard time keeping their opinions from showing up on their faces. But, despite the taste, they are always polite and complimentary.

"Okay, I'll pick you up about eleven," I told her. "The judging will start at 11:30 and I want to get a good seat."

"I'll be ready." She paused as if a thought had occurred to her. "I read in the *Paradise Progress* this morning that Ray Connerson passed away. You know we used to sit together at church and went out to dinner a few times last year. I had to break it off though; he was ten years older than me and I need a younger guy."

I know that Aunt Edith's dating calendar is more full than mine, but I guess Mr. Connerson didn't meet her relationship criteria.

"Anyway, his viewing is at Simpson's Funeral Home on Saturday from two to five. Would you mind taking me there, so I can pay my respects?"

Oh, boy. When Aunt Edith "pays her respects," I really have to keep an eye on her. She was almost banned last month from Morton Brothers Funeral Home. One of the partners, Billy Morton, caught her with her comb out rearranging Juanita Blair's hair. A week earlier, while Aunt Edith was at another viewing, Clara Bacon's hairstyle mysteriously changed.

When I questioned her about it, she insisted that she had known those ladies for more years than the Morton Brothers had and that the restyling gave them a more natural look. The two ladies in question had been regulars every Monday morning at Gladys' Mane Event, the hair salon where Aunt Edith has a standing appointment.

"I'll take you to Mr. Connerson's viewing, but you have to promise that you won't try to change his hair," I said.

"Oh, don't worry about that. You must have forgotten that he's almost bald. Besides, Simpson's let's the relatives make the decisions about the hairstyle and makeup. Those Morton Brothers hired some young floozy to do it, and she does 'her own thing.'" She moved her fingers up and down in a quote-unquote fashion.

Mentally shaking my head, I picked up my bag and headed toward the back door.

"Okay, I'll plan on seeing you at eleven on Saturday," I said. "Enjoy your television program, and please tell Miss Daisy and Uncle Clarence I said 'hello.'" Giving her a quick hug, I walked outside, got into the car and headed home.

As I turned onto the street where I live, I realized I was too wiped out to work on furniture. Mid-winter dusk had already settled in, and all I wanted to do was take a warm bubble bath and watch *The Apprentice*. Only ten candidates remained, and my favorite was still in the running.

Earlier, I had told my grandparents that I intended to call Traci. Hawaiian time is four hours behind Oklahoma's. Looking at my dashboard, the clock read 7:15. Traci would still be at school, since it was only 3:15 there. I decided I would call her after the show. I knew she had been watching it, too, so it would be fun to tease her that I already knew who had been fired.

Driving by the Davises' house, it looked ominous in the dark. Through the windshield, I could see a red ember and wisps of smoke coming from the area of their porch swing. Passing on by, I pulled into my driveway. As I got out of my car, I could hear the squeak of the neighbor's swing as it moved back and forth.

While gathering up my things, the squeaking stopped. I looked in that direction and could see Luke sauntering across his yard toward me. I quickly locked the car, then rushed to my front door. I didn't feel like another encounter tonight.

I pushed my key into the lock, but it wouldn't turn. Jiggling it loose, I pulled it out and tried again. Glancing behind me, I saw that Luke was still headed my way. He was already across Mrs. Googan's yard. The key still wasn't cooperating, so I jerked it out. I inserted it again, and this time I pulled on the door while turning the key. Relief swept over me when I heard the lock release.

As I clambered inside, I threw my stuff on the floor, then slammed and locked the door. I stepped to the window and peeked through the shades. Luke was standing beside my car looking toward the house. Since the room was dark, I knew he couldn't see me, but I was pretty sure he knew I was watching him. He stared at the window for several minutes, then tossed the cigarette butt into my yard and walked away.

My heart was hammering as I pulled the shades closed. I walked across the room and turned on a lamp. The light cast aside eerie shadows and made the room feel warmer. Still a little shaken, I decided to fix some tea.

While waiting for the water in the teakettle to boil, I was determined not to let Luke Davis ruin my evening. Heading to the bathroom to start the water running for my bubble bath, I saw the red light blinking on my answering machine. The bath water could wait a couple of minutes longer.

I slid down into my favorite chair, a large, cozy recliner, and kicked off my pumps. I reached over to the machine sitting on the end table and pushed the button.

The first message was from my cousin Kristin. She said she had missed me after school, but wanted to see if I would be interested in going to a movie the next night. Also, she told me that she had received a letter from her husband, Kevin, who serves as chaplain for a group of fifty soldiers in Iraq. She said she would tell me more about it at school on Friday.

Kevin sends letters every week to Kristin and their son Joey. Once a month, he also includes a separate page or two containing short messages from the soldiers. Our two classes have been pen pals with Kevin's unit for several months.

The second message was from Traci. As I listened to her voice, I felt a little ache inside, realizing how much I miss her.

"Hi, Allie. I didn't know if you would be home yet. It's 4:30 Oklahoma time. Since you aren't, I guess you're still working hard at school. I have a surprise for you, so please give me a call sometime tonight. I can't wait to hear back from you; this is so exciting! Love you."

At the end of Traci's message, I thought of how we had shared everything while growing up. We had been inseparable and often wore the same hairstyle and each other's clothes. Though I had adjusted to the many miles separating us, tonight I could use a face-to-face conversation with her.

I heard the teakettle calling me, so I padded back into the kitchen and poured the boiling water over the teabag. It could steep while I took a bath. The cuckoo in the clock chirped once, telling me it was 7:30. Hearing it, I realized I had better get a move on or I would miss the first part of *The Apprentice.*

I walked down the hall, stripped off my clothes and began filling the tub. I lit a couple of vanilla scented candles, then slipped into the warm, sudsy water. The commercial that said "Calgon, take me away" floated into my mind from somewhere as I let the magic bubbles melt away the stress of the day.

Cocooned in warmth, I became more curious about Traci's message. She said she had some exciting news, and since I already knew about the pregnancy, I couldn't imagine what she might be referring to. Perhaps she was expecting twins? That would really be something!

Still wondering about it, I released the water from the tub, toweled off and slathered scented lotion onto my body. I cleaned up the mess in the bathroom, then wrapped myself in a fluffy towel and trotted to my bedroom.

After putting on my pajamas, a robe and a pair of thick socks, I caught a glimpse of myself in the full-length mirror on the closet door. I wasn't making a fashion statement in this attire, but until I had a husband to keep me warm at night, the ensemble served its purpose.

Despite the fact that my family owns a company that produces oil and natural gas, it didn't prevent high heating costs from being passed on to me. I had been keeping my thermostat a few degrees lower all winter.

When I got back into the kitchen, I stuck a bag of popcorn into the microwave. While it was popping, I sweetened the tea and plopped in some ice cubes. When the popcorn was finished, I took the bag and my drink to the living room and settled into my recliner to watch the show.

As I pulled a blanket over my legs, I reminded myself of a little old woman with her snacks, remote and lap robe. All I lacked was a cat curled up on my lap!

I raised the footrest on the recliner, then turned on the television. With five minutes to spare before the show began, I munched on the popcorn while watching the commercials. I was watching an ad about Ford trucks and drifted off to sleep. When I woke up, Donald Trump had already fired someone. I had missed the whole show!

I sat up in the chair and found pieces of popcorn strewn across my lap.

A couple of pieces were hanging in my hair. The ice cubes in my tea were almost melted, and my cuckoo clock was telling me it was 9:00.

Aggravated that I had fallen asleep, I picked up the spilled popcorn and carried the bowl and glass to the kitchen. I stretched and moved around the room, trying to wake myself up before calling Traci. Not only could I not tease her with my knowledge of who got fired, she was going to know before me! *Sheesh!*

I took my cell phone to the bedroom and stretched out on the bed. I dialed her number, and after the third ring, she picked up the phone and said, "Aloha. Morris residence."

"Aloha, yourself, island girl," I said. "I was planning on calling you tonight, but you beat me to it. I guess great minds think alike."

"Of course they do," she said. "I got home from school about an hour ago and started fixing manicotti, which I know is one of your favorite dishes. Why don't you run over and eat with Tommy and me tonight?"

"Yeah, I could do that. Just let me crank up the old jet, and I'll be there in a flash."

"I do wish you were here, because when I tell you my surprise, I'd like to see the look on your face."

"What in the world is this surprise of yours? It must be something big for you to call me from school."

"I had just received some great news from our principal, Miss Kahala, and I couldn't wait until I got home to share it with you."

"You sound like you're about to burst."

"Oh, Allie, you aren't going to believe this," she said. "Our school is one of two sites chosen to conduct summer classes for the leeward side of the island for second and third-graders. A lot of teachers are going to be needed for the four-week June session, and Miss Kahala is having a hard time filling all the positions. I can't work because Tommy and I are planning to come to Oklahoma the last part of June to see our parents."

As I listened, I thought it was a little unusual that she was going into so much detail about summer school, especially since she wouldn't be teaching. Eager to hear about her big surprise, I said, "I'm sorry she's having trouble finding teachers, but I'll be glad to see you and Tommy when you come here in June."

Traci didn't say anything for a moment, then blurted out, "No, Allie, you don't understand! Do you remember when your cousin Michael was in the student exchange program in high school?"

Now she had really thrown me for a loop! First summer school and now back to my childhood.

"Yes, he stayed with a family in Hawaii for a few weeks," I said. "Then the boy from that family came here and stayed with Michael. His name was Richard. I was only eleven, but when a handsome guy from across the ocean pays attention to you, you don't forget it."

"Well, I recently found out that Miss Kahala is Richard's aunt," Traci said. "When I told her that I had a good friend back home that is an excellent third-grade teacher and happens to be Michael Winters' cousin, she asked me if you might consider coming for an interview for one of the positions."

I sat there speechless, trying to take in what she had just said.

"Well, say something! Wouldn't you love to come to Hawaii for the whole month of June? Even though you'd be conducting classes for four hours each morning, you'd have the rest of the day off to see the sites, go to the beach and hang out with me. In other words, live it up!"

A month in Hawaii sounded like a dream, but I didn't think Traci had considered everything. Where would I live, and how would I pay for the airline tickets? Lots of expenses figured into a trip like that.

"Traci, I appreciate the fact that you talked to your principal about me, but it would cost a lot of money for me to come. A teacher in Oklahoma isn't paid as well as teachers in Hawaii."

"That's the good part, Allie," she said. "A grant has been awarded to Prince Kuhio Elementary for the purpose of 'helping mainland teachers become more culturally aware of the Polynesian student's study habits.' What better way to do that than to have mainland teachers observe and interact with the students right here in Hawaii?"

She went on to say that the grant pays for travel expenses of prospective candidates for the interviewing process as well as travel to and from the island for the June session. A meal stipend of seven hundred dollars would be given to each person hired, and the school system had vehicles available for their use.

"Okay, I agree, it sounds fabulous, but where am I supposed to stay? The food, travel and transportation are provided, but would I have to pay for a hotel? That could run well over a hundred dollars a night."

"The grant will pay host teachers a five-hundred-dollar stipend for providing a room in their home," she said. "That is much less than the cost of a hotel and it would give the island teachers the chance to interact with their mainland counterparts. I told Miss Kahala that you could stay with me."

I was trying to absorb all the information that Traci was feeding me.

"Oh, Allie, just think of the great fun we can have while you're here! Even though Tommy and I are planning to come to Oklahoma the last part of June, you're welcome to stay in our apartment, and it won't cost you a cent!"

"It sounds enticing," I said. "Can I think about it for a day or two? When does Miss Kahala need an answer?"

"She's going to interview candidates the first two weeks of March. I told her Oklahoma usually has spring break in mid-March. When is your break this year?"

"We're out the week of March 7th," I said. "If I come for the interview, can I stay with you and Tommy?"

"Of course, silly! I'd be mad if you didn't. Think about it for a couple of days, then call me back. Even if you aren't chosen for one of the positions, coming to Hawaii for spring break would be a dream vacation, wouldn't it?"

"It would be fabulous! I would love to see you, relax on the beach and soak up some sun for a few days."

We shared the latest news about our families and talked about the new baby that would soon be entering their lives. I mentioned that I had thought her "big surprise" might have been that she was expecting twins. That comment made her gasp for air.

"Our little apartment will be crowded enough with one new addition," she said. "I can't imagine how cramped it would be if we brought twins home."

We were on the phone for over an hour. Before hanging up, I told her I would call her back by Sunday evening. That way, she would know what to tell her principal on Monday morning.

With our conversation buzzing inside my head, I brushed my teeth, turned out all the lights and nestled down in bed. As I watched the shadows dancing on my ceiling, I had to admit that being considered for a job in Hawaii was flattering. I didn't think it would take me until Sunday to make my decision, but I didn't want to be too hasty. I'd bounce the idea off some of my family members this weekend.

I drifted to sleep, dreaming of warm ocean breezes and brightly colored macaws perched in swaying palm trees.

CHAPTER 4

Friday morning arrived with a vengeance. I was awakened by thunder vibrating the walls of my bedroom. The room showed only a hint of daylight, then was made brighter for a moment when a streak of lightning lit up the sky. I glanced at my clock and saw it was only 6:30, so I had thirty more minutes to sleep.

Groaning at the thought of going out into the cold rain and wind, I put my pillow over my head. I tried to go back to sleep, but the reverberating thunder protested my efforts. Deciding it was futile, I got out of bed and wrapped myself in a quilt that Nana Kane had made for me for my sixteenth birthday. Though slightly worn from years of use, it still offered me warmth and comfort.

Wrapped from neck to toe, I made a quick stop in the bathroom to turn on the overhead heater. I closed the door so it would be warmer when I dressed in there later, then went to the kitchen to make some hot chocolate. I had never acquired a taste for coffee, though I had grown up around coffee drinkers.

Dawdling at the window while the microwave heated the mug of milk, I could see that the heavy thunderclouds were threatening to release their watery contents. The sun and warmth we had been blessed with the previous day was only a memory.

When the microwave beeped, I took out the hot milk and stirred in some Nesquik. After carrying the cocoa back to the bedroom, I set it on the dresser. I pulled out a heavy, cable-knit sweater from the bottom drawer, along with a coordinating turtleneck from the closet. Each Friday at school is "jeans day," so I grabbed my last clean pair from the hanger.

Gathering up the clothes and the mug, I darted into the warm bathroom to get ready to face the day. Thank goodness it was Friday!

By the time I was ready to leave, rain was pouring down in sheets. I fought with my umbrella from the moment I stepped out the door. The wind whipped the silky material as I ran down the sidewalk, and by the time I reached my car, it had turned inside out.

Raindrops pelted my face as I pulled open the car door. Once inside, I slammed it on the umbrella. While dodging the drips, I pushed the door open again and brought the mutilated object inside.

Tossing it onto the floor of the passenger's side, I sat there for a moment, trying to compose myself. My shoes were soaked, so I kicked them off. I reached into the glove compartment and pulled out some napkins. I used them to dab my shoes inside and out. By the time I finished, they were still wet, but wearable.

I backed out of the driveway and uttered a prayer. "Dear Lord, though this day hasn't started out well, please help me to have a good attitude so that it will be a productive day."

As I continued driving, I thought I needed to add an amendment to the prayer. "Also, You know that Traci called me last night. I would appreciate some help in making the decision about the interview. It sounds like a great opportunity to me. What do You think about it?" Though I didn't hear His answer right then, I felt confident that He would let me know.

It was only sprinkling by the time I reached the school. Since my umbrella was in shambles, I left it and held my totebag over my head as I darted to the building. It was a good thing I had twisted my hair into a knot on the top of my head this morning, or it would be a kinky mess by now.

Before going to my classroom, I walked to the kindergarten wing to see if Kristin had arrived. She was busy hanging construction paper George Washington figures from wires attached to the ceiling. Her students had been talking about the Father of our Country, and had been hard at work with scissors and paste. The entire kindergarten was planning an ice cream party in honor of the president's birthday on the twenty-second.

"Good morning," I said as I walked up behind her.

Turning around, she looked at my wet clothes and said, "What happened to you? I thought it had stopped raining."

I relayed my dilemma about my car being parked outside and the umbrella fight with the wind. The incentive to get the Mustang back into the garage went up a notch.

"If you don't have other plans, I'd like you and Joey to come over for lunch after church on Sunday to see the new furniture," I said. "It should be done and in place by then, if I can get Doug's help moving it inside. It's not very heavy, so if he's not available, do you think you and I can handle it?" I gave her one of my charming smiles.

"I'll help you move it in if you can't recruit Doug. But I'll expect a special lunch for my trouble," she teased. "How about some of those Oriental wraps that Joey and I are so fond of?"

"I think I can manage that," I said. "I have chicken breasts in the freezer, and I'll pick up some cilantro and chow mein noodles at the store before then. I already have the tortillas and other ingredients on hand."

"You've got a deal, then."

"You said that you received a letter from Kevin. How is he doing?"

"Not too well, I'm afraid. He wrote that he's concerned about the depression in the unit. Due to injuries from insurgent bombings, there have been a lot of wounded Iraqi children brought in. Most of them are recovering, but the distress of the situation is weighing on the medics. Kevin has tried several different things to boost the morale of his troops, but nothing seems to be working."

I put my hand on her shoulder. "Kevin is a smart guy," I said. "He'll figure out a way to encourage them. Hang in there; you'll see."

"I'm sure he will," she said. "I guess I just needed a shoulder to cry on. Thanks for yours."

"You're welcome to cry on my shoulder anytime. Did Kevin include any news to share with our students?"

"Yes, I made a copy of the page this morning." She walked to her desk, picked up the photocopy and handed it to me.

"Thanks. I'll look it over on the way to my room." I glanced at the clock on the wall. "I'd better get going. The bell is about to ring and I'll have kids looking for me." I touched her arm and gave it a little squeeze. "Don't worry. Kevin will be fine."

"Thanks again for your support."

"Do you still want to see a movie tonight?" I asked.

"Absolutely. Let's have an early dinner, then go to the Cinema Six. Joey is going to spend the evening at your brother's house playing with

Brittany." My oldest brother, Jamie, has two daughters. Brittany is six and Ryan is eighteen months old.

"There are three different films I've been wanting to see, and they all start around 6:30. We can decide on one when we get there," she said.

"Sounds like a plan. I'd better run," I said, then headed out the door.

❀   ❀   ❀

I read Kevin's letter to my class before lunch time, and as always, they were glad to get news from him. He had included a bit of information about the Iraqi children but had kept the news light. After I finished reading it, I asked if anyone had any questions or comments about it.

Jeremy Smart expressed his sadness for the children, then said, "Miss Kane, I wish there was something we could do to help those kids and the soldiers, too." Several of the students nodded in agreement.

Rufus held up his hand and asked, "Why can't we do something for them, Miss Kane? I saw something on television the other night about people sending stuffed animals to the soldiers to hand out to the kids. Could we do something like that?"

"I saw that same news clip, Rufus. There's a website where soldiers list items that they would like to have, but need help from the public to get them. Are any of the rest of you interested in putting together a package for Kevin's unit?" I asked. Every child's hand went up.

"Okay. I'll talk to the principal, and if she agrees to it, I'll get a letter ready to go home to your parents."

During the lunch hour, I visited with the principal, Mrs. Graves, about the project. My students had insisted on naming it "Care for Soldiers and Children" and she was impressed that they wanted to do it. She said that if my students didn't mind, she would like to bring it before the entire faculty to see if any other classes might want to participate. A meeting was planned that day after school. I told her it was fine with me and thought the children would be in favor of the idea as well.

After lunch, I brought up the issue with my class. At first, some of them were resistant about sharing the project, but after some discussion, they decided that more items would come in if other students participated.

"I think it's a good idea to let the whole school in on it," Heather said.

"I'll talk to my mom about the stuffed animals. She sells them in her gift shop, so maybe she'll help out."

"That's a nice offer, Heather. I'll give her a call and explain the details to her," I said. "Now, let's brainstorm about some items to include in our package." Within a short time, a variety of non-perishable snacks, small toys, paperback books, magazines and other items were listed on the board.

The afternoon flew by, and it was time for the kids to go home. Wanting to leave as soon as the meeting was over, I gathered up some ungraded papers, straightened the desks, then went to the library where the meeting was to be held.

I walked to the table, where Kristin and a couple of other teachers were already seated and pulled out a chair. Mrs. Graves came in followed by a woman I had never seen before.

"Thanks for coming, everyone," the principal said. "We've all worked hard this week and are anxious to start the weekend, so I'll make this quick. Allison's class is starting a project called 'Care for Soldiers and Children.' As you know, Kristin's husband, Kevin, is serving in Iraq, and I think it would be great if we could send a large package filled with items they want."

I hadn't had a chance to share the idea with Kristin, so she was wide-eyed with surprise at Mrs. Graves' announcement.

"Allison has agreed to draft a parent letter to go home on Monday outlining the plan," she continued. "I'm going to give her a chance to share some of the details with you now."

I mentioned some of the items my students had come up with to send. As I talked, the teachers' nods and notetaking were encouraging. After answering a few questions, I turned the meeting back over to Mrs. Graves.

"Please let me see a show of hands from those of you who are interested in joining her class in this effort," Mrs. Graves said. Every hand in the room went up. "Alright, Allison, after the letter is ready, please give it to me and I'll sign it, then have the secretary run the copies. You indicated that you thought a February 28th deadline would be sufficient time for things to come in, and I agree. With the experience I've had over the years with Elliott Kane parents, I suspect we'll have several boxes of goodies to send to Kevin's unit. Now, let's get to the last item on the agenda."

Before she could continue, Kristin stood up and said, "Mrs. Graves, I'd like to say something, if you don't mind."

"Certainly, Kristin, go right ahead."

"I think it's wonderful what you're proposing to do for Kevin's unit. You've all been so supportive and kind to me since he's been gone and I appreciate it so much. Thank you for caring and for your prayers. We're both grateful."

"Kristin, we are the ones who should be grateful for the sacrifice both of you are making for us. This is only a small token of our appreciation to him and his unit. It's the least we can do for our own," she said. "Now, on a lighter note, I'd like to ask Mrs. Carpenter and Miss Miller to please stand."

Jennie Carpenter, who is eight-and-a-half months pregnant, struggled to her feet with the help of hands around her.

"Jennie's blessed event is due in about a week, and I believe she has gone far beyond the call of duty to still be teaching this long. Let's all give her a round of applause," Mrs. Graves said. "While she's on maternity leave, DeLana Miller will be taking over her first-grade class. She was kind enough to come in this afternoon to go over plans and meet the students, despite a mishap with her car in getting here. She was anxious to meet all of you as well. Before you leave, please take a moment to come up and introduce yourself to her. Have a nice weekend everyone."

She walked over to Miss Miller and shook her hand as other teachers started toward them.

"Let's go meet Riley's temporary reading teacher," I said to Kristin. I pushed my chair under the table. As we made our way to the front, the room was emptying quickly. When we reached the substitute teacher, I stretched out my hand to her. "Hi, welcome to our school. I'm Allie Kane, and I teach third grade down the hall."

"Kane? Are you related to the person that this school was named for?"

"Elliott Kane was my great-great grandfather," I said. "He was the founder and teacher of the first one-room schoolhouse in this area."

"And I'm Kristin Sinclair, Allie's cousin," Kristin said, stepping forward. "I teach kindergarten. If there's anything you need, or if you have any questions, you'll find the teachers here are helpful and friendly. We're glad to have you on board."

Miss Miller smiled and said, "Please call me DeLana. I already feel at home here, and I haven't even reported for work. I'm looking forward to filling in for Mrs. Carpenter. She's been terrific at showing me around, and she's so organized. I hope I can do her students justice."

Jennie waddled over and said, "I know you'll do fine. I have a great group of kids. As I told you, the students change classes for reading and I have the accelerated group. One of the brighter ones is Riley Winters, who is a cousin to both Kristin and Allie. She knows where I keep things and has offered to help you if you need it."

The four of us walked toward the door leading from the library.

"Ladies, I'm ready to start my weekend. How about you?" I asked. Among murmurs of, "You bet," and, "I sure am," we waved goodbye, and Kristin and I walked to the parking lot.

"Why don't I follow you home, then we'll take my car to dinner and the theater," Kristin said.

"Fine with me."

Traffic was light, and we reached my neighborhood in no time. When I drove by the Davises' house, I glanced over and saw Luke using a shovel to pound the dirt in the flowerbed where Ginger had been digging yesterday morning. The birdbath had been moved from the center of the yard to the bed and was crowded among last summer's dead foliage. He looked up and grinned at me. I turned my head and sped toward my house.

I pulled into the driveway and got out and locked my car door. Kristin pulled in behind me.

As I climbed into her car, she said, "What was that all about? That scraggly-looking guy had a smile on his face a mile wide."

"Let's drive out the other direction and I'll fill you in about him."

I proceeded to tell her about the bloodied shoe, the confrontation at the car wash and about the incident in the yard the night before.

She pulled up in front of the Mexican restaurant and parked. "I know you're independent and like to handle things yourself," she said, "but if I were you, I'd call Frankie and ask him to check out those people."

I thought about it for a minute. "You might be right. He kind of owes me a favor."

My cousin, Frankie Janson, is a detective in the Paradise Police Department. The favor I was referring to had to do with an incident that happened last fall.

Just before Halloween, some of the cars on my street were being hit with eggs. Every morning for a week, several of my neighbors were finding runny goo on their vehicles. Though the officers were doing more patrolling, they hadn't caught the culprits. Aunt Edith and I decided they needed some help. She is the head of the Neighborhood Watch on her block, but nothing was happening over there. Itching to do something, she offered to help in my neighborhood.

One night after dark, we sat in her four-wheel drive pickup, watching for the egg throwers. We played *Eye Spy*, sang our own version of "Ninety-Nine Bottles of Root Beer on the Wall" and ate a whole bag of cheese doodles. About 9:00, as we were polishing off some cream-filled chocolate cupcakes, I spotted a rusted green Chevy Nova coming toward us with all four windows down. The arms of the occupants were hanging out on both sides, even though it was only forty degrees outside.

"Aunt Edith, look," I said. "Don't you think it's a little cool for those boys to be cruising with all the windows down?"

"You've got a point there," she said as four eggs flew through the air and hit Mrs. Scaletta's minivan.

"It's them! Now what?" I asked. Though we were great at stakeouts, we hadn't formulated the plan of action if we saw the people involved.

"You call 911 and I'll stop them," she said. She started the truck and shifted into drive.

While I was dialing, I said, "Wait a minute. What do you mean, 'stop them?'" The words were lost in the air as my head slammed back against the headrest.

The truck reached forty miles an hour in less than sixty yards, then fishtailed. Sitting sideways in the street, blocking the path of the Nova, I heard a voice on my phone saying, "911, what's your emergency?"

"Rita, this is Allie. Please get a patrolman over to my street right away. We've caught the kids that have been throwing eggs all week."

"Allie, what do you mean, 'we've' caught them? Please don't tell me you and your Aunt Edith are playing vigilante again."

"Well, we happened to be out here and kind of cornered them," I said. "But we really need one of your guys to take it from here."

"There are two units a few blocks from you. I'll tell them to get over to your street right away. Don't do anything until they get there!"

As I was about to tell her that we wouldn't, Aunt Edith opened her door and climbed out.

"Aunt Edith! Get back in here! The police are coming!" All I saw was the top of her curly white head bobbing as she walked toward the Nova.

"Tommy Rosser, is that you in the front seat?" she hollered as she marched up to the passenger side door. "Who else is in there with you? Is that Tim and Jim Wallace in the back? You boys get out here this minute! Come on, I haven't got all night."

The passenger door opened and Tommy climbed out of the car. "Come on you guys. I'm not taking the blame for this alone," he said.

I was surprised when the remaining three boys got out and sauntered to the front of the old car. Towering over Aunt Edith, they stared down at the ground, still several steps from her.

"I'm disappointed in you boys," she said, stepping closer to them. "Do your mothers know what you've been up to?"

Two patrolmen that I recognized pulled up. Feeling better now that professionals were on the scene, I got out of the truck.

"Mrs. Patterson, who have you got here?" Carl Floyd asked, climbing out from behind the wheel of his cruiser.

"I guess these youngsters haven't had enough to keep them busy, Carl, so they've been egging cars," Aunt Edith said.

"I think we can take it from here. You boys turn around now, so we can put the cuffs on you. Tommy, I don't expect your daddy is going to be too happy when he has to come down to the station to get you." He and the other officer starting putting handcuffs on them. "Now you go with Bert here, and he'll get you settled in the patrol cars. I need to visit with these ladies for a minute."

"How's your grandmother, Carl?" Aunt Edith asked. "Still having trouble with her arthritis?"

"She's doing a little better, Mrs. Patterson. I'll tell her you asked about her," he said. "Now I'm concerned about you two being out here looking for those boys. What if they hadn't been so cooperative? You might have gotten hurt. I wish you'd leave the policing to the experts."

"Carl, I've known those boys all their lives. I taught them in Sunday school when they were young tots. They know better than to backtalk me.

They just made some bad decisions this week, that's all. Allie and I were glad to help you guys out."

I guess Carl knew it was pointless to argue with her, so he told us goodnight, then got into his car and left.

Frankie had called me later that night and thanked me for our help in the arrest. But he told me that if I ever did a fool thing like that again, he'd tan my hide.

I decided I would get in touch with him this weekend. It was time to collect on the favor.

CHAPTER 5

After filling up on Tex-Mex, Kristin and I drove to the Cinema Six. We decided on a comedy, and after getting our tickets, I bought a box of popcorn with extra butter and a root beer at the concession stand. Since it was Friday night, the theater was already filling up, but we managed to find two seats halfway down in the middle.

Looking at my treats, Kristin said, "You just ate three tacos, rice, a burrito and drank a large lemonade. I don't know how you could possibly hold another bite."

"You know I can't resist theater popcorn, even if it is covered in artery-clogging butter," I said. "Here, have a handful."

Taking the box from me, she took out some kernels and tossed one into the air, catching it in her mouth. Not willing to be outdone, I threw one up, caught it, and then repeated the motion. The kernel bounced off my cheek and landed in the ponytail of the man sitting in front of me.

Kristin looked at me and started giggling. I reached forward to lift it from the strands of his hair, but then he sneezed, embedding it deeper.

She covered her mouth with her hand to muffle the laughter. I was starting to get tickled myself, but was determined to follow this through.

An older couple next to us saw what had happened. The woman was trying to hide her smile, while the man sitting by me offered some advice. "You might try the straw," he whispered.

His wife elbowed him and hissed, "Stay out of this!" Ignoring her, he winked at me and nodded toward my cup, moving his hand in a scooping motion.

I pulled the straw from my drink and licked off the droplets hanging from it. If I could get it beneath the popcorn, maybe I could flip it off.

Leaning forward, I tried a couple of times, but the rough edges of the kernel were stuck.

While watching Ponytail Man talk to his companion, an idea struck me. I leaned across and told Kristin, "I'm going to try to suck it out."

"You've got to be kidding!"

"Watch me," I said, then leaned toward the man's head. I put the straw against the kernel and starting sucking, forming a vacuum. After a bit of maneuvering, I lifted the piece out and dropped it into my hand. I held it up for Kristin to see. "Not bad, huh? Where there's a will, there's a way."

"You never cease to amaze me," she said, shaking her head.

The man sitting beside me said, "Good job."

I had drawn some curious stares from folks around me, but I didn't care. The mission was accomplished.

"Now I can enjoy the film," I said, taking a gulp of my root beer.

The movie was hilarious, and Kristin and I laughed our heads off. Walking outside to her car after it was over, she said, "This evening has been fun, but your show beat the one we paid for."

"Thanks. Glad I could help."

"For once, I was able to stop worrying about Kevin's situation. And speaking of that, why didn't you tell me about the 'Care for Soldiers and Children' project before the meeting today?"

"I never got the chance. All the credit for the idea goes to my class and Mrs. Graves. With the whole school participating, we should get a lot of neat things to send."

"Kevin and his parents will be thrilled when I tell them," Kristin said.

"In the letter to the students' parents, Mrs. Graves asked me to add a note that cash donations will be accepted. The money will be used for shipping costs, and if enough comes in, she wants to buy some hand-held video game systems and games to send."

"I'm sure the soldiers would love to get some of those. Kevin says downtime can really be boring."

Heading back to my house, Kristin asked, "Have you started making any plans for spring break? Kevin's folks have asked Joey and me to come to their house for a few days that week, and I'm considering it. We haven't seen them since Christmas, and the change of scenery would be nice." Kevin grew up in southern Oklahoma, about two hundred miles away from Paradise.

"I got a call from Traci Morris last night. Her principal is looking for some teachers to teach summer school, and she is trying to get me to apply for the remaining third-grade position." I told her all I knew about it, then asked, "What do you think? Should I go for the interview?"

Glancing at me, Kristin said, "You're telling me you have the opportunity to go to Hawaii for a month, get most of the expenses paid, stay with your best friend and teach a grade that you're familiar with?" Pausing, she shook her head. "I can't believe you haven't already said, 'Yes, I'll do it,' and, 'How soon can I come?' Spending a week there for the interview alone would be terrific!"

When she put it that way, I realized I was overanalyzing an opportunity of a lifetime. By the time we got to my house, I was so excited about the prospect, I didn't know if I would wait until Sunday to call Traci back with my answer.

As we pulled into my driveway and I started getting out of the car, Doug came out his front door. I could see shiny black eyes and wet noses jiggling under each arm.

Heading toward me, he said, "Just the person I wanted to see."

"Allie, this doesn't sound good," Kristin said, stepping out of the car and walking around to hug their cousin. "Hi, Dougie."

"Hi, Kris. Don't worry, this is a good thing," he replied. "I've been helping treat a young boy at the clinic for several weeks now, and today his mother said they just couldn't afford to keep these guys. We agreed on a price, and now I'm a proud dog owner."

"Oh, Doug, they're precious!" I said, taking one of the puppies from him.

"They're sweeties alright. But on the way home I happened to remember that I have a date tonight and wouldn't feel right leaving them alone their first night in new surroundings," he said to me. "So, how about sharing custody?"

Always a sucker for cute animals, I held the puppy closer as it licked my chin.

"I guess I'd be willing to do that. How old are they?"

"They're four months old. The one you're holding is the male." He passed the second pup to Kristin. "That's the little girl. I haven't named them, yet, so I'll let you two decide on what to call them."

"Have you bought anything for them?" I asked.

"As a matter of fact, I have. I went to Pet's Market on the way home and bought a basket bed, some puppy chow, some food and water dishes and a couple of chew toys." He held up his hand, and two fingers were wrapped in gauze. "But two toys may not be enough."

"Okay, if you'll bring over their supplies, I'll keep them the first night."

"I was hoping you'd say that, so I took the liberty of setting everything in your kitchen a few minutes ago." Doug and I had exchanged keys to each other's units when we first moved in.

"That was nice of you, Doug," Kristin said, grinning. "Come on, Allie. I'll help you get your new children settled."

"If you think of anything else they need, let me know, and I'll pick it up tomorrow," he said. "My date is expecting me at 9:00, so I need to run."

As he walked toward his car, I called out, "Doug, I've got to take Aunt Edith to a viewing tomorrow afternoon, so you'll need to baby-sit."

"That's fine. I'm going to install a doggie door in the garage, so I'll be around. I bought one for your side door, too, in case you wanted it."

"That's a good idea. That way they will be able to go in and out of our garages from the backyard. Good thinking."

"I thought so," he said, getting into his car. We waved at him, then carried the puppies inside.

Kristin filled their dishes with food and fresh water while I started getting acquainted with them. Sitting on the floor next to them, I watched the male devour his cup of food while the female daintily chewed hers.

"That one is precious," Kristin said. "That would be a good name for her."

"Yes, it would," I said.

I watched the puppies explore their new surroundings. The female didn't stray far from the kitchen, but the male began nosing at some magazines on the floor in the living room. When one slid off the stack, catching his front paw, he started barking at it like it was an enemy. He didn't hush until I walked over and started stroking his head.

"You're a rowdy little guy, aren't you? Don't worry, this mean old magazine won't hurt you," I told him as I put it back on the stack.

He continued staring at the pile as if daring it to move. Content that he had won the battle, he pranced over and laid down next to his sister.

"I guess I'll go home," Kristin said. "I'm going to e-mail Kevin with the news about the project. It's bound to lift his spirits. See you at the cookoff tomorrow."

After seeing her out, I locked the front door. Turning to the pups, I said, "Let's go outside and I'll show you your new bathroom. The sooner you're potty trained, the better."

Opening the kitchen door leading to the fenced backyard that Doug and I shared, I coaxed them outside. They were cautious at first, but soon began wandering around the small perimeter, staying close to each other until they found a spot suitable to do their business.

I heard Mrs. Googan's back door open, and Ginger came bounding off the porch. When she saw the puppies, she came over to the fence to investigate. Newly weaned, the puppies must have been missing their mother, because they cozied up to the area of the fence where Ginger was sticking her nose. Reaching through the fence, I scratched her between the ears while she and the puppies got acquainted.

"Ginger, it's time to come in now," Mrs. Googan called from the backdoor.

"She's over here with us, Mrs. Googan," I hollered. "Doug brought home two dachshund puppies, and she's getting to know them."

Mrs. Googan stepped off the porch and walked across her yard. "Ginger is quite motherly. She sleeps with an old rag doll and often carries it around the house. But lately, she's been acting more like a puppy, digging out beneath the fence and going to Grumpy's next door." She pointed to the Davises' house. "I hope she doesn't teach your dogs her ornery ways."

"I'm glad you told me. I'll let Doug know that we may need to reinforce the bottom of our fence if they start digging out."

"Just so that you are aware, I called the police on the new neighbors last night," Mrs. Googan said. "It was about midnight, and you never heard such yelling and foul language in your life! It sounded like someone was getting killed."

"I guess they're still alive, or we would have heard about it. Maybe the visit from the police will do them some good," I said, picking up the two pups. "Well, it's time we said goodnight."

"Goodnight, Allie. Sweet dreams." She and Ginger turned and walked toward her backdoor.

The puppies and I got to know each other a little better while watching the late local news over a bowl of butter pecan ice cream. I made a mental note to pick up some dog biscuits, but, not wanting to hurt their feelings by eating in front of them, I gave each of them a lick off my spoon. Just as we finished our snack, the phone rang.

"You weren't in bed, yet, were you?" Michael asked.

"No, we were just watching the news and eating dessert." I set the bowl on the coffee table and plopped down on the floor. Both puppies settled into my lap, allowing me to scratch their tummies.

"We? Do you have a guest tonight?"

"Not anything that dramatic. Doug bought two puppies, then talked me into sharing ownership. He had a date, so I have them tonight. I'm already getting attached to them, and it will be nice to have someone meet me at the door when I come home."

"Riley has hinted about wanting a dog, but I've been able to hold her off by adding more bird toys from time to time," he said. "Speaking of which, she said you wanted her to bring Flip and Fluff for show-and-tell sometime."

"It would be a great ending for our unit. It will probably be the week of state testing, but I'll give you an exact date later."

"That's fine. Thanks again for carting her around yesterday."

"I was glad to do it."

"So, what else is going on?"

I filled him in about Aunt Edith's elixir dilemma, and we laughed about Riley's "winky" remark. I also decided to share my news about the spring break interview.

"What a great opportunity! Now you'll be able to get some sun and maybe meet a handsome surfer or two in the bargain," he said.

Leave it to Michael to bring up the lack of male companionship in my life.

"Traci and I will probably go to the beach, but I don't plan to attach myself to any surfers. I'm missing her a lot, and it will give us some time to catch up."

"Do you remember Richard Kahala, the exchange student from Hawaii?" he asked.

"As a matter of fact, Traci told me that his aunt is the principal at her school. I remember he was cute, and the two of you teased Kristin and me mercilessly when he was here."

"Oh, yeah, we did, didn't we? Anyway, we still keep in touch, and I'm sure he'd get a kick out of seeing you again. I'll give you his phone number. You should give him a call while you're over there."

"It seems funny to be making plans and I haven't even got the interview, yet."

"Knowing Traci, I'm sure she'll get you in," he said. "Then after you get there and show the charm you inherited from the Winters' side of the family, you'll get the job."

Listening to Michael, I remembered that modesty wasn't a Winters trait. Before hanging up, he told me he wouldn't be at the chili cookoff the next day because he had been rear-ended at lunch time and was taking his car to get a couple of estimates.

When I got off the phone and was getting ready for bed, I decided to set the alarm for 2:00. I figured the puppies would need to go out for a potty break by then. I placed their basket next to my bed, and after they each pawed the cushion and circled it a few times, they curled up together and fell asleep.

I took a quick shower, then climbed into bed, burying myself beneath the cozy comforter.

Trying to breathe through a straw in a pool filled with popcorn, I was disoriented when the alarm went off. Shaking myself from the dream, the only light in the room was the illumination from my clock, and it took me a minute to remember why I had set it for 2:00. Reaching over the edge of the bed, I touched the head of a sleeping puppy, but couldn't find the second one.

I switched on my bedside lamp and saw Precious looking up bleary-eyed at me, but scanning the room and under the bed, I had no luck finding her brother.

Grabbing my robe from the end of the bed, I slipped on the sneakers I had removed earlier and knelt down next to the basket. "Sorry to pull you out of bed at this time of night, little girl, but you need to go outside. Let's go find your brother."

I carried her down the hallway, and as we got closer to the living room, I could hear a scratching sound. It got louder as I walked around the back of my recliner. When I turned on the lamp by the chair, a surprised puppy with a mouth full of padding stared back at me.

"Oh no, you don't," I said as I scooped him up with my free arm. "You've got chew toys, and you're not going to tear up my furniture, you little squirt."

He had torn a small piece of foam loose from the seat, and, after retrieving it from his mouth, I set it on the kitchen table. I could see something wet on the floor and realized he had had an accident.

"We're going outside," I told them. "I don't want any more puddles tonight."

I unlocked the sliding glass door and carried them into the backyard. A strong wind had come up, so after setting them down, I retied the sash on my robe. Realizing I needed to go to the bathroom myself, I said, "Hurry up, guys. You don't need to check out the whole yard."

Precious finished her chore, then laid down at my feet. While we waited for her brother, he started barking and running toward the fence. I caught sight of a movement in the Davises' yard. In the shadows, I could see a glowing cigarette and realized we were being watched.

Following the pup to the fence, I reached down and scooped him into my arms. "Okay, buster, time is up."

Holding him against my chest, we started toward the back porch. I glanced back and saw that the man had moved out of the shadows and into the alley that runs behind our yards. Grabbing Precious on the way, I hurried inside, then closed and locked the door.

"Well, that's done," I said, setting them on the floor. They both trotted over to inspect their dishes. Until my nerves settled, I knew that sleep was out of the question, so I walked to the pantry and scooped out some kibble for each of them. While they ate, I cleaned up the accident on the floor.

When they finished eating, I coaxed them back to their basket in the bedroom. Once the lights were off, I tried to get comfortable and go to sleep, but I couldn't shake the uneasy feeling I had about my neighbor.

Before Thursday, I'd never seen the guy. Now he kept turning up like a bad penny, and I wasn't sure it was a coincidence.

It seemed like I had just dozed off, when the puppies woke me. Daylight was filtering through the shades and as much as I wanted to sleep in, I knew it wasn't fair to make them wait to go outside. I followed them to the back door and felt it would be safe to let them venture out on their own. When I opened the door, they dashed out when they saw Ginger in her yard. Yipping all the way to the fence, I decided Rowdy was a perfect name for the boy.

I went back to the bedroom to get dressed, and I found a lot of empty hangers when I opened my closet door. Sure that the laundry fairy wasn't coming, I sorted two loads and carried them to the laundry room that was connected to the kitchen. As I passed by the window, I checked on my charges. They were busy exploring the yard, so I started the washer, tossed in some detergent and some colored clothes. I left the remaining socks, pajamas and underclothes in a basket next to the machine.

The puppies began scratching and barking at the door to be let back in. "Okay, hold on, I hear you," I said, walking toward the door.

They bounded through the kitchen, straight to their empty bowls. They looked up at me like neglected children, so I pulled their food from the pantry and put some in their dishes, adding a few extra morsels. I re-filled their water dishes, then poured myself a large glass of orange juice and took my vitamin.

As the puppies were finishing breakfast, I checked on the washer and was anxious to get to the furniture in the garage. I remembered that the sweats I had worn while working on it a few nights ago were still lying on the chair in the bedroom. I went to put them on, then grabbed a large bar-rette from the top of my dresser and clipped my hair out of my face.

I walked into the kitchen and said, "I'm going to be busy for a little while. You two be good and take a nap or play with your toys."

Acting as if they understood exactly what I had said, they both wagged their tails and barked.

Within thirty minutes, I had finished all the sanding. Wiping my hands on some rags, I walked back into the kitchen and saw Precious chewing on one of the toys. When I didn't see her brother, I called, "Here Rowdy; come here, boy."

I walked to my bedroom, thinking he might be asleep in their basket.

He was in it, but not asleep. While grasping one of my bras with his front paws, he was ripping it with his teeth. One cup was torn from the under-wire while the other cup hung in shreds.

"I'm going to scob your knob," I said, pulling it from him. Fortunately, it wasn't one of my best bras, but I was low on underclothes and would now be forced to go shopping for more.

Having lost his toy, he stood on his back legs and began lunging at a dangling strap. I saw a pair of panties beneath him, with strings of elastic ripped from the waistband.

"Okay, that's it. First my recliner and now my clothes. I'm going to tell your Uncle Doug that we've got to have a crate for you to stay in when I can't watch you."

Precious had come to the bedroom door to check out all the commo-tion, then walked over and began licking my ankle.

"Why can't you be nice, like your sister?" I said, rubbing her head.

Grabbing the panties from the basket, I tossed them and the ruined bra into the trash can next to the dresser. Just then the doorbell rang and they bolted toward the door, barking at the visitor.

"Saved by the bell," I said as I followed them into the living room.

I opened the door, and Doug walked in carrying two bags.

"Good morning, Aunt Allie. How was your night with these cuties?" He knelt and patted Rowdy's head, then stroked the back of his sister.

"The night wasn't bad, if you don't count the hole in my recliner and one accident. On top of that, I just caught Rowdy shredding a set of my underclothes."

"Rowdy, huh? Sounds like the name fits him. I'm sorry he's been tearing up stuff. I'll look into some obedience lessons for them."

"That's a good idea. But, I have to admit they are great company. It's kind of nice hearing the click of little toenails in the house."

Holding up the bags, Doug said, "I brought some donuts for us and some doggie biscuits for them. I also bought a large carrying crate, which I put in my garage. It sounds like it will come in handy when we're not around to watch them, don't you think?"

I took the donuts from his hand and said, "Great minds think alike."

Before joining me at the table, Doug laid several biscuits in each of the puppy's dishes, then peeled off some paper towels from the dispenser on the counter. I had put saucers and tumblers at our places and carried over the carton of milk before sitting down. Diving into the sack of donuts, neither of us said much until several had been devoured.

"Thanks, that hit the spot," I said, licking the last of the chocolate icing from my fingers.

"My pleasure. I only bought a half dozen this time because we'll be eating chili in a couple of hours."

Looking at the cuckoo clock, I said, "I still need to put the last coat of varnish on the furniture in the garage so it can be drying. That way you can help me move the pieces into the spare bedroom tomorrow after church. Also, I've got laundry going, and I'll have to shower before picking up Aunt Edith."

"Okay, I get the hint. I need to do a few things before the luncheon, too." He picked up the puppies and started toward the front door. "I'll take these two off your hands for the rest of the day. Just keep all the stuff I gave you. I bought more this morning to keep at my place." He stepped onto the porch, then turned back to look at me. "Since I'm going to help you with the furniture, how about fixing lunch for me tomorrow?"

"I've got it covered," I said. "I've invited Kristin and Joey to come over, and I'm going to fix those wraps we all like." I made a mental note to myself to stop at the store after Mr. Connerson's viewing.

"Sounds good," he said. "See you later."

Closing the door behind him, I knew if I didn't get some clothes dried, I wasn't going to have anything to wear to the luncheon. I tossed the wet load into the dryer, added a softening sheet and then headed back to the garage to finish the furniture.

I was admiring my finished project when I heard the dryer buzzing. I had already cleaned up my mess and thrown away the stained papers, so I went inside to wash my hands. Glancing at the clock, I realized I only had thirty minutes before I was supposed to pick up Aunt Edith.

I emptied the dryer, tossed in the second load, then rushed to the bedroom. I threw the clothes on the bed, opting to fold them later. Stripping off my sweats, I headed toward the shower to wash my hair.

Out in three minutes flat, I wrapped myself in a towel, zapped my hair with the blow dryer, and then pulled it into a ponytail. I dabbed on a little blush and mascara, then headed to the bedroom to get dressed.

While standing by the bed, I heard the sound of a door closing. I listened for a few seconds, thinking that maybe Doug had come back for something for the puppies.

"Doug, is that you?" Met with silence, I pulled the towel tighter around me, then walked toward the living room. "Doug?"

I didn't see anybody, so I thought I must have imagined the sound or heard a noise from outside. "Okay, Allie, now you're hearing things."

I turned to go back down the hall and gasped when I saw ashes on the floor near my recliner. I hurried over and checked the front door and found it unlocked. It is my habit to keep the door bolted when I'm alone, but I didn't recall doing it after Doug left. I locked it, then peeked out the front window. Seeing no sign of anyone, I realized that an intruder could still be in here with me.

Beside my front door, I have a peace lily in a huge brass pot. Still trying to hold the towel together, I heaved the flowerpot up onto my hip. The rooms in my place are large and open, except for the bathrooms and spare bedroom. Since I had just come from my bedroom, that only left the other two rooms where someone could hide. While lugging the plant down the hall, I flipped on the light in the guest bathroom, but didn't see anyone there. Turning around, I tiptoed toward the guest bedroom. When I reached the closed door, I put my ear against it, but couldn't hear anything.

Okay, it's now or never, I thought. Tucking the end of the towel so that it would stay put, I clutched the flowerpot tighter, then turned the knob and shoved open the door.

Relieved when I found the room empty, I sank to the floor, still holding the plant in my sweaty hands. I hadn't wanted to bop someone on the head with the pot, but hey, sometimes a girl has to do what a girl has to do. Looking toward the doorway, I saw another reason to be thankful that no one was here. My towel was lying in a wad on the floor.

CHAPTER 6

Driving to Aunt Edith's, I decided it was time to call Frankie.

"Paradise Police Department."

"Hi, Rita. It's Allie. How's it going?"

"Actually, pretty slow for a Saturday morning, and that's just how we like it. No reports of domestic disputes, which is rare, but hey, the day is young."

"Is Frankie around?"

"As a matter of fact he is. He was out earlier, but came in about twenty minutes ago. Hold on, and I'll transfer you back there."

"Thanks. I appreciate it."

While waiting for Frankie to come on the line, I pulled into Aunt Edith's driveway and did the honking thing.

She came out the front door and walked down the steps. Getting into the car, she looked at me and said, "Don't you look spiffy."

Still holding on the phone, I said, "Thanks, but I feel kind of thrown together. You look nice. Is that a new dress?"

"Yes, I was downtown dropping off some stuff at Goodwill and passed by Mary Jane's Boutique. She had a sign on the window that said 'Think Spring,' so I went inside to see what new stuff she had. I found a nice dress for Easter as well as this one. Also, I splurged and got this pretty little pillbox hat." She patted each side of it and smiled. "They were all bargains, and she offers a senior discount, too."

I heard a clicking on the line. "Please excuse me a second, Aunt Edith."

Frankie came on and said, "Isn't this a surprise. What's going on?"

"Can't a girl call her cousin without having a special reason?"

"Yeah, she can, but with you it's rare."

I knew he was right, so I said, "Well, this is one of those rare times. Aunt Edith and I are on our way to the chili luncheon. If you'll come, I'll buy your lunch."

"Well, I hadn't planned on lunch today, but I can't pass up an invitation like that."

"We'll be there in a few minutes, so I'll go ahead and buy our tickets."

"This must be important if you're willing to buy my lunch. I'll meet you in a few minutes."

"See you then," I said, then switched off the phone.

"A friend coming to meet you?" Aunt Edith asked.

"That was Frankie. Since he's working today, I thought I'd treat him to lunch."

"Well, isn't that nice. One of Paradise's finest will be eating at our table."

When we reached the Senior Citizen's Center parking lot, I had to drive around three times before I found a spot. This is a popular event, and even though the judging and serving didn't start for a while, people were already flooding in.

Aunt Edith and I walked in with some seniors using walkers and canes. I held the door for them to go ahead of us. As I fell into step with her, she whispered, "I'm sure glad I don't have to use one of those things. That would cramp my style."

When it was our turn at the ticket table, I saw Frankie walk in the door. "You go ahead, Aunt Edith. I'll be there in a minute."

She nodded at me, then walked away. I saw her wave to my parents and other family members already seated at one of the long tables.

"Just in time," I said as Frankie walked up beside me. "Here, have a ticket."

"Thanks. Don't mind if I do." He took hold of my arm and led me a short distance away from the ticket line. We stopped near a small table that had some *Senior Living* magazines laying on it. Two plush chairs were pushed under the table. He pulled out one of them. "Here, have a seat and tell me why you called."

"You get right to the point, don't you?"

As I relayed the information about my recent encounters with Luke

Davis to him, he started frowning. When I reached the part about the ashes and searching for an intruder on my own, he let me have it.

"What in the world were you thinking? You could have been hurt, or worse, if you had found someone." He paced back and forth for several seconds. "If you suspect someone is in your house, get out of there! If you have your cell phone, call 911. If you don't, run to Doug's or Mrs. Googan's. Don't wait; just do it!"

In hindsight, I guess I hadn't made the best decision, but at the time, it didn't seem so wrong.

"Okay, so I made a little mistake in judgement," I said. Frankie's stern expression didn't waver. "Okay, a big mistake. Since Mrs. Googan has already called the police to come out once, can you tell me anything about this guy?"

"I'll look at the report when I get back to the station, but you know that I can't tell you much about it."

"I know, confidentiality and all that. But you can at least let me know if he's an ax murderer or out on parole for some crime." I decided to try a more persuasive tactic. "You know I have a right to this information, since I help the Neighborhood Watch Commander on our block." This was stretching it a little. I would have to be sure and attend the next meeting and volunteer more.

"Really, since when?"

Standing up, I said, "The length of time isn't important. You know I've always had a keen interest in keeping my neighborhood safer." He couldn't argue the point, because he knew it was true.

"Okay, I'll see what I can find out."

Feeling better now that Frankie was aware of the weird things happening on our street, I looped my arm through his. "Now, that's enough business. Let's go join the family and have some of Gramma's chili."

I laughed with my cousins until my sides ached and ate so much food, I had to unbutton the top button on my slacks. The judging of the various types of chili was hilarious. My dad tried to control his facial expressions after eating Mrs. Hastings' jalapeno blend, but after drinking his entire glass of water, he grabbed mine, then my mother's. After all of that, I saw him by the dessert table gulping down a can of Pepsi.

On the other hand, Grandpa never drank more than his own glass of water, but I overheard Nana say, "A.J.'s trying to act macho. He'll be asking me for the extra-strength Maalox as soon as we get home."

After saying our good-byes, Aunt Edith and I left a little before 2:00 for Mr. Connerson's viewing. Grandad and Uncle Clarence were planning to come, too, but were driving over a little later. All three men had served together on the "Helping Hands" committee at church, doing handyman type home repairs and painting projects for widows and the senior members.

Driving to the funeral home, Aunt Edith said, "I'm going to miss hearing Ray's bass voice in the church choir. Even at his age, he could sing better than a lot of other people."

"He did have a nice voice," I said. "I enjoyed his solo during the Christmas cantata."

When I pulled into the parking lot at Simpson's Funeral Home, I saw several other church members getting out of their cars. I waved at those closest to me as Aunt Edith fell into step with Daisy Johnson just ahead of me.

"It's so nice that you took time to bring Edith here today, Allie, but I'll be glad to take her home," Daisy said. "I'm sure a pretty girl like you has lots of things planned on a Saturday with young people your own age."

Though she didn't say it, I knew she meant "young men." "Thanks for the offer, Miss Daisy, but I'll stick around until she's ready to leave."

Ever since Aunt Edith forgot to renew her driver's license almost a year ago, she catches rides from another family member, Miss Daisy, or myself. Despite not having a license, she has been known to drive herself to church, or to the store, claiming she doesn't want to trouble anybody to come and get her.

But Miss Daisy isn't a great alternative, either. She's eighty years old and drives forty on the highway. She often hits curbs and doesn't slow down at yellow lights. One time, she and Aunt Edith drove to Tulsa and were all the way to the turnpike before they realized they had missed their exit eight miles back. Therefore, I try to do the majority of Aunt Edith's chauffeuring, and she seems to enjoy our time together.

We had just walked in the front door of the funeral home and signed the guest register when, out the window, I saw Grandad's pickup pulling into the lot. "I'll wait here for Grandad and Uncle Clarence if you and Miss Daisy would like to go on back," I told Aunt Edith.

"Yes, I think we will," she said. "I'm sure Ray will have a lot of visitors."

I watched the two ladies walk down the hallway, past the chapel and into one of the rooms. When Grandad and Uncle Clarence came in, they were going to have to wait several minutes behind other guests to sign the register. I chatted softly with them as they moved forward in the line, then directed them to the room that Aunt Edith and Daisy had gone into earlier. I told them to take their time and I'd sit in one of the chairs by the chapel and wait for them.

After they left, I sat down and watched people walking by. I exchanged a few words with the folks I knew. Within fifteen minutes, Grandad, Uncle Clarence and Daisy came walking back down the hallway toward me.

"Where's Aunt Edith?" I asked them when they reached me.

"She left us about ten minutes ago for the ladies room," Daisy replied. "I thought she'd be out here by now."

Getting an uneasy feeling in the pit of my stomach, I said, "I think I'll go check on her to make sure everything's alright."

As I headed toward the restrooms, I heard a blood-curdling scream, then someone yell, "That body moved! Help someone! That body moved!"

This couldn't be good. I hurried toward the room from where the scream had come, and just as I reached the doorway, a large woman came barreling through it, mowing me down. She never looked back and continued yelling as she ran down the hallway. I sat dazed on the floor.

I took some deep breaths, then grabbed the doorknob and pulled myself up. Inside the room, the walls were lined with caskets. This wasn't a viewing room, but rather a storage room.

All the coffins were open except for one. In the far corner, the lid was closed on a pink one that was decorated with roses on the handles. Moving toward it, I heard a tapping sound and felt the hair on my neck bristle. I stopped in my tracks when I saw the lid slowly rising. A wrinkled hand appeared and started waving at me.

I nearly wet my panties when a voice behind me barked, "Hey, you're not supposed to be in here!"

Spinning around, I saw Jessie Simpson standing with his hands on his hips. Jessie and I had gone to high school together, and I hadn't seen him since our five-year reunion. Since then, he had gained at least fifty pounds and looked like a sack of potatoes in the black double-breasted suit. The pants were too short, and his white socks glowed in the fluorescent light.

As recognition set in, his scowl was replaced by a smile. "Hey, Allie, long time no see," he said, moving toward me.

"Hi, Jessie." I tried to think of a reasonable explanation to give him for being in there. "So how are Myrna and the kids?"

"Oh, the old ball and chain is pregnant again, and all four kids are growing like weeds."

"I forgot you worked here."

"It takes a lot to feed a family of six and one on the way, you know." He grinned and moved one hand in a sweeping motion. "But, I've got a sweet job here with Uncle Tony, so I don't have to worry. I'm training to take over the business when he retires, so I'm set for life."

More like set with death, I thought.

"We're big into pre-planning here; never too early, if you ask me. Looks like you're shopping, so let me show you this little beauty that just came in last week." He started walking toward the pink casket. "Really feminine, this one is. In fact, my grandma is getting one of these."

"I didn't realize your grandma passed away." I stepped in front of him, blocking the path to it.

"Oh, no, she's still chipper over at the Paradise Retirement Center," he said. "But she can be making payments on it now, so it won't be hard on us family members once she kicks the bucket."

"She's lucky to have such a caring grandson, like yourself, Jessie." *Sheesh!* Just then, I heard a squeaking sound behind me.

"Hey, did you hear something back there?" Jessie asked as he tried to look around me.

"No, I didn't hear a thing." Taking hold of his elbow, I turned him toward the opposite wall. "You know, maybe I should start thinking about pre-planning. How about showing me what you have over here?"

As we started walking, there was a *squeeeak* and then a *bang!* Spinning toward the noise, Jessie's eyes grew wide, then he slumped to the floor.

"Man, it was getting hot in there!" Aunt Edith said. "Allie, can you please give me a hand?"

Jessie was out cold, so I released his arm and moved toward the pink coffin. I got there just as Aunt Edith's legs swung over the edge. "Aunt Edith, what were you doing in there? You nearly scared us to death!"

"Just trying it on for size," she said. "After I left the ladies room, I was passing by and saw the door open and thought, 'No time like the present.'"

Standing next to me, she brushed some wrinkles from her dress and adjusted her hat. Stepping over Jessie and proceeding through the door, she said, "Well, I'm ready to go now. How about you?"

I was tempted to follow her, but when I heard Jessie stirring, I changed my mind and thought I had better make sure he was all right.

"What happened? What am I doing on the floor?" he asked.

As I reached down to give him a hand, he nearly pulled me over before he was able to steady himself. He rubbed the back of this head where it had hit the floor and began to look around the room.

Afraid he would put two and two together, I said, "You scared me when you collapsed like that. Do any other of your family members have fainting spells?"

"I don't think so, but maybe I'd better check into it," he said, still rubbing his head. "But now that I think about it, something weird in here caught my eye. Then the next thing I know, I'm looking up from the floor."

"Hmmm. Well, you might want to take it easy the rest of the day."

"Yeah, that's a good idea. I'll tell Uncle Tony I need to take the rest of the day off. I'll go home and have Myrna fix me a nice big dinner, then I'll relax in front of the TV all evening with my feet up."

Lucky Myrna, I thought. "I need to be going, Jessie. Take it easy."

"Thanks, Allie. Remember, when you get ready to start your burial planning, be sure and come back and let me help you."

"Thanks. I'll keep it in mind."

Walking toward the entrance, I saw my family standing in the front foyer talking with some other visitors. When I reached them, Daisy looked at me and said, "Here's Edith, dear. You must have missed each other. Did you get lost?"

Aunt Edith kept her eyes averted when I said, "No, I was talking with Jessie Simpson. Trying to smooth some ruffled feathers, you might say."

"He's such a nice young man with such a promising future," Daisy said. "Too bad he's got a wife."

Considering pregnant, overworked Myrna, I thought, *Yes, it's too bad.*

Giving Grandad and Uncle Clarence a hug before we left, I told them I'd see them at church the next morning. On the ride to her house, Aunt Edith talked about how nice Mr. Connerson looked. We both avoided talking about the incident in the storage room. I knew there was no need to rehash it. Aunt Edith would always be Aunt Edith, and I was used to it.

I dropped her off at her house, then drove home.

Pulling into the driveway, I saw Doug in his garage, crouched down by the side door. As I walked inside, he reached into his toolbox and pulled out a large screwdriver.

"How is the installation of the doggie doors going?" I asked.

"Just tightening the last screw on the frame."

Standing up, he brushed off the knees of his khakis, then with a sweeping of his hands, sang, "Tah dah."

I walked past him and bent down to examine his handiwork. Doug has always been good with his hands, so I wasn't surprised to find a job well done.

"Good, job. Have you already done the door on my side?"

"Yes, I started there. I put the dogs in the backyard with an old beach ball that I found in the closet because they kept getting in my way."

"I think I'll walk around back and check on them," I said.

Opening the door and stepping into the backyard, I called to the puppies. When they didn't come running, I continued around the corner of the garage. They were busy digging a hole under the fence.

Walking toward them, I said, "What are you two doing?" Precious acted like she had been caught with her paw in the cookie jar. However, Rowdy was so intent on his digging, he didn't notice me until I reached down and touched his tail. He yipped and jumped a foot from where he had been tunneling.

"I see you grew tired of the beach ball and started getting into mischief. You've got this whole, big backyard to explore and play in. The grass isn't always greener on the other side of the fence." I thought about the new neighbor two doors down. "Come on. Let's go tell Uncle Doug what you've been doing and see if we can nip this in the bud."

With their tails tucked, they followed me back into the garage. Doug was putting away his tools and gathering up trash.

"We need to reinforce the bottom of the fence, or I'm afraid Heckle and Jeckle are going to escape," I told him. "Ginger has been coaching them in the fine craft of digging, and it won't take much of a hole for them to get out."

I took Doug out back to see what they had done. He said that, on Monday, he would go to the feed store and pick up some chicken wire to put around the sections that led to the street and alley. It didn't matter if they dug into Mrs. Googan's yard, because it was fenced.

"You guys are getting expensive," Doug said while holding their chins and looking them in the eye. "If you're not careful, Aunt Allie and I will be having some super-sized hotdogs for dinner." He ruffed up the hair on their heads, and I could tell they weren't worried a bit.

"Speaking of meals, do you have a request for dessert tomorrow?" I asked.

"If it's not too much trouble, how about baking a pie?"

Mentally extending my shopping list, I said, "Okay, how about coconut cream? I know it's one of Kristin's favorites. If Joey doesn't like it, I have some cookies he can eat."

"I love that kind," he said.

"Coconut it is, then." I looked down at the dogs. "Come on, kids. Let's go home."

Leading them through the open garage to my front door, I grabbed the mail before going inside. I closed and locked the glass door and left the wooden door open. It was such a beautiful day, I wanted to let in some sun.

The dogs followed me into the bedroom, where I changed back into my sweats, then I hung up the rest of the laundry lying on the bed. I retrieved the remaining load from the dryer, folded and put it away, then changed my sheets. Still in the domestic mode, I tackled both bathrooms and ran a dustcloth over all the furniture.

"Ready for a break guys?" I asked. I realized they hadn't been under my feet for a while, so I went looking for them. I guess they were tuckered out from watching me do all that work because I found them curled up together in their basket, sound asleep. I touched each head, then went to the kitchen for some root beer.

With my drink in hand, I switched on my stereo, then stretched out in my recliner. "Surfin' Safari" by the Beach Boys was playing. Staring out the glass door at the clear blue skies, I thought about ocean waves and sandy beaches. After a few minutes, I felt two wet noses nuzzle my hand.

"Did you two have a nice nap?" I asked, reaching down to scratch their ears.

Without answering me, they trotted over to the sliding door. Either they were catching onto the potty training idea, or they loved their new backyard. At any rate, there were fewer accidents on my floors.

"I'll call Uncle Doug and ask him to keep an eye on you while I go to the store," I told them, sliding open the door. "Behave yourselves and remember, no digging."

I knew they would probably do whatever they wanted to do, despite my admonishment. After calling Doug to watch them, I drove to the store.

When I reached Wal-Mart, I found a spot close to an entrance and went inside. Drawn by the smells from the deli, I couldn't resist picking up some fried chicken and macaroni salad for supper. I picked up the things I needed to finish Sunday's lunch, along with some frozen dinners, milk and shampoo. Then I headed to the speedy checkout line.

Scanning the tabloid headlines while waiting my turn, I felt a hand basket bump into my leg. A voice said, "Sorry about that."

I turned and was startled to see Luke standing there. Though the store was crowded, I felt uneasy by his close presence.

"That's okay," I said, facing forward, relieved that I was next in line.

"Did you find everything you needed?" the young associate asked me.

"Yes, thank you."

Not willing to be put off, Luke said to me, "Why is a pretty girl like you grocery shopping on a Saturday evening? You should be out dancing and partying and having a good time."

I ignored him and pretended to be occupied reading the label on one of the frozen dinners I had chosen.

He moved closer to me. "I've got a job tonight, but I'd be happy to take you out some other evening, Miss Kane. I could show you a time you'd never forget."

Not in this lifetime, I thought.

The associate looked at me, then at him, probably wondering what kind of relationship we shared. She must have noticed my troubled expression because she said, "I sure am glad the rain stopped for a while. How about you?"

Focusing my attention on her, I said, "Yes, it was a pleasant change today."

"That comes to $21.52, please," the girl said.

I handed her some bills, then she gave me my change. "Thank you for shopping at Wal-Mart. Have a nice evening."

"Thanks, you, too," I said, gathering the bags from the spindle.

"Yes, you have a real nice evening, Allie," Luke called out. I headed toward the door, and never looked back.

I hurried toward my car and saw that his wrecker was parked next to it. Tossing the bags in the front seat, I got in and locked the door. After pulling out of the parking space, I looked in my rearview mirror and saw him walk out of the store. He raised his hand and waved.

"And don't forget to bring st___ ___ ___ ___ others," Ruth's hollered ___
___ one started out the door.

"Thank you, Ruth," I said. "See you tomorrow."

Quiet settled over the room, and I ___ ___ I sorted sets of papers. When
I finished, I walked to the workroom ___ ___ into ___ a new shirt, hidden
in ___ that I had bought. Before ___ ___ ___ ___, ___ was turned out ___.
___ ___ out of the workroom, I ___ ___ ___ ___ ___ ___ tucked ___
___ inside the door.

"How did your first day go? ___ ___ ___ ___," I said as she walked
toward me.

"It was great," she said, smiling. "I ___ been teaching first graders,
and these kids are eager to learn. I ___ ___ to ___ ___ _We Were Not the
Only Ones_ _How We No Good, Long Road_, ___ ___ to ___ ___ ___ ___ reading
group I work on, and it's one of my favorite ___."

My third-graders enjoy their ___ ___ too ___.

"Two of the kids needed ___ ___ ___ ___ ___ ___ the vocabulary, and
___ ___, Riley, proved to be ___ ___ ___ ___ ___ ___ ___ comfortable
___ ___ with them, and it gave me the ___ ___ ___ ___ ___ ___ each of the ___.
She also helped me find the ___ ___ ___ ___ ___ ___ ___ ___ that we
needed for the store scene in Riley ___."

"I bet she was thrilled to g___ ___ help, ___ that you're enjoying the ___.
They're ___ at that age," she ___, "___ ___ ___ ___ ___ third-graders."

Delana glanced at the wall clock ___ ___ ___ ___ ___ rude, but I ___ ___
___ appointment with your cousin ___ ___ ___ ___ o'clock for a car." She
___ ___ pink message slip. "The girl ___ ___ ___ message for me to call ___.
I hope my insurance company ___ ___ ___ ___ I ___ plumber's about ___ ___
___."

"I've got to get going, too," I said. "See you in the morning."

"Have a nice evening," she said ___ ___ ___ moving to the front door.

I carried the bulletin board I made ___ ___ ___ ___ ___ ___ in I set them on the
___ ___ table, then gathered my ___ purse and jacket, heading to the office
___ ___ but I remembered that ___ ___ ___ ___ ___ ___. Aunt Faith had asked
me to call her. It had slipped my mind ___ ___ ___ ___ ___ ___ ___ I would pick
up some of our favorite Chinese food and take it over.

A block from the restaurant, I ___ ___ ___ ___ ___ to be sure she wasn't
already cooking something. She picked up after ___ ___ ___ "Hello?"

"Hello?"

CHAPTER 7

When I got home, I emptied the sacks and heard the puppies barking outside. I glanced out the kitchen window and saw them running the fence with Ginger.

I started mixing pie ingredients and boiling chicken. Things went smoothly until I knocked over the canister of flour and had to drag out the vacuum sweeper to clean up the mess. By the time I had mopped the kitchen floor and wiped off the cabinets, it had grown darker outside. I looked out the glass door, but saw no sign of the puppies. I figured Doug had brought them in.

I walked into the living room and turned on the television to watch the evening news. The pie was cooling on a wire rack, and all the lunch items were ready and back in the fridge.

There was a knock on the door. When I opened it, Doug was standing there with the two dogs. He was dressed in a pair of black slacks, a blue shirt and striped tie.

"Boy, it smells good in here," he said. "Do you need me to sample something, perhaps the pie, just to be sure it's edible?"

"Sorry. You'll have to wait until tomorrow. You sure look nice. Your date tonight must be a special girl."

"I clean up pretty good," he said, ignoring my remark about the girl.

Doug had never been stuck on his good looks, nor bragged about his dates. Despite his busy social life, he was conscientious about making good grades in medical school, and he had told me that he wasn't ready for a permanent relationship.

"The pups dug another hole under the fence, but I saw it and filled it with dirt," he said. "You might not want to leave them out alone too long tonight."

"Thanks, I won't."

"Well, I'd better get going. Don't want to keep the lady waiting," he said, stepping onto the porch. "See you at church in the morning."

"Good night. Have fun."

After he was gone, I turned out the porch light and pulled all the shades. I fed the dogs, then took the deli food from the fridge. Though tempted to cut the pie for dessert, I knew Doug would be all over me if he saw a wedge missing when he came back tomorrow.

I let the dogs out, then I ate while working on the letter for school. Engrossed in the composition, I lost track of time until I heard the pups scratching at the door.

I opened it and Precious trotted inside. Rowdy stayed outside tugging on something.

"What have you got there, boy?" I asked, stepping onto the porch.

His teeth were clamped onto an object as big as he was. Looking closer, I recognized the sneaker from Luke's porch. Though the pup was reluctant to give up his toy, I managed to pry it from his jaws. I guess he thought that his prize was in good hands, so he ambled inside and laid down.

With the help of the kitchen light shining through the glass, I could see that the outside of the shoe was caked with mud, while the insole was soaked with a red slimy goo. Not wanting the nasty thing in my house, I dropped it on the lawn chair. I went into the kitchen and scrubbed my hands, then put on some rubber gloves. I switched on the porch light, then grabbed some paper towels before going back outside.

With the added light, I could see a scrap of white beneath the tongue of the shoe. I reached inside and pulled the cloth free. It was a sock wrapped around something with a horrid smell.

Setting the shoe back on the lawn chair, I started peeling back the shreds of cloth. *Thud!* I gasped and stepped back when I saw a big toe lying on the porch. I couldn't believe my eyes! Starting to feel light-headed and queasy, I sat down on the step and put my head between my knees. I wasn't crazy about touching the thing again, but I certainly didn't want it on my porch. Using the sock, I picked up the toe and stuffed it back into the shoe.

Knowing I could have contracted any number of diseases, I peeled off the gloves and tossed them into the trash can under the sink. I scrubbed my hands with hot water and disinfecting soap, then dried them on a paper towel. Tossing the paper towel into the bag, I tied it up and carried it out to the large container in the garage.

When I got back to the porch, I stared at the shoe with the white lump sticking out and tried to decide what to do next. Any rational person would call the police right away, but my curiosity was outweighing rationale.

I walked back into the kitchen. "I'm going to be gone for a few minutes," I told the pups. "You two stay out of trouble."

I grabbed a flashlight and a trowel from the garage, then headed out the front door. It was very dark outside due to the thick cloud cover. I switched on the flashlight, then cupped my hand over it to reduce the glare. I walked across Mrs. Googan's yard and stopped when I reached the hedge. Logic was telling me to turn back. Ignoring its pleas, I plunged ahead.

The Davises' house was dark and quiet as I knelt by the flowerbed. The storms had dug deep valleys in it, and when I shined the light into the hole where the shoe had been, I saw some long, white threads. Taking the trowel, I dug deeper into the hole, revealing a piece of dirty cloth. Sure that it was more of the sock, I reached in to pull it out.

Just then, I heard the rattling of the wrecker and saw its headlights coming up the street. I fumbled to turn off the flashlight, then started looking for a hiding place.

With time running out, I dove under the hedge. I tried to hold down the springy branches to conceal my light clothing. The beams from the headlights swung across the yard. When the truck was parked, I fought to quiet my heavy breathing as its occupant emerged from the cab. In the shadows, I could see him pulling some cables on the back, then he walked to this side and adjusted some ropes.

Intent on holding down the branches, I dropped the flashlight. I watched it roll from beneath the hedge and hit a metal figurine sitting nearby. The loud *ding* broke through the stillness of the night.

Luke had been walking up the sidewalk, but stopped and turned toward the noise. He looked at the bushes. Sure that I was caught, I shifted my legs and prepared to roll out and start running. But instead of advancing toward me, he took a step toward the azaleas and bent down. Standing back up, he looked around the yard, then walked to the porch. As he ascended the steps, he was patting his thigh with my trowel!

When I heard his front door close, I waited for what seemed like forever to come out from my hiding place. Crawling out from under the hedge, I picked up my flashlight and hightailed it home.

"You have *what?*"

"I have a sneaker with a man's toe in it," I repeated for the third time. I had already explained where it had come from, how the shoe got here, and how I had come across what I thought to be the rest of the sock in the flowerbed. Why he was having me repeat it again was beyond me.

"Just keep everything where it is," Frankie said. "I'll call a judge and get a warrant to search that yard, then I'll be right over."

"Okay, see you in a bit," I said.

While waiting for him to arrive, I gathered up the Sunday school materials that I would need for my class the next day. It was hard to concentrate on the lesson because the image of the bloody toe kept coming back to me.

Relieved when I heard the police cars out front, I flipped on the porch light and opened the door. I saw Frankie and a man in green scrubs walking across my lawn.

Once they were inside, Frankie introduced me to the county forensics specialist, Walter Lane. Getting right to the point, Walter said, "If you'll lead the way, Miss Kane, I'd like to see what you've got. I'm sure you'll be glad to get it out of your way."

That's an understatement, I thought. "Come right through here," I said.

We walked through the kitchen to the back porch. I stayed out of the way while they inspected the shoe. Wearing latex gloves, Walter placed it and the contents into a large plastic zipper bag. He scribbled something on a white label that he had removed from his pocket and stuck it to the bag.

As we all walked back to the front door, Frankie said, "We're going to serve this warrant and see what we can turn up. If we make an arrest, I'll need you to come down to the station and give a statement."

"I want to go over there with you," I said.

"You can't interfere with a police investigation, Allie."

Looking out the door, I could see several neighbors standing around watching the police in the Davises' front yard. "I'll just stand out there with the other neighbors and observe. I promise I won't get in the way."

Looking at the crowd forming, he relented. "Okay, you can watch with Mrs. Googan and the others for a while. Then, I want you to go home, go to bed and get some sleep."

Walking with Frankie and Walter across Mrs. Googan's yard, I joined Davy and his parents, along with the elderly couple from across the street. They were huddled near the hedge where I had hidden earlier.

I watched Walter get into his car with the "package." Frankie joined a patrolman and another detective talking to Luke on the porch. I shifted my attention to the flowerbed. There were two policemen setting up flood-lights around it, and two more were starting to dig out the azaleas.

"What do you suppose has happened, Allie?" Mrs. Googan asked.

While watching every scoop coming out of the bed, I told Mrs. Googan about the shoe, the toe and my suspicions about the senior Mr. Davis.

"You think Luke killed his father? Oh, how awful!" she said.

Just then, the two men in the ditch yelled at the detectives. The patrolman moved closer to Luke while Frankie and the other man walked toward the plot. Kneeling down, Frankie said something to the men, then pulled out his cell phone.

I was itching to see what they had found and was finally able to catch his attention. He started walking toward us, disconnecting his call as he reached our group.

"Well?" I asked him.

He took hold of my arm and pulled me a short distance away from the neighbors. "They uncovered a leg. I just called the medical examiner."

A leg? Oh, brother!

"We won't dig any further until the M.E. gets here and the crime technicians get what they need."

"Frankie, how could anyone kill his father and bury him in front of their house? That's sick!"

"Don't jump to conclusions. We asked Luke about his father, and he claims he's in Missouri visiting relatives for a few days. We'll check it out and wait to see what forensics says about the items that you gave us. Now would you please help me out and go tell your neighbors that you're going home to bed and suggest they do the same? It may be awhile before the M.E. gets here."

"Okay, I'll see what I can do."

With the trying events of the day, I was drained. It was all I could do to put one foot in front of the other. It was after midnight, and I wanted to go to bed and leave the stress of the day behind me. I walked back to the yawning group still milling around the yard. I told them that I was going home and recommended they do the same. After a few "Good nights," they all went their separate ways.

As I stood there alone, Frankie came over and put his arm around me. "I'm sorry about this, kiddo. I know it must have been a shock."

Clinging to him, I felt the emotional dam burst, and tears rolled down my cheeks. Brushing them aside, I stepped back as the medical examiner pulled up next to us.

"Please let me know what you find out," I said.

He nodded at me, and I turned and walked to my house. Once inside, I locked the door, turned out all the lights and went to the bedroom. After pulling off my muddy clothes and slipping into my pajamas, I went into the bathroom to scrub my face and the remaining traces of dirt from my hands.

The puppies were asleep in their basket as I knelt beside the bed to say my prayers. Exhausted, I crawled under the covers and fell into dreamless sleep.

It was another sunny day when I awoke on Sunday morning. The episode of the night before was a foggy memory. While the dogs took care of their business outside, I showered and fixed my hair. They were excited to find breakfast waiting in their bowls when they came back in. While they gobbled it down, I took time to eat a piece of toast with apple butter on it and drink a glass of milk. When I finished, I brushed my teeth, put on my makeup and dressed for church.

It was time for me to leave, so I brought in the crate from the garage and set it by the sliding glass door. "You two are going to stay in here while I'm gone," I told them.

Their floppy ears wiggled as they scampered over to me, not realizing what was in store for them. I felt guilty cooping them up, but I wanted some furniture free of holes when I returned from church. I reached inside the crate and pulled out some new rawhide bones.

"Here you go. You can have fun chewing on Uncle Doug's gifts while you look out the glass door."

Once they were inside the crate, they began howling when they realized I was leaving them there. But by the time I had gathered together my Sunday school papers, they had quieted down and were chewing on the bones.

As I drove by the Davises', the mound of dirt and deep ruts made by vehicles the night before created an ugly scene. A world away from this destruction of life, I was anxious to get to the warm refuge of my family and friends at church.

After arriving, I walked down the hall toward my classroom. I could hear the choir practicing for the morning worship service. Humming along, I was busy setting papers and crayons on the small tables for my students and didn't hear my parents come up behind me.

"We hear you had quite a scare yesterday," Dad said. "I wish you had come to stay with us last night."

Turning to look at them, I could see the concern on their faces. "I take it Frankie called you."

Nodding at me, Dad said, "He called this morning after questioning that Davis fellow at the station most of the night."

Mom put her hands on my shoulders and kissed my forehead. "You're an independent young lady, and we know you love adventure, but please remember we're always here for you."

"I know you are, and I appreciate it."

Some of my students were beginning to arrive. "We'd better get to our own class, Maggie," Dad said. "It's Sister May's turn to bring breakfast, and I'm starving."

The ladies from their Sunday school class take turns bringing breakfast treats. You can smell the coffee and hear laughter coming from that room long before the starting bell rings.

"See you in the sanctuary later," I said.

Turning my attention to the students, I taught the lesson about Paul and Silas singing in prison. We enjoyed snacks and did crafts, then the time was gone. I gave each child a parting hug, then after picking up the room, I joined Kristin and my parents in the sanctuary. Michael led praise and worship, and the sermon was about "all things working together for good." By the time it was over, I felt encouraged and ready to conquer another week.

While Kristin went to retrieve Joey from Kid's Church, I mentioned Traci's call to my mother. I told her that I was planning on going to Hawaii for the interview.

"That's exciting, Allie," she said. "Why don't you come over for lunch and tell us all about it?"

"I appreciate the invitation, but I'm fixing lunch for Doug, Kristin and Joey. I'll come by the shop in a couple of days and fill you in."

"I'll look forward to it," she said. "Now, I'm going to see if I can find your father and drag him home."

I spotted him, along with Grandpa A.J., Uncle Clarence and Grandad, across the sanctuary in the middle of a group of other men. They were laughing and having a big time, so I knew that Mom and my grandmoth ers would be hanging around for a while longer. People talk about women being gabby, but we don't compare with the men in our family.

I waved at Gramma, Nana and Aunt Edith, who were standing in the aisle a few yards away visiting with some ladies from the quilting circle. They all waved back, then Aunt Edith put her hand to her ear and mouthed, "Call me."

I nodded, then went to join Kristin, who was motioning to me from the side door.

She and Joey followed me home. I could hear the puppies barking from inside the crate before I got the door unlocked.

"Okay, okay, I know you want out. Just a second," I said. I walked over and unlatched the door.

You would have thought they had been imprisoned for days—instead of a few hours—the way they came darting out. As they jumped on my legs and begged for attention, I rubbed their heads. After a few moments, they noticed Kristin and Joey and bounded over to meet the guests.

"Mom, look! Aren't they terrific?" Joey said. On his knees in a flash, it was love at first sight. "What are their names, Allie?"

"The boy is Rowdy and the shy one is Precious."

Watching her son roughhousing with the dogs, Kristin said, "They're cute, alright. If it's okay with Allie, why don't you go into the backyard and play with them while we get lunch ready?"

"Good idea," I said. "I'm sure they need to go out. Joey, there's a beach ball out there, if you want to throw it for them."

He headed toward the door and slapped his hands on his thighs. "Come on, Rowdy and Precious. Let's go play ball." The three of them ran out the door, never looking back.

"He sure likes dogs, doesn't he?" I said. I started removing food from the refrigerator and setting it on the table.

"Dogs and every other kind of animal," Kristin replied, taking plates from the cabinet. "When he stayed at your brother's Friday night, they watched the *Homeward Bound* video, and all I've heard since picking him up yesterday is how much he wants a pet. But with my allergies, dogs and cats are out of the question."

"He's welcome to come over here and play with the puppies anytime he wants to, and I'm sure Riley would share Flip and Fluff with him." Just then, there was a knock on the door. "That's probably Doug. Would you please let him in?"

Kristin set the plates down and started toward the door. Before she got there, it opened and Doug's head popped inside.

"It's me. You forgot to lock your door again."

Remembering yesterday's ashes on the floor and everything else that had happened, I should have learned my lesson. "I'm feeling a little more secure, I guess, since our neighbor is locked up."

"Locked up?" Kristin asked, looking from Doug's face to mine.

"Allie had quite a night last night," Doug said. He sat down at the table and helped himself to some olives. "Didn't she tell you about it?"

I relayed the events to them as if it was any other day in my life. But I knew I wasn't fooling them with my nonchalant attitude.

"At least that strange guy is in custody now," Kristin said. "Maybe you won't have to deal with him anymore."

"I hope not," I said. "Lunch is ready. Do you want to see if you can tear Joey away from the puppies long enough to eat?"

While Kristin coaxed her son inside, I asked Doug about his date. As usual, he didn't offer much information. He said her name was Cheryl, that he had met her in medical school and that he had taken her out a few times over the past two weeks.

Seeing his chance to switch the subject when Kristin and Joey came back inside, he asked, "Have you heard from Kevin lately?"

Kristin is always delighted to talk about her husband. She was looking over Joey's shoulder at the sink to be sure all the grime was being washed off. "I got a letter last week. He misses us as much as we miss him, and he's eager for his two-week leave. Unfortunately, that won't happen for at least a couple of months."

After the rest of us sat down at the table, Doug said grace, then we passed around the Oriental wraps. I had also fixed a chicken Caesar salad and warmed some pork and beans. From our loaded plates, it looked like none of us had eaten in days.

After several minutes of quiet as we assuaged our hunger, Doug said, "This is delicious, Allie." Kristin and Joey nodded in agreement. "I see on the counter you have coconut pie for dessert. I get dibs on a big piece, because I know once Kristin gets hold of it, that's all she wrote."

"Look who's talking," Kristin said. "It's a good thing the rest of us got some wraps right off the bat, because you had five of them."

"Hey, I'm a growing boy, but you have to watch your girlish figure. When Kevin comes back on leave, you want to walk, not roll to the plane to meet him."

"Don't fret yourself about that, Mr. Growing Boy," Kristin replied. "I've actually lost eight pounds since seeing him at Thanksgiving."

Not wanting her to dwell on Kevin's absence, I said, "We're starting to work on a project at school, Doug. We hope to collect lots of goodies to send to Kevin's unit. With extra money that comes in, the principal wants to buy a couple of Game Boys to send."

"That's great," he said. "In fact, I'd like to make the first contribution. I've got several games for those units that I haven't played in ages. If you don't mind sending used games, I'll give you four or five of them."

"Thanks, Doug, that's sweet of you," Kristin said.

"Yes, that's very generous. I hadn't thought about asking for used games. I'll add that to the letter that's going home. Now, who wants pie?"

By the time the four of us had finished with dessert, only crumbs were left in the pie plate. I scraped them into the puppies' dishes, along with a few scraps of leftover chicken. Cleanup was a breeze since everyone pitched in.

With the kitchen clean, we went into the living room. Doug sat down in my recliner and was soon snoring. Joey played on the floor with the puppies. Kristin and I lounged on the couch talking, then when we realized Joey and the dogs were curled up asleep, too, we decided to take naps ourselves.

When Doug woke up an hour later, he stretched and said, "Wake up, everybody. That furniture's not going to move itself in here."

Rousing ourselves from sleep, we all trudged to the garage. The pieces weren't heavy, but they were bulky, and it took some maneuvering to get them through the doorways without scratching them. Joey's job was to keep the dogs out of the way.

Once the dresser was in place, Doug and Kristen carried in the headboard and bed frame. Doug asked me where I wanted the headboard to go, and I pointed toward the west wall.

He set it down in the middle of the floor. "Hey, Joey. If this was your room, where would you want the bed to go?"

"I'd want it over there," he said, pointing to a different wall. He acted like it made him feel important that he had been consulted; I could tell because his chest puffed out a little.

"Me, too," Doug said.

I looked at Doug, then at Joey. "Why there?"

"So the sun wouldn't shine in my eyes through that window and wake me up," Joey said. Doug nodded his head in agreement.

I realized they were right. "Good thinking, guys. Let's put the bed over there."

Doug winked at Joey, and I helped him and Kristin set it in place. Surveying the finished room, I said, "I appreciate everyone's help today. I'll order a mattress set this week so that my nieces and cousins can sleep over anytime they want to."

"That will be great, Allie," Joey said. "I'll be glad to come over anytime and help you take care of Rowdy and Precious."

"I'll keep that in mind," I said.

Kristin winked at me, then turned to Joey. "We'd better get going, son. Gramma Winters told me at church this morning that she has a big jar of her chili leftover from the contest that she wants to send home with us. By the time we stop there for a few minutes, it will be close to dark before we get home."

"Terrific! Now I'll get to tell Grandad about the puppies and how I helped you all today." He walked over to his mother and started pulling on her hand. "Come on, Mom, what are you waiting for?"

"Thanks for lunch and a great afternoon, Allie. We've enjoyed it," Kristin said, giving me a hug. "And it was nice seeing you, too, Growing Boy."

"Yeah, I had a good time, too," Doug said. "I might have to borrow that recliner of yours sometime, Allie. It's great for naps."

We all walked onto the front porch, and I watched Doug chase Joey to the car. He tickled him while helping him with his seatbelt. As Kristin pulled into the street, Doug pointed a finger at me from the driveway. "Lock your door."

"I will, don't worry," I said. I watched him walk up his front steps, then I went inside and secured my door.

The cuckoo clock had just struck five, so I decided there was time before dark to take the dogs on a quick walk. I try to walk or ride my bicycle several times a week, but with all that had happened in the last few days, I hadn't been able to do either. I walked into the bedroom and changed from the dress I had worn all day into some sweats. After lacing up my jogging shoes, I grabbed the leashes from the pantry.

Since Doug and I had owned the dogs, they hadn't been walked on a leash, so I didn't intend to go far. Clipping the straps onto their collars, I said, "Let's get some fresh air, you two." Locking the door behind me, I attached the door key to a springy cord around my wrist, and off we went.

At first the dogs pulled against each other, but it didn't take them long to get the hang of what they were supposed to do. We stopped a lot because they wanted to check out every new odor they found, but we still made decent time.

"Let's go around the block and back home from the other direction," I said. They were game, so we turned the corner and plowed ahead. I stopped to chat for a few minutes with the neighbor who lives behind me, then we continued on our way.

When we turned the corner that put us back on our street, I had no apprehension about passing the Davises' house. It felt good to relax for one night while Luke was being held at the police station.

The sun was setting and darkness was closing in. When we were in front of their house, I thought I caught a glimpse of light coming through one of the shades. Since no one was supposed to be there, I decided it must be the last rays of sunlight hitting one of the panes of glass.

As we started up our driveway, I saw Davy helping his mother carry in groceries. I turned around when she called to me. She motioned for me to come over, so I led the dogs across the street, where she met me at the end of her driveway.

Standing near the streetlight, she asked me a few questions about the body that had been found the night before. I could tell she was nervous about the whole thing, so I assured her that Frankie and the other officers wouldn't rest until the case was solved. I said goodnight, and then the dogs and I went home.

After unleashing them, I turned on the lamp next to my chair to ward off the gloom of darkness that had enveloped the room. As I walked into the kitchen, I said, "How about some dinner, guys?"

Without waiting for their reply, I walked to the pantry for their food, then rinsed and refilled their water dishes. I made myself some tomato soup and a grilled cheese sandwich, then carried it all on a tray to the living room. Switching on *60 Minutes,* I watched a story about conjoined twins, then turned over to a funny home video show. As soon as it went off, I set my dishes in the sink, then went to my computer to check on some flight times to Hawaii.

With some choices in hand, I flopped down in my recliner to give Traci a call. When she answered, I said, "Yes, I want to come, and how long can I stay?"

"You don't mince any words, do you?" she said, laughing.

"If you had been in my shoes the last couple of days, you'd be ready to fly off to paradise, too," I told her. I filled her in about the toe and the events of the night before.

"This calls for a change in scenery. I'll talk to Miss Kahala first thing in the morning."

"I can't wait!" I said. "Do you think you can put up with me for a week?"

"It will be a sacrifice, but I'll try," she teased. "The interview with Miss Kahala will only take an hour or two, then the rest of the time you're here will be your own."

"There's a flight leaving Tulsa at 9:00 a.m. on Saturday the twelfth, and it reaches Honolulu about three."

"I'll pass that information along to her so her assistant can get it booked," she said.

Our conversation turned to what kind of clothing I would need to bring and places we might visit. She told me that she planned to take me to a quiet beach that she and Tommy had found on Saturday.

After hanging up, I grabbed some paper and a pencil from the kitchen and started a shopping list of things I would need for the trip. Before going to the bedroom to inventory what outfits I already had, I walked to the front windows to close the shades. Glancing out, I was shocked to see Luke Davis!

He was leaning against the streetlight in the Scaletta's yard, smoking a cigarette. While staring at me through the window, he saluted with a pointed metal object. My knees grew weak when I saw that he had my trowel! He tossed the still glowing butt across the street and into the edge of my yard, then turned toward his house. I flung the shades closed, leaving them swinging in protest.

I jumped when the phone started ringing. My heart was beating a mile a minute, so I took a couple of deep breaths, then walked over and picked up the receiver. When I tried to say "hello," only a squeak came out of my mouth.

"Allie? Hello? Allie, are you there?"

My shoulders relaxed a little when I recognized Frankie's voice. "Yes, I'm here." I took another deep breath. "I just saw Luke Davis staring at my house from across the street. Why didn't you let me know he was out of jail?"

"I've tried to call you ten times in the last hour, but your line was busy," he said. "If I hadn't reached you this time, I was driving over to tell you that we had to release him. His story checked out about his father being in Missouri. We asked the St. Louis police to go to the address of the old man's brother, and sure enough, he's been there for over a week. He told them that he's coming back to Paradise on Friday."

"So if the body isn't Luke's father, who is it?"

"I hope we'll find out more when the DNA report comes back from the lab, but right now we're looking at someone associated with the previous tenants. The landlord gave us an emergency contact number for a cousin of the woman who used to lease the house. She lives in Tulsa, so we'll try to find the former tenants through her."

"You mean the Sanders," I said.

"Did you know them?"

"We would wave if we saw each other, but I was only in their house one time. Last fall, Mrs. Sanders gave me some clothing to put in the church rummage sale. While I was there, I met her husband and his Uncle Fred. I had seen the uncle in their porch swing a few times, and he always smiled and waved when I drove by."

Frankie was quiet for a moment. "The body was buried in peat moss. Peat is aseptic and kills a lot of the bacterium that causes decomposition. Along with the help from the cold weather, the facial features are still intact. I hate to ask you this, but would you be willing to go to the morgue with me and see if it's the same man you saw on the porch?"

I don't like to look at dead people. Even though I take Aunt Edith to viewings, I don't go into the rooms with her. It's not that I'm afraid, I just like to remember the person still full of life.

"What about Mrs. Sanders' cousin? Why don't you ask her to identify the body?"

"We did, but she refused," he said. "She doesn't like to look at dead people."

I was silent for a moment. "Okay, I guess I can do it. When do you want me to come?"

"The sooner the better. How about on your lunch hour tomorrow?"

Oh, great. Eat a sandwich and look at a dead guy. "Okay. I'll meet you at the morgue about twelve."

"Thanks, Allie. By the way, I let Luke Davis know that we're aware of his interest in you and warned him to keep his distance. That's probably why he was on the other side of the street. We could pick him up for loitering, but he could say he was just taking a walk."

"It's okay. I'll let you know if he does anything more than look. See you tomorrow."

"I'll be waiting for you," Frankie said. "Good night."

Several questions popped up, along with comments from the guys — it's not safe for a girl to travel alone, so they offered to come along as bodyguards. Most of the girls were excited for me, though feigning fears that I would come back brown as a biscuit while they remained lily white. Aunt Emily cornered Uncle King and wanted to know why he didn't ever take her somewhere exotic like Hawaii. Of course, Dad, Michael and Doug gave me a hard time about keeping my head and not letting some Polynesian Romeo steal my heart away.

"I think it's time for dessert," I said, trying to turn the attention away from me.

Taking my lead, my aunts stood up to start gathering up the dirty plates, while Gramma and Nana were told to go sit and not to join in on the sweets. While picking up dishes and setting out silverware from the drawer, I overheard Uncle Jake ask Michael if his Lincoln was in the shop again.

Not yet," Michael replied, "It's almost finished. Before I got word from the agency who put me that her insurance company was going to allow Barney to do the job, his was the lowest estimate... and the one who I was almost sued that it was rejected in the first place. I am leaving the car off in the morning and get a loaner car."

Jamie came in from the living room carrying my niece, Ryan. I took her from him, and she started fingering the buttons on the front of my blouse. I planted kisses on her soft, downy curls.

"You need to stop doing that," my brother said to me. "You're going to make her hair fall out."

Ha ha, you're so funny," I said, nuzzling her silky strands. "It will grow in thicker now that you're messing it."

Sitting down across the table from Michael, Jamie said, "Is the woman you're after you a blonde, Michael?"

He looked up and stuck out my tongue at him. Since I'm a blonde, as none of the cousins are, it's rare that a new blonde joke isn't told at the family dinners.

Giving me an innocent look, Jamie said, "What?"

No, she has auburn hair," Michael said. "But she dropped an envelope outside her car that had a picture of two blonde kids in it. Does that count?"

"Close enough," Jamie replied. "Did you learn about the pretty blonde

CHAPTER 8

I pulled into the parking lot behind DeLana Miller on Monday morning and waved at her as I parked my car next to hers.

"Ready for the big day?" I asked as we met at the front of her car. I noticed her crumpled front fender, but didn't say anything about it.

"Excited, willing and able." She motioned toward the fender. "This is what happened on my way out here last Friday. Unfortunately, the other guy's car looks worse."

As we walked toward the building, she told me that she had had a lunch date with her brother, who works at a downtown bank in Tulsa. She had been looking for a parking spot when the Lincoln she was following stopped at a red light and she rammed his back bumper.

"That's too bad," I said. "I hope no one was hurt."

"Just my pride. I've had a perfect driving record, until now. The guy didn't say a lot, but behind those brown eyes, I could tell he was upset, and I don't blame him. He was dressed in a beautiful black suit, and his car was spotless. He had too much class to put me in my place, though he had every right to."

As we walked into the building, I said, "I hope you get everything straightened out. My cousin Pauley is a great mechanic and works at a body shop here in town, if you need an estimate for your insurance company."

"Thanks," DeLana said. "I might let him take a look at it."

While we were in the office signing in, I gave the Care project letter to one of the secretaries for Mrs. Graves' approval. Turning to go to my classroom, I told DeLana, "Off to the trenches. Have a good first day."

The morning lessons went well. Some of the students had brought snack items and sports magazines to kick off the campaign. During my planning period, I found some boxes and made a banner to put up near the display case as a constant reminder of the project.

After taking my students to the lunchroom, I drove the short distance to the morgue while sipping on a cold Diet Pepsi. In light of the task ahead, I wasn't up to eating. As I pulled in, I saw Frankie waiting for me at the bottom of the steps leading to the service entrance. I parked my car, then walked over to join him.

"I appreciate you taking your lunch time to do this," he said. "We haven't had any luck tracking down the Sanders, yet. The cousin said they moved to southern California, but wasn't sure what city."

Walking into the cool, dark building, I fought the urge to turn around and run. Goose bumps were forming on my arms and legs, and it wasn't the temperature causing them. Trying to shake off my uneasiness as we walked down the hall, I asked, "Have they determined how the man died?"

"The coroner didn't find any superficial markings from a stab or gunshot wound," Frankie said. "We're still waiting for all the lab results to come back, but he's confident it's cirrhosis of the liver. The indicators point to the guy drinking himself to death. There were some hairs that weren't his on the clothing, so we're hoping they belong to the person who buried him."

We stopped outside two large aluminum doors, and I took a deep breath. Frankie turned to me. "This shouldn't take long, and I'll be right there with you."

I nodded, then followed him into the large room. The first thing I saw was a stainless steel autopsy table in the center. Off to one side, there was a glass cabinet full of scalpels and other tools of the trade. An empty gurney rested perpendicular to the wall holding the refrigerated compartments. There were eight drawers in it, and I found it disconcerting that any or all of them could be holding dead bodies.

After Frankie greeted the medical examiner, he led us to drawer number six, which was marked with a white tag that read "unidentified white male." Releasing a latch, he pulled out the drawer with a draped form lying on it. The doctor looked at me. "Are you ready?"

Not really, I thought, but nodded anyway. As he pulled back the sheet, I directed my gaze to the man's chest, then plunged ahead and looked up as far as his neck. Taking a deep breath, I forced myself to look directly into his face. The closed, sunken eyes were enveloped by pasty skin. Thin, stringy hair clung to the scalp, and bits of stubble covered his chin. As I continued staring at him, I half expected him to jump up and ask me if I was getting an eye full. Taking a step closer, I looked him square in the face. "I don't know this man," I said.

With a puzzled expression, Frankie looked at me. "Are you sure? There has been some decomposition, so maybe you should take a second look."

Willing to give it another shot, I leaned over until my nose was only about a foot from the corpse's. Spider veins, like roads on a map, covered his cheeks and nose. I stepped back and said, "That's not Fred Sanders. This guy isn't big enough to be him. Besides, Mr. Sanders had thick, white hair and this guy is nearly bald."

"Well then, we're back to square one," Frankie said.

He thanked the doctor, then we walked back through the double doors and out the way we had come in. When I pushed open the outside door, I breathed in fresh air and tilted my head up. Sunlight never looked so good!

As Frankie walked with me to my car, I asked, "Now what?"

"We'll keep trying to find the Sanders. The medical examiner placed the time of death at about four weeks. That was before the Davises moved here, but before the Sanders moved out."

"Since there was no evidence of foul play, why would someone bury a body in their flowerbed instead of letting the authorities take care of it?"

Frankie shook his head. "People do all kinds of strange things. We're hoping that once they're found, one of the Sanders can shed some light on this."

"I better get back to school," I said. "Let me know if I can do anything else."

"Will do. Thanks again for coming down today."

The afternoon sped by. Each of the three reading groups were working on stories they enjoyed, so after lively discussions, they settled down to do some drawings of their favorite scenes. A science test was the last item for the day, and after collecting them, I let the students have some Drop Everything And Read, or DEAR time. Five minutes before the final bell rang, I passed out the project letters, and everyone stuffed them into their homework folders.

"Don't forget to finish putting your spelling words in alphabetical order tonight," I reminded them.

"And don't forget to bring stuff for the soldiers," Rufus hollered as everyone started out the door.

"Thank you, Rufus," I said. "See you tomorrow."

Quiet settled over the room, and I graded several sets of papers. When I finished, I walked to the workroom to laminate a new spring bulletin board set that I had bought. By the time I was done, it was almost 5:00. Coming out of the workroom, I saw DeLana in the office, so I stuck my head inside the door.

"How did your first day go? You stayed late," I said as she walked toward me.

"It was great," she said, smiling. "I just love teaching first-graders, and these kids are eager to learn. Mrs. Carpenter chose *Alexander and the Terrible, Horrible, No Good, Very Bad Day* by Judith Viorst for the reading group to work on, and it's one of my favorites."

"My third-graders enjoy that book, too," I said.

"Two of the kids needed some extra help with the vocabulary, and your cousin, Riley, proved to be a great assistant. They seemed comfortable reading with her, and it gave me the opportunity to monitor the rest of the class. She also helped me find the red and blue construction paper that we needed for the story scene mobiles."

"I'll bet she was thrilled to get to help. I'm glad you're enjoying the kids. They're fun at that age, but I'm still partial to third-graders."

DeLana glanced at the wall clock. "I don't mean to be rude, but I made a 5:00 appointment with your cousin Pauley to take a look at my car." She held up a pink message slip. "The guy I hit left a message for me to call him. I hope my insurance company isn't giving him problems about fixing his car."

"I've got to get going, too," I said. "See you tomorrow."

"Have a nice evening," she said, turning toward the front door.

I carried the bulletin board materials to my room and set them on the activity table, then gathered up my purse and jacket. Heading to the office to sign out, I remembered that, yesterday at church, Aunt Edith had asked me to call her. It had slipped my mind until now, so I decided I would pick up some of our favorite Chinese food and take it over.

A block from the restaurant, I decided to call her to be sure she wasn't already cooking something. She picked up after the second ring.

"Hello?"

"Sorry I didn't call you last night," I said. "To make it up to you, how about some pork lo mein and sweet and sour chicken for supper?"

"And some of those shrimp egg rolls?" she asked.

"You bet. I'll order four of them."

"You're forgiven. I'll give you some money when you get here."

"No, this is my treat. Now neither one of us will have to eat alone while watching *Wheel of Fortune*."

"Sounds good to me," she said. "Drive carefully."

I pulled up to the drive-in window of the restaurant and ordered, then couldn't resist adding two cups of egg drop soup as well. When I took the heavy bag from the attendant, I knew it was twice the amount of food we would eat tonight. But neither of us minded eating it reheated, and now we wouldn't have to cook tomorrow night, either.

When I pulled into her driveway, I was surprised to see Uncle Clarence's 1984 red Dodge pickup. Over the years, it had experienced lots of mishaps, and he had never been in a hurry to get it repaired. There were still some rusted dents and scrapes that I remember being there since I was a kid. The back bumper was hanging low on one end, while the right mirror had a big piece of gray duct tape across it. Getting out and walking by the driver's side, I could see that the running board had rusty baling wire holding the left side up. The afghan that Gramma gave him when I was in the sixth grade still covered the seat.

He opened the door as I stepped up on the porch.

"Hi, Uncle Clarence." I gave him a one-arm hug while holding the bag of food with the other one.

Returning the embrace, he said, "Hi, Allie. Just stopped by to bring Edith some walnut brownies your grandma made today. I don't want to interfere with the feast you two ladies are having."

"Interfere? Would you listen to that?" Aunt Edith said, walking in from the kitchen.

My mouth dropped open at the sight of her hairstyle. Ever since Gladys decided to start working part-time, sometimes Tammy Tuttle does Aunt Edith's hair. Today's hairdo looked like some of her work. Her usual short curls had been lengthened, and she reminded me of a white-haired Goldilocks.

"Of course, you'll stay and eat with us," she said. The long, springy curls bounced with every move she made. "You know the China King gives super-sized helpings of everything. I made strawberry slushies, and with Sarah's brownies for dessert, there will be more than enough for all of us."

"Yes, Uncle Clarence, please stay," I said. "There's plenty of food, and we haven't visited in ages."

"Okay, you talked me into it. But only if you'll let me take the two of you out to eat some night."

"You've got a deal," I said.

"Count me in, too," Aunt Edith said. "Now come on, and let's eat while it's hot."

Walking behind her toward the kitchen, I watched the recoiling tresses. "That's a new look for you, Aunt Edith."

"You know, Daisy and I were watching *Braveheart* with Mel Gibson on television the other night, and I commented to her that his hair was longer than I'd ever seen it. From the front you could tell it wasn't a wig and Daisy said it was done with hair extensions. I'd never heard of such a thing, so I asked Gladys about them. She said it was the latest thing in Hollywood and that I might like to give them a try."

"That's sounds like Gladys," Uncle Clarence said.

I had to admit that the hairdresser sometimes came up with some odd suggestions.

"It just so happened she had some white ones, so while Tammy T. washed and set my hair, Gladys curled some up with the curling iron." She paused to admire her reflection in the microwave door. "I think I might stick with them. A change is good once in a while if you want to catch a man's eye."

While pulling food out of the bag and setting it on the kitchen table, I said, "You may be right. With my track record, maybe I should go down and let Tammy have a crack at my hair."

Stopping midstream while filling tumblers with strawberry slushies, she looked at me. "Why, Allison, your hair is gorgeous! I've always envied the pretty blonde color and how thick and healthy it is. You can wear it in so many different styles, while I have to keep mine short to make it look decent."

"And you don't worry about the lack of men in your life, young lady," Uncle Clarence said as he set the forks and napkins on the table. "The right one just hasn't found you, yet. But when he does, it will be the best thing that ever happened to him. I was twenty-five before I found my Emma, and she was the light of my life."

With everything spread out, we sat down to eat. Uncle Clarence said grace, then we dug in.

"You're still young, Allie, and you've been smart not to have settled for just anybody," Aunt Edith said as the curls boinged against her neck. "I'd be willing to wager that Mr. Right is waiting just around the corner, but you may need to look beyond the corners of Paradise."

"Pickings are a little slim here, all right," Uncle Clarence said.

Wanting to avert the subject from my lack of a love life to something else, I looked at him and asked, "So what have you been up to this week?"

Wiping a drop of sweet and sour sauce from his chin, he said, "Your granddad and I have been working in the garden. Since the rain let up, we've been breaking up the large clods and have tilled the whole thing a couple of times. It was in pretty good shape, since last fall we worked in some extra organic matter that we got from your Grandpa A.J.'s place."

"The garden" is an acre plot of ground on Grandad and Gramma's place used to grow vegetables and strawberries. Each year, enough is grown to supply every member of the Kane and Winters clans, as well as many friends. When Grandad plowed it years ago, it was about one-fourth the size it is today, but as the families grew, so did the garden. The organic matter is the cow manure from the Circle K, the eleven hundred-acre ranch that Grandpa owns.

His grandparents, Elliott and Paulena Kane, were the first settlers in this area and named the town Paradise. Paulena was a full-blood Osage Indian and was given four sections, or almost twenty-six hundred acres of land, in 1885. Upon their deaths, their two offspring, William and Rosella, each inherited two sections. William and his wife Caroline had Andrew James, or A.J. as he was called, and another son, John.

Grandpa and John worked with their dad to build the largest cattle ranch in Oklahoma at that time, with over eight thousand head. John never married and died from pneumonia in his mid-forties, so the ranch became Grandpa's.

Within a year of his and Nana's wedding, Grandad and Gramma married and bought one hundred fifty acres from them. Grandad made a comfortable living raising soybeans and a family of seven children. After Aunt Emma died, he gave an acre of his land to Uncle Clarence. Together with the help of several other family members, they built him a small house.

"We're going to plant two rows of onions and a row each of asparagus, cabbage and broccoli this week," he said. "Then in a couple of weeks the threat of frost will be past, and it will be safe to plant carrots, radishes and potatoes. It wouldn't surprise me if it snows again, so we aren't getting in a hurry with the last three varieties. It's too much work planting all of it to let it freeze."

I've lived through enough plantings to know that the cold-hardy plants he mentioned would thrive as long as they weren't planted more than four weeks before the last frost. By late February, the ground is gradually warming, so even if it snows, the seedlings make it fine. In Oklahoma, it's not uncommon to have March snowstorms.

"How long are the rows this year?" I asked.

"About the same as last year, a hundred feet long. We should be able to plant about seventy rows and still have room to expand the strawberry patch."

There's nothing like sweet, juicy strawberries picked fresh from the garden. Since we were kids, my cousins and I have been the delegated pickers, though our grandparents know that we eat as many as we drop in the buckets. By the time the berries are gone, I usually have a rash and a sore mouth from eating so many of them.

Stuffed with Chinese food and getting a brain-freeze from the drinks, I pushed back my chair. As Aunt Edith reached for a walnut brownie, one of her long curls fell on the floor.

"I'm not sure if I can live with these hair extensions, after all," she said, reaching down to pick it up. "What do you think Clarence? Should I keep them?"

I noticed that Uncle Clarence hadn't said anything about her hairstyle and was pressing his lips into a thin line. As he cupped his hand in front of his mouth and coughed into it, I realized he was trying hard not to laugh.

"Edith, whatever you like just tickles me to death. I like the short way you've been wearing it, but maybe that's just me. You do whatever makes you happy."

Standing and picking up her plate and glass, she said, "It's been fun, but I think I'll go back and let Tammy redo it in the morning."

Uncle Clarence winked at me and mouthed, "Thank goodness."

As we cleaned off the table, Aunt Edith said, "So, Allie, I heard you had lots of excitement in your neighborhood Saturday night, finding that big toe, then the body and all. Sorry I missed it."

"Word gets around fast, doesn't it?" I said.

"The buzz at the barber shop is that it might be Fred Sanders," Uncle Clarence said.

"No, I went with Frankie today to see if I could identify the body, and it's not Mr. Sanders," I said. At their insistence, I gave them a few more details about that night, but left out everything pertaining to my encounters with Luke Davis.

"I told them at Gladys's that it was your dogs that dragged in the toe and that you were the one who led the police to the body," Aunt Edith said. "Everyone at the shop will want more details next week, so keep me informed."

Not sure how I felt about providing information for the rumor mill, I didn't say anything.

When the kitchen was straight, we went into the living room and watched *Wheel of Fortune*. The winning contestant walked away with over twelve thousand dollars.

"Not a bad hour's work for that guy," Uncle Clarence said, standing up. "Girls, this has been nice, but I need to get to bed early tonight. At church yesterday, Jud Spillman invited some of us to go fishing at his dock on Grand Lake early in the morning. Since the rain stirred up the water, he said the bass and crappie have been biting like crazy."

"I need to be going, too," I said. "I enjoyed the food and the company."

As Uncle Clarence and I walked to the front door, he said, "Thanks for letting me join you. I'd like to return the favor by taking the two of you to that new seafood place that opened on Highway 13. How does Friday night sound?"

"You don't need to do that, Uncle Clarence."

"I know, but I want to," he said. "How about it?"

"Friday is good for me," Aunt Edith said.

"Fine with me, too," I said. "I'll be happy to drive. I can pick both of you up here about 6:00."

"We'll be ready," he said, smiling.

"Amen," Aunt Edith said.

After we said good night, Uncle Clarence and I walked down the steps. Pausing next to his pickup, he patted the hood. "She may not be the babe magnet she once was, but she still runs like a dream. See you Friday night."

Smiling, I walked to my Mustang and climbed inside. As I backed out of the driveway, I saw Uncle Clarence run his hand across the dash of his truck. *It must seem like an old friend to him,* I thought. And old friends are sometimes hard to come by.

CHAPTER 9

When I left for school on Tuesday morning, the skies were leaden and the air was brisk. Perhaps Uncle Clarence's prediction of snow wasn't unfounded, though the weatherman wasn't forecasting it.

Student behavior is affected anytime there is an abrupt change in the weather. The kids are often louder, and attention spans are shorter. Today was one of those days. Three students didn't have their homework done, two got into a scuffling match in the restroom, and the noise level in the classroom before lunch was only slightly below a roar.

My patience was running thin by the time Rufus slammed his locker door for the third time. I was glad to see the lunch hour come, even though I had recess duty, which isn't my favorite thing to do. Jennie Carpenter and I had shared the same duty day, but now that DeLana was substituting for her, it would give me a chance to get to know her better.

In the cafeteria, the students lined up as the lunch duty teacher dismissed them, then we shepherded the two hundred students down the long hallway and onto the playground. They scattered in all directions, running and yelling like a group of banshees.

"They're wild today, aren't they?" I said to DeLana as we moved to a centralized area where we could see everyone.

"Yes, I can tell that a cold front came through," she said. "First thing this morning, two boys got into a fight with the finger paints, and very little was accomplished by anyone during center time."

I felt arms loop around the tops of my legs and heard a young voice say, "Guess who?"

Recognizing the voice, but knowing that she enjoyed teasing me, I said, "Are you wearing a dress?"

"No," she replied.

"Are you a boy?"

"Eeewww, no way."

"I think this is a ticklish girl named Riley," I said, running my fingers up and down her arms.

Giggling, she released me and ran out of the reach of my tickling fingers.

"What are you up to today?" I asked. "Keeping out of trouble?"

"Of course I am," she said. "Some of us were over there playing hopscotch, but I wanted to come over and tell you 'hi.'"

I saw a group of second-graders playing tag and getting a little rough, so I whistled at them to get their attention. Jennie had always been the one to get the bull horn when we had duty, and I hadn't thought of it. I whistled again as one of the students fell to the ground and started crying. Before I headed toward the group, I said, "Riley, would you please go to the office and ask for the bull horn and bring it to us? We need some extra volume out here."

"Sure, I'll be right back with it," she said, then started running toward the building.

Heading toward some first-graders climbing up backwards on the slide, DeLana said, "I'll take care of the group over there."

I checked on the injured student and sent him to the office for first aid, then warned the roughnecks to take it easy. Riley was handing the horn to DeLana as I reached the blacktop. She grinned from ear to ear when DeLana thanked her and complimented her new purple outfit.

The girls at the hopscotch grid were hollering for Riley to come back and play. She waved at us and said, "They need me. See you later."

"She's such a sweet little girl," DeLana said. "From what I've seen so far, she seems to be reading near a fourth-grade level. Have her parents had her tested?"

"She was tested and is in the gifted program this year. Her father will be meeting with her regular teacher soon about accelerated classes for next year. Her mother is out of the picture for the most part."

Seeing some kids climbing on the fence, I pointed toward the horn that she still held. "May I use that? The kids over there seem to have forgotten the fence rule."

"Sure," she said, handing it to me.

After the kids jumped down and ran in another direction, I said, "Did you take your car by Pauley's shop yesterday?"

"Yes, he worked up an estimate, then was kind enough to fax it to my agent. It was the lowest price of the two, so I'm sure they'll let him repair my car. I wish the guy that I hit would come to him, but I have no idea where he lives. To make things worse, my agent called me this morning to say that he had misread some of the numbers and rejected the bid he had submitted. My agent hasn't been able to reach him to explain his mistake. That just gives him one more reason to be upset with me."

"That's too bad," I said. "Surely he'll realize it's not your fault."

"I imagine he thinks everything about it is my fault."

"Can you call him and explain the mix-up to him? Maybe if he hears it directly from you, he won't think you're trying to sabotage him."

"I guess it's worth a try, and I kind of enjoy talking to him," she said, smiling.

"Oh, really. That's interesting."

"He's not like anyone I've every met before. Despite our run-in—no pun intended—I can't seem to get him out of my mind. But because of this car business, I'm afraid that anything beyond a business relationship isn't going to happen."

"You never know until you try. Who knows? Maybe the accident happened for a reason."

"It would be nice to think that something good will come from it, but it seems remote."

I looked down at my watch. "We'd better take the kids back inside. They've had an extra ten minutes as it is."

I pressed the button for the siren on the horn to sound. As the students found their individual class lines, I handed it to DeLana and asked her to pick someone to take it back to the office. I saw her motion to Riley, then hand it to her. As I led the way, Riley fell into step beside me.

"I think I'm one of Miss Miller's favorite students, Allie. Isn't she terrific?" she said.

"Yes, she's pretty great," I said, smiling at her, "and she seems to think you're special, too."

Once we were inside, the afternoon went better than the morning had. The students stayed on task and were quieter. The extra recess time had given them the chance to expel some pent-up energy.

When the final bell rang and they were out the door, I turned on my cell phone to call one of the parents about a conference. There was a voicemail from my mother asking me to please come by Paradise Petals. I had promised her on Sunday that I would tell her about my plans for Hawaii, and this would give me the chance I needed. I grabbed my purse and coat, then headed down the hall.

When I got to the shop, the parking lot was packed, and I had to wait until someone else pulled out to get a parking space. As I opened the door, I saw wall-to-wall shoppers and a line of people at the counter placing orders.

Mom looked up and motioned to me to push through. When I reached the front, Aunt Emily waved at me while talking to someone on the phone.

Aunt Cynthia came from the back carrying two huge arrangements in crystal vases and handed them to a couple waiting near the door. As she walked by me toward another customer, she said, "Glad you're here, Allie. We can use your help."

Moving behind the counter toward Mom, I said, "Kind of busy, aren't you?"

She handed an order she had just taken to one of her co-workers. "Swamped and a little overwhelmed is more like it," she replied. "Would you mind helping out for an hour or two? Ethel Bennett passed away this morning, and orders have been pouring in from people who know the family. She had eleven children and thirty-some grandchildren, so it seems that everyone in the county wants to send flowers. On top of that, Misty Rainwater is getting married in three weeks and wants to come in at 5:00 to order her arrangements. I'll need to spend about an hour with her and her mother, so if you could help Emily with orders, I would appreciate it."

"Sure, I'll be glad to help out. I didn't have anything going on tonight anyway. Maybe when things settle down after you close, I can tell you about my trip."

"Yes, I want to hear all about it. Also, your father gave me a little something to give to you."

Just then, Misty and her mother came through the door. "You go meet with your clients. We can talk later."

She walked over to the Rainwaters and escorted them to her office in the far back of the shop. A lady waiting in front of me cleared her throat. I picked up an order pad and shop catalog, then proceeded to show her some of the latest arrangements and prices.

After helping customers non-stop for two hours, I was ready for a break.

"Whew, what a day," Emily said as she locked the door and turned over the closed sign. "I took at least twenty phone orders, and more than half of them were for the Bennett service. You were a lifesaver, Allie. Before you got here, I was getting the evil eye from some people wanting help at the counter, but the phone kept ringing."

The Rainwaters were all smiles as they walked out of Mom's office. I knew she must have wowed them with some of her wedding ideas. She has a knack for making every bride feel as if her wedding is the most important one of the year. More brides than ever before are letting Mom plan their special days.

Mom let them out and relocked the door.

"They looked happy," I said.

"I think they are," she said as she walked toward us. "She's invited over three hundred guests and wants the very best arrangements. I was able to help her trim the quantity of them by adding some other smaller touches to help save her parents some money. Her mother was pleased with that, and since no quality was compromised, Misty was pleased as well."

"You give them the best, Mom. That's why you're so busy all the time. But don't you think you ought to consider hiring another full time person so you don't have to work fifty hours a week?"

"You sound just like your father. But I have been giving it some serious thought because he wants to travel more. Your brother Jamie is starting to take on more responsibility at Kane Energy, and your dad feels comfortable leaving it in his and your Uncle Philip's hands. I'll try to get around to writing up a want ad and put it in this Sunday's paper."

"I think that's a great idea," I said. "I think it's high time you and Dad travel more."

"Now, that's enough about me. Sit down, and tell us about your interview."

Everyone was gone except for my aunts and us, so we grabbed some soft drinks from the cooler, then sat down at a table in the backroom.

After I answered a lot of their questions, Mom walked over to the counter and got her purse from beneath it. She pulled out an envelope and handed it to me. "I mentioned to your dad that you were going to Hawaii, and even though I didn't know the details, he wanted me to give you this. He said he wanted you to have the things you needed."

Tears filled my eyes when I opened it and pulled out five one-hundred-dollar bills. I never ask my parents for money, but Dad has told me several times how proud he is that I've made it on my own. Even so, he has let me know that it is his prerogative as my father to give me gifts whenever he wants to.

I leaned over and hugged Mom. "Thank you so much. I'll go by the house, or call Dad and thank him, too. I started a shopping list, and now I'll be able to splurge and buy some new outfits."

"You're welcome," she said, "and thanks for coming in and helping today. We all appreciate it. Now, girls, it's time we all go home."

Tossing the soft drink bottles in the recycling bin, we gathered up our belongings, turned out all but the security lights and walked together to our cars.

With each passing day, the Care boxes were filling up. By Friday, I had taken six full ones to the storeroom and put out three more empty ones. The final day to bring items was the following Monday, and with Friday being payday for some parents, I expected the three boxes to be full before the project ended.

Mrs. Graves told me that over two hundred dollars had been turned in and she planned to use most of it to shop for Gameboys and games that weekend. The rest of it, and any additional money that came in, would be used for the postage to send the boxes.

I enjoyed a nice dinner on Friday night with Uncle Clarence and Aunt Edith. The hair extensions were gone, and Uncle Clarence bragged about the fish he and Grandad had caught at the Spillman dock earlier in the week.

On Saturday, I took the gift from my parents and went shopping. I bought two new swimsuits, a netted cover-up and sandals at a specialty shop in town, then drove to Tulsa. Lots of new spring items had come in at my favorite department store. I bought three pairs of shorts with coordinating tops—one in baby blue, one in crimson and another one in lavender.

I drove to a nearby mall and checked out a new dress shop that had just opened. I bought a gold striped sundress that would be perfect for a night out. In the same complex, there was a variety store where I picked up some sunscreen, new sunglasses, and a few other accessories. I had some nice shorts and tops that I had bought the summer before to fill in the gaps. Since I would only be in Hawaii for seven days, the remainder of the gift money would come in handy for souvenirs for family members. After carrying my treasures to the car, I started back to Paradise, more excited than ever about the trip.

When I turned onto my street, I saw Luke Davis in his wrecker, pulling out of his driveway. He stopped crosswise in the street, making it impossible for me to get by. I stopped a few yards from the driver's door waiting for him to pull around, but he seemed oblivious to my presence. My window was open and I could hear his father shouting obscenities at him. For some strange reason, he was also calling him Larry.

I debated honking to get his attention, when he looked straight at me. He pulled forward a few feet, allowing enough space between the wrecker and the curb for me to get by. As I started inching around him, he backed up and I had to stomp on the brake to keep from hitting him.

He got out of his vehicle and sauntered toward me. I knew I could jump the curb and get around him, but in broad daylight I didn't think he would dare try anything. My doors were locked and I debated rolling up the window, but this time I intended to show him I wasn't going to be intimidated.

He rested his hands on my door and glanced into the backseat. "Well, hello there, Miss Kane. Been shopping, have you?"

I was nervous about his close proximity, but was determined not to show it. I nodded, then said, "I'd like to get home. Would you mind moving your truck, please?"

He glanced at the wrecker, then back at me. He seemed to be enjoying the cat and mouse game. "I'll tell you what," he said. "I'll be glad to move my truck, if you'll go out with me tonight. It's Saturday, and I feel like having a good time with a pretty girl. How about it?"

There was no way on earth I was going to go out with Luke Davis, and I wanted him to understand he was wasting his time asking me. Adhering to my upbringing, I decided to take the more polite, diplomatic route. "Thanks, but I've had a busy day. I'm going to spend a quiet evening at home."

Moving his head closer to the opening in the glass, he said, "That sounds better than going to some crowded place. I'd enjoy having you all to myself, if you know what I mean."

I was sure I knew what he meant and the thought made me ill. *So much for diplomacy*, I thought. I looked at him and said, "It's never going to happen, Mr. Davis, so you're wasting your time and mine. Now, I'd appreciate it if you'd get that wrecker out of my way!"

Mr. and Mrs. Scaletta were out in their yard and were watching our exchange. Luke stepped closer, where his mouth was almost touching the glass. "What's the matter?" he snarled. "Do you need to get permission from that cop cousin of yours before you can go out with a real man?"

"I don't see a real man around here," I said, revving my engine.

Throwing the car into reverse, I backed up a few feet, then shifted into drive and hopped the curb. He watched as I drove around the back of the wrecker and into my own driveway. Raising the garage door, I barely cleared the back bumper before lowering it.

I was angry but determined that Luke wasn't going to ruin the nice day I had had. I took some deep breaths, then reached for the sacks in the back seat. As I walked to the door, I could hear the puppies howling inside their crate.

"What's the matter, guys? Did you think I had forgotten you?" I asked, setting my packages on the table. They were scratching at the door and whining as I knelt down to let them out.

They jumped up on me like I was a long lost friend. Feeling bad that they had been confined most of the day, I said, "Are you ready to run? Come on; let's go outside and play."

I took them into the backyard and threw the beach ball for them until we were all huffing and puffing. Sitting down on the grass, I could feel that the tension inside me from the encounter with Luke had drained away. After scratching the dogs' tummies for a few minutes, we went back inside, and I gave them some food and fresh water. While they were eating, I stuck a frozen dinner into the microwave to heat. I gathered the sacks into my arms and carried them to the bedroom to look through later.

It was my turn to play the organ for the Sunday morning worship service, so after teaching my class, I hurried to the sanctuary. Kristin was at the piano pulling out some upbeat songs for us to play while people came in. After a few rounds of "I'll Fly Away" and "I Feel Like Traveling On," the musicians were pumped and ready to go by the time Michael led the choir in.

After church, most of the family gathered at Grandpa and Nana's ranch for dinner. I hadn't made anything to contribute, but had brought along some bottles of pop. Since many of us stay all afternoon, lots of soft drinks are consumed.

With the adults seated at the big table and the kids at two tables in the kitchen, Grandad was elected to say grace. We try to grab him or Grandpa before Gramma starts praying, because their prayers take a fraction of the time that hers do. She has been known to pray for the missionaries in Russia and the Congo while saying grace.

When we were thirteen, Kristin, Doug and I went behind the barn at Gramma and Grandad's place and smoked our first and only cigarettes. At the next family dinner, when Gramma said the prayer over the meal, she asked God to please deliver us from the evils of smoking. It was a shock to us that she even knew about it, and since our parents didn't know either, all three of us got into big trouble when we got home.

"Everyone, please bow your heads," Grandad said. "Heavenly Father, we thank You for this food. Please bless those who prepared it and those who consume it, and keep us in Thy care. Amen."

The moment the prayer was finished, the sounds of clattering bowls and clicking utensils filled the room. When platters of food are passed, you have to be quick, or you'll get left behind. One time, when I was fourteen, I was reaching for the last pork chop and Michael accidentally poked me in the back of the hand with his fork.

With a group of over thirty people, lots of conversations were going on, but when Dad asked me about my upcoming trip, the room grew quiet.

"Some of you already know about it, but for those of you who haven't heard, I have the opportunity to interview for a summer school job in Hawaii. The flight expenses will be paid by the school, so even if I don't get the job, I'll still have a fabulous vacation over spring break."

Several questions popped up, along with comments from the guys that it's not safe for a girl to travel alone, so they offered to come along as bodyguards. Most of the girls were excited for me, though feigning jealousy that I would come back brown as a biscuit while they remained sickly white. Aunt Emily cornered Uncle Roger and wanted to know why he didn't ever take her somewhere exotic like Hawaii. Of course, Dad, Michael and Doug gave me a hard time about keeping my head and not letting some Polynesian Romeo steal my heart away.

"I think it's time for dessert," I said, trying to turn the attention away from me.

Taking my lead, my aunts stood up and started gathering up the dirty plates while Gramma and Nana walked into the kitchen to bring out assorted sweets. While picking up dirty napkins and silverware from the table, I overheard Uncle Jake ask Michael if his Lincoln was in the shop, yet.

"Not yet," Michael replied. "It was late Friday before I got word from the lady who hit me that her insurance company is going to allow Pauley to do the job. His was the lowest estimate, and that was why I was confused that it was rejected in the first place. I plan to drop the car off in the morning and get a loaner car."

Jamie came in from the living room carrying my niece, Ryan. I took her from him, and she started fingering the buttons on the front of my blouse. I planted kisses on her soft, blonde curls.

"You need to stop doing that," my brother said to me. "You're going to make her hair fall out."

"Ha, ha, you're so funny," I said, nuzzling the silky strands. "Actually, it will grow in thicker now that I'm watering it."

Sitting down across the table from Michael, Jamie said, "Is the woman who hit you a blonde, Michael?"

I looked up and stuck out my tongue at him. Since I'm a blonde, as many of the cousins are, it's rare if a new blonde joke isn't told at the Sunday dinners.

Giving me an innocent look, Jamie said, "What?"

"No, she has auburn hair," Michael said. "But she dropped an envelope outside her car that had a picture of two blonde kids in it. Does that count?"

"Close enough," Jamie replied. "Did you hear about the pretty blonde woman who went to the Halo Heights addition looking for work?" Halo Heights is the ritzy neighborhood in Paradise where the upper class lives.

"No, I guess I missed it," Michael said, resting his arms on the table.

"She knocked on the door of this well-to-do family, and when the man answered, she asked, 'Do you have any work that I can do for you?' The man felt sorry for her, so he said, 'Well, how much would you charge me to paint my porch?' The blonde said, 'Let me take a look at it and I'll let you know.'

"After about five minutes, she came back to the door and said, 'How about fifty dollars?' Knowing he was getting a heck of a deal for the big porch, the man said, 'Sure. The white paint is in the garage, along with a roller and brush.'

"An hour passed by, and the blonde comes back and knocks on the door again and says that she has finished. The man knew it was impossible to have covered that much area in so little time, so he asked, 'Are you sure you painted the entire porch?'

"The blonde said, 'Yes, but it's not a porch; it's a Lincoln.'"

Several of my relatives burst out laughing, and I had to fight back a smile. Dad gave Jamie a slap on the back, then winked at me.

"Fortunately, I know the difference between a porch and a Lincoln, Michael," Pauley said, standing in the doorway grinning. He tossed some keys across the table to him. "Those are to the black Grand Marquis sitting by the door of the shop. Sorry it's not the high society car you're used to, but maybe it will meet your needs for a few days."

"Okay, smart aleck. You just be sure you don't scratch my baby while you have her. Here's my keyless entry code," Michael said, writing the numbers on one of his business cards. "I'll leave the keys under the floor mat and lock it, since you late risers won't be there, yet." The body shop doesn't open until 7:30.

"Don't worry. I'll have her looking like new in no time," Pauley said, taking the card from him.

Michael stood up and pushed back his chair. "Now who's ready for some music?"

Nana and Grandpa have a five-thousand-square-foot house and on one end of the second story there is a huge music room containing Nana's baby grand piano, a full set of drums and a Hammond organ. Since Nana and Gramma grew up playing instruments, they were determined that their children and grandchildren would have the same opportunity. Mandatory piano lessons are given by one of them for two years when a child reaches seven years old. After that, he or she has the choice of whether or not to pursue an instrument.

A few of my cousins chose to switch from keyboard to trumpets, clarinets or flutes, while Kristin and I, along with a few others, stuck with the piano and organ. Drums and guitars are also available, as long as some formal lessons are taken. Most of us studied for many years and mastered one or more of the instruments. We also participated in school and church choirs and won our fair share of awards at contests.

Sunday afternoon jam sessions are the norm. Years ago, Grandpa and Grandad added extra shelves and built some cubbyholes in one of the closets in the music room that were perfect for the horn players' instruments. The room temperature is regulated and Nana makes sure it stays as spotless as the rest of her house.

Like the Pied Piper, Michael led some of us upstairs. He took his place at the drums, and soon the warm-up sounds of flutes and clarinets filled the room. Some of the younger cousins, who hold first chair in their school bands, were fussing about whose turn it was to sit in the first chair here.

The Blessing twins, Angel and Amber, were trying to dump their youngest brother Patrick out of a chair. He was clinging to it yelling, "Mom!"

"I'm not going to have to come up there, am I?" Emily called out from downstairs.

As I headed toward the organ, there were answers of "Patrick won't share" and "I'm telling Mom."

Patrick is eleven and the youngest of the five Blessing siblings. He has won more awards in contests for his instrument solos than any of the rest of us. If he continues at the pace he is going, he is sure to get a full music scholarship to an Ivy League university. He is the closest thing to a child prodigy that I have ever seen.

Doug also plays the trumpet, but falls short when he tries to outperform his younger brother. No one has booted Patrick from first chair since he first began band classes at age seven. He was the youngest student in the history of Paradise to get to take band before the fourth grade. An exception was made for Patrick when the junior high band director heard him horsing around with one of the twins' clarinets at a football game. He was only in the first grade at the time. The director convinced his parents to let him try the trumpet, and since then, he's taught himself to play trombone, cornet and French horn.

"Patrick, why don't you come and play the organ with me," I said. "Let one of the girls have first chair for a while." With the piano lessons he had taken from Gramma and the techniques that I had shown him on the organ, he was doing well on the keyboard, too.

"Okay. I'd rather sit by you, anyway," he said, making a face at the twins.

I scooted over to give him some room. "Why don't you play the lower panel, and I'll take care of the upper keyboard and the pedals?"

He nodded as I reached for a stack of new music lying on top of the organ. Thumbing through the top selections, I asked Michael, "So, maestro, what do we start with today?"

Since Michael is the oldest, we tend to look to him to get things going. As the afternoon progresses, we all put in our two cents worth.

"How about Packet Five," he said. From time to time, he puts together packets of songs that are in the same key or that easily flow from one song to the next. The packets may be rock, country or gospel music. Awhile back, at the insistence of the "grownups," who listen to us from the family room downstairs, he put together some classical, blues and jazz packets. Anyone can suggest a song for new packets, but before it can be added, a vote is taken among the group, and the majority rules.

"Alright, kids," I said. "Start passing out Packet Five." It's the job of Riley, Joey and Brittany to pass out packets to everyone.

While they handed them out, Uncle Clarence slipped in with his alto saxophone. "Thought I'd join you youngsters," he said. "It's more fun in here than it is sitting down there listening with the old folks."

"The more the merrier," Jamie said as he stretched out the arm on his trombone. "Pull up a chair next to Doug and me. If it wasn't for the three of us, this group would be in sad shape."

When everyone had the music on his or her stand, Michael hit his drumsticks together, and the first song began. Brittany, Joey and Riley clapped and danced. When we were well into the fourth song, Mom slipped in with Ryan. Wiggling her way out of her grandmother's arms, she started running in circles and hopping up and down to the beat of the music.

"Makes me dizzy just to watch her," I heard Nana say from the doorway.

By the time the songs were played, Gramma, both grandpas and a couple of aunts had joined us. Ryan entertained her growing audience and squealed with delight when Dad came in and scooped her up, tossing her in the air.

The three kids collected our packets, then started passing out a different set.

"Give me a B-flat chord, Allie," Gramma said.

I was pretty sure I knew what was coming next. Gramma started singing one of her favorite songs, "When We All Get To Heaven." Most of us can play by ear, as well as by note, so we harmonized with her as she led us in all three verses, then the chorus twice.

When the song was finished, instruments were shifted around, and I got up and let Nana have a turn at the organ. Michael moved and let Frankie take the drums, and he sat down to play bass guitar. After another hour of music, we started winding down, and it was time to put everything away.

While we straightened the room, Gramma, Aunt Cynthia and Mom made chicken salad sandwiches and put out bags of chips and paper plates on the table. We gathered around, Dad said the blessing, then we dived into the food. Jamming is kind of like swimming; you can really work up an appetite.

When everyone was finished eating and starting to gather up dishes, coats and kids, I felt someone's hands on my shoulders. I tilted my head back and looked up into Jamie's face. His eyes were closed and he was fighting back a smile.

"What in the world do you think you're doing?" I asked.

"The Bible says that Moses laid hands on Joshua, imparting the spirit of wisdom into him. I'm doing the same thing, so you'll make wiser choices and let the police take care of dangerous situations."

Frankie was standing close by, and I knew he must have told Jamie about my recent encounters with body parts and Luke Davis.

I smiled sweetly at Jamie. "I appreciate your effort, big brother, but Moses had something in his head to impart, unlike you who only has emptiness between the ears."

"Ouch!" Doug said. "Afraid she's got you there, cousin."

I motioned for Frankie to sit down next to me. "I haven't heard a word from you all week. Have you identified the body yet?"

"Since I've been working a lot of overtime, Kailyn and I took a few days to go see her parents in Dallas. We just got back last night." He looked down at his pager that was going off. "I told them not to contact me today, unless it was important. I'll call you later tonight and fill you in on the latest."

Pulling out his cell phone, Frankie said goodbye to the few remaining people in the room, then motioned to his wife to join him at the front door.

I kissed my nieces and my parents, then after hugging my grandparents, I joined the stream of cars leaving the ranch and headed toward home.

CHAPTER 10

On Sunday evening after watching *Dateline*, I went into the kitchen to microwave a baked potato for my supper. While it cooked, I poured some precut romaine salad mix into a bowl and topped it with ranch dressing. When the potato was done, I slit it down the middle and slathered it with butter, salt and sour cream. I poured a glass of tea from a pitcher in the refrigerator and was all set. There are many nice things about the family dinners; one of them being that minimal cooking is required that evening.

Carrying my food on a tray into the living room, I sat down in my recliner. Just as I took a big bite of hot potato, the phone rang. Washing it down with some iced tea, I reached over and picked up the phone on the fourth ring.

"I didn't catch you at a bad time, did I?" Frankie asked.

"No, but I had food in my mouth. Since it's only you, I'll continue eating while you talk."

"I can't believe you can hold any more food after all you ate at Nana's today. Did you fill your plate two or three times?"

"Don't think you're going to make me feel guilty, Frankie Janson. There were three pieces of fried chicken lying next to the roast, baked beans and mashed potatoes on your plate. Besides that, I saw Kailyn heaping four kinds of dessert on another plate for you."

"Hey, what can I say? I'm still a growing boy."

"That's the same thing that Doug says. But, you're twenty-eight years old, so that excuse won't fly. If you're not careful, you're going to get the middle-aged spread."

"Not a chance," he said. "Now, do you want to know what the lab told us about the mystery man?"

"Let me have it."

"His fingerprints matched an old military file dating back to the Korean War. His name was Lester Crane, a homeless man seen in various locations over the past twenty years, with the latest being in Paradise. During really frigid weather, the workers down at the shelter said he would sleep there. As it turns out, he met Fred Sanders when Fred did some volunteer work there several years ago. According to the shelter director, Lester and Fred formed a friendship over checker games."

"Do you think Fred Sanders killed Lester?"

"The coroner confirmed that he died from cirrhosis of the liver. The reason I was paged today was because the Sanders were located in Santa Barbara. I called and spoke with Mrs. Sanders and told her what we had found. From the description that I gave her, she said it sounded like Lester Crane. The last time she saw him, he was playing checkers in their dining room with Uncle Fred. She left to go shopping for a couple of hours, and when she came home, he was gone."

"Can't you ask Fred about him?"

"She said the old man has Alzheimer's and has been going downhill over the last few months. But, I've contacted the authorities out there, and I'm going to fly to Santa Barbara to try to talk to him. It's worth a shot."

"What happened to Lester? Is he still at the morgue?"

"No, we found a name on a piece of paper in his back pocket, that turned out to be a brother in Kansas. He came down and claimed the body and took it back up there for burial."

"At least he'll be near family now," I said. "Thanks for filling me in."

"No problem. I'll talk to you later."

After talking with Frankie, I looked at my half-eaten potato and decided to stick with the salad. Kailyn would stay with Frankie even if he ballooned to twice the size he was now. However, I didn't have the luxury of adding on extra pounds, especially if I wanted to look good in the new swimsuit and shorts I had just bought.

I rinsed my dirty dishes and graded some papers for a while, then let the dogs outside to do their nightly chores. After I got ready for bed, I let them back in, and we called it a day.

On Monday, we had a brief teacher's meeting after school, and I announced that eleven boxes had been filled to send to Kevin's unit. Twenty used Game Boy games had been donated, and Mrs. Graves had purchased two systems over the weekend. She told us that three more new systems had mysteriously appeared on her desk during the lunch hour. I knew that Kristin had gone out to lunch with her mom, so I suspected that she and Uncle Philip had donated the units. With eighty dollars left to be used for shipping costs, the project had been a remarkable success.

After the meeting, Kristin and I taped and labeled all the boxes and got the two-wheeler to load them into our trunks. We had just replaced the handcart and were checking out at the office when Michael came in the front door. Raising a hand in greeting, we waited for him to get closer, then I asked, "What are you doing here?"

"I'm meeting with Mrs. Miller about Riley's accelerated class options for next year. She and the counselor have come up with some suggestions, and she asked me to come by to discuss them with her."

"I'm glad they've got the ball rolling on that," I said. "Riley needs more challenge."

"Well, lately, she's been acting like she doesn't want to leave first grade. She has fallen head over heels in love with Mrs. Miller," he said. "The way Riley describes her, she must have lost a lot of weight and dyed her hair. Every time I turn around, it's Mrs. Miller this and Mrs. Miller that."

Kristin and I gave each other a puzzled look. "Becky Miller hasn't lost any weight," she said. "In fact, she was telling us in the lounge the other day that she has put on ten pounds since Christmas and is going to try that low carb diet everyone is on."

"And her hair is as black as it's always been," I said.

"Riley was driving me nuts last week telling me she's been showing her teacher where things are and that she got to fetch the horn for her at recess," he said. "If you ask me, a teacher should know where she puts her own stuff."

A light bulb went on over my head. I looked at Kristin and said, "Riley's not talking about Becky. She's talking about Jennie Carpenter's substitute." I took hold of Michael's hand and started leading him toward the first-grade wing. "Come on. Before you have your meeting with Riley's regular teacher, I want to introduce you to someone."

We walked down the hallway and stopped by the closed door of Riley's reading class. I knocked, then opened it and stuck my head inside. The lights were off and no one was there.

"It looks like she's already left for the day," I said. "This woman's name is *Miss* Miller, not *misses*, and from what I've seen so far, she's as wild about your daughter as Riley is about her. She often stays as late as I do, but she may have had an appointment of some kind today."

"Mr. Winters?" We turned toward the voice and saw Riley's classroom teacher standing in her doorway. "Are you ready for our meeting?"

"I'll see you later," I told Michael. "Kristin and I have to get the packages we're sending to Kevin's unit to the post office before it closes."

Before following the teacher into the classroom, he said, "I'll bring Riley and the birds to your place about 7:15 Friday morning. She can't wait to show them off to your class."

"Thanks for the reminder. With all that's been happening lately, show-and-tell slipped my mind." With a final wave, I hurried back down the hall to join Kristin.

We got some help at the post office unloading the heavy boxes from our trunks. Since they were going to troops in Iraq, we were given a special rate. Each class had included a letter or picture, and it felt good to see the packages on their way at last.

The next three days at school were dedicated to state testing. The process is as hard on me as it is on the students. Even though I'm able to grade papers while they are working, the change in routine takes its toll.

On Friday, with the testing done and spring break beginning the next day, the third-grade teachers decided to combine classes and show a video. After lunch, the recess duty teachers were nice enough to allow the students to have some extra playtime. They seemed refreshed when they came back inside and were ready for show-and-tell.

I had brought Flip and Fluff in their travel cages that morning and had set them on a table near the window so they could look outside. Their expandable tree perch was sitting in a corner ready to be used when Riley came down to show them. During the day, the kids had enjoyed hearing the birds talk and were eager to get a closer look at them.

Some of the students had also brought something to show, so we did that first, then I sent Sammy Jacobs to get Riley from her class. While we waited for them to get back, I put newspapers in an open area in the front of the room, then set the tree perch and birdcages in the middle of them.

When Riley walked through the door, Flip whistled and said "Yoohoo, pretty girl." The kids laughed as she walked to the front of the room.

After introducing her, I said, "Riley, do you want me to help you get them out of their cages?"

"Let me show you the best way to do it." She took a pair of leather gloves and a small mirror from the bag she had brought in with her. Handing one of the gloves to me, she walked to Flip's cage and unlatched the door. Putting her gloved hand inside, she held the mirror a few inches away and said, "Flip, out." The large bird hopped onto her wrist and bent his head as she brought him through the cage door.

"Now you try it," she said to me, motioning to Fluff.

Since the bird wasn't used to me, I was a bit apprehensive about sticking my hand into the cage. Riley must have picked up on it because she said, "It's okay. Fluff is gentle, and she won't hurt you."

Taking her word for it, I slipped on the glove, pulled it on my wrist as high as I could, then unlatched the door. "Do I need a mirror or a toy to coax her out?"

"No, just say, 'Fluff, out,'" Riley replied. "Flip is stubborn sometimes, but he can't resist shiny objects."

Some of the students were enjoying seeing me squirm in this unusual situation, while others were shrieking, "Miss Kane, be careful," or, "Don't let her bite you, Miss Kane."

Determined that I could do it if Riley could, I held my hand to the open door and said, "Fluff, out." The bird cocked her head but didn't move. I wasn't sure if she was going to take the plunge and let me take her out. But then she looked at Flip and seemed to be more secure with him close by. She hopped onto my wrist, and I slowly lifted her out.

"Way to go, Miss Kane," Rufus said. The students applauded, then laughed when I bowed.

Riley asked me to carry Fluff across the room, then turn around to face her. "Hold your arm out like this," she said, extending her arm to the side.

Following her directions, I was surprised when she said, "Soar, Fluff," and the bird left my wrist and landed on Riley's head. The kids were ecstatic at the feat, and I thought it was pretty amazing myself.

"Are you ready for Flip to come to you?" she asked me.

"I guess so. Do you want me to say what you did using his name?" At her nod, I braced myself and said, "Soar, Flip," and ready or not, the bird leapt off Riley's wrist and landed on my head.

Riley brought Fluff down from her head to her wrist and started telling the students facts about the birds. I felt silly standing there with a bird on my head, but Flip didn't stay there long. He spotted a box covered with shiny paper on the activity table that is used to store crayons and markers. Before I realized what was happening, he jumped from my head and flew to the table, landing just inches from the box. He waddled over and started pecking at the paper and seemed oblivious to anything else going on in the room.

"I'll have to go back there and get him," Riley said. "He ignores commands when he's playing with shiny things."

After retrieving the bird, Riley used the scrap of paper he had torn from the box to get him to do more tricks. When they were finished, she let both birds fly to the perch. The students asked some questions, and by the time we got the birds back into their cages, it was almost time for the final bell to ring.

"Class, let's give Riley, Flip and Fluff a round of applause to thank them for their performance today," I said.

As Riley was walking toward the door to go back to her own classroom, Flip whistled and said, "Goodbye, pretty girl."

"Goodbye, Flip," she said. "I'll see you later."

Turning my attention to the class, I said, "It's only a few minutes until spring break begins, so you need to get your desks cleaned out. Please put all graded papers into your backpacks to go home, and be sure to throw away any trash." While the students cleaned, I wadded up the newspapers on the floor and deposited them into the trash can.

Within minutes, desks were straightened and everyone had their backpacks on. Anxious to get out the door, they were lined up ready to leave when the bell rang. I gave them hugs and wishes for a good holiday, then I stood chatting with Mrs. Blake, the teacher from across the hall, until all the stragglers were gone.

"Don't look now, but you have a handsome visitor sneaking up behind you," she said.

Feeling large hands on my shoulders, I turned my head and looked up into Michael's smiling face.

"Don't let him hear you say that; compliments make his head swell," I said, grinning.

After being introduced to the other teacher, he said, "I'm sorry if I'm interrupting, but I've come to get the feathered friends."

"See you after your trip, Allie. I hope you have a great time," Mrs. Blake said as she turned to walk back into her classroom.

I turned and walked with Michael into my room. "Riley and the birds were a smashing success. She does an excellent job handling them, considering she's so small."

As Michael picked up both cages, I gathered up my things and grabbed the perch, now separated into two pieces. We walked down the hall together, and as we reached the teacher's workroom, DeLana came through the door carrying several bundles of papers. She bumped into Fluff's cage, sending the bird into a squawking frenzy. Startling DeLana, she dropped the papers that were in her hands.

"I'm so sorry," she said, stopping short as she looked up at Michael. "Oh, it's you."

He had a surprised look on his face. "What are you doing here?" he asked.

She knelt down and started gathering together the scattered papers. "I work here. What are you doing here?"

He set down both cages and began helping her pick up the mess on the floor. Realizing I was standing there like a dunce, I bent down and grabbed some sheets that had slid under one of the chairs.

"Don't trouble yourself; I can do this on my own," DeLana said to Michael.

"It's no trouble," he replied. "These papers are a mess. Let me help you get them organized." He took the sheets from her and added them to his own. Heading to a nearby cafeteria table, he started sorting them into stacks.

Puzzled at their exchange, I said, "I take it you know each other."

"You could say that," Michael replied.

"We had a close encounter last week," DeLana said.

"That reminds me, I still have something that belongs to you," Michael said. He pulled an envelope from his jacket pocket and handed it to her. "I'm sure you've wondered where your children's pictures went to. You must have dropped them while you were digging out your insurance verification card."

She looked inside the envelope. "Thanks for returning these, but they aren't my children. They are my niece and nephew."

"So this is the person you had the wreck with," I said, not addressing either one of them specifically.

They both looked at me and together said, "Yes."

"DeLana, let me introduce you to my cousin and Riley's father, Michael Winters," I said. "And Michael, this is the teacher Riley has been raving about for the past week, DeLana Miller."

As Michael stood staring at her, Riley came bouncing up behind him. "Daddy, I'm glad you're finally getting to meet Miss Miller," she said. "Isn't she beautiful?"

As color crept into DeLana's face, Michael looked down at Riley. "Yes, sweetheart, she certainly is."

I gathered up the papers from the table and handed a stack to each of them. "Riley, why don't you and your daddy help Miss Miller take these to her room. Flip and Fluff will be fine where they are for a few minutes. I've got to go because my plane leaves in the morning, and I have things to do before then."

Composing himself, Michael looked down at the papers that I had slid into his hands. "We'll be glad to help her, won't we Riley? I'm sure Miss Miller has plans this weekend, too."

"Well, not really," she said as they started walking toward the first-grade wing.

I heard Riley say, "Daddy, why don't you ask Miss Miller to come with us when we go to the Circle K tomorrow?" On most Saturday afternoons, weather permitting, relatives ride the horses kept in the stables there.

"The Circle K? Oh, yes, riding tomorrow," he said.

Leave it to Riley to come to the rescue. Now that her dad and DeLana had met, I suspected that she wasn't going to let the matter rest until they got to know each other a lot better.

❀　　❀　　❀

When I got home, I let the dogs out, then tossed in a load of laundry. Since my suitcase would be loaded with dirty clothes when I returned, I wanted to be sure everything else was clean before leaving.

I went to the garage and pulled my large suitcase from the storage closet. Since I hadn't traveled in a while, it was dusty. I used an old rag to wipe it down, and then I carried it inside. In the bedroom, I examined every piece of clothing for tears or stains before packing it. There was only one top that needed a button sewn back on.

Laying it aside, I searched through the drawer for a needle and thread, then set to work fixing it. After the button was back on, I folded the shirt and placed it in the suitcase on top of the other clothes.

I heard the puppies yipping to be let in, so I padded to the kitchen.

"I'm going to miss you guys while I'm gone," I told them as they scrambled inside. They sniffed their empty bowls, so I dumped some food into the dishes. "You be good for Uncle Doug, and maybe he'll let Joey come over and play with you."

As I tossed the clothes into the dryer, the phone started ringing. When I answered it, I heard "Aloha Oeeee, Aloha Oeeee, until we meet again."

Giggling, I said, "Nice sendoff, Frankie. A hui hou."

"What?"

"A hui hou. In Hawaiian it means, 'until we meet again.' I thought I ought to learn a few basic Hawaiian phrases, so I bought a dictionary online a few days ago."

"Leave it to a teacher to study for her vacation," he said.

"What's up?"

"I just got back from California last night, and I thought I'd fill you in on the latest details of the case. I talked with Fred Sanders and his nephew's wife, and they told me that checker games with Lester Crane had become an important part of their uncle's routine. In nice weather, they would sit on the porch and play for hours. Fred said that Lester loved the azaleas when they were blooming and that they reminded him of his mother's garden when he was a kid. Apparently, he told Fred that when he died, he'd like to have azaleas planted on his grave."

Uh oh. I was beginning to see where this was going.

"The best we can piece together, Lester died in the middle of a game while Mrs. Sanders was out shopping," Frankie continued. "Uncle Fred wanted to grant his friend his wish, so he put Lester under his bed until sometime that night. Then, while everyone was asleep, Fred dug a shallow grave under the azaleas and put Lester in it. Mrs. Sanders said the old man was upset when they told him they were moving to California, and I guess it's partly because he didn't want to leave his friend behind."

"I assume he's going to be in trouble for this," I said. "Isn't there some law about burying people in your yard?"

"Oklahoma has a statute regarding the burial of human remains in regulated cemeteries. In part, it's due to public health and safety issues. But with the age and medical condition of Mr. Sanders, I doubt if he'll be charged with anything."

Frankie and I talked for a few more minutes, then I went back to my packing. I was glad the matter was resolved and that all the body parts would be put in a proper place. Also, I hadn't had any more trouble with Luke Davis lately and assumed he was giving up. That was just fine with me.

CHAPTER 11

The next morning, my alarm clock woke me at 5:00 after a restless night's sleep. From the time I was a little girl, I was always too excited to sleep before a trip.

I took a quick shower and spent some extra time applying my makeup. After curling and fixing my hair, I put on a royal blue pantsuit. The flight to Hawaii would take almost twelve hours, with layovers in Salt Lake City and Los Angeles. I tend to get antsy on long trips, so I stuck the novel I had been reading, along with a crossword puzzle book, into my carryon bag. With the reading material and a good in-flight movie or two showing during the five hours over the ocean, I'd be fine.

By 6:30, I had my bags packed and sitting by the front door, waiting for my dad to come and take me to the airport.

"Rowdy, Precious, let's go to Uncle Doug's," I said as I washed my orange juice glass. I had made arrangements with him to keep the puppies, and Kristin had offered to water the plants and pick up my mail while I was gone.

The dogs had already been outside, but didn't seem too pleased about me waking them from their naps. They took their time stretching before I could get them into their crate. Once they were inside, I carried them across the yard, then set them down on Doug's porch.

Out of breath, I told them, "Either you two are putting on weight, or I need to exercise more." I rang Doug's doorbell and heard Mrs. Googan calling to Ginger.

"Now you don't go next door, do you hear me, Ginger?" she said. "That man threatened to skin you and put you in a pot of stew if he caught you pooping in his yard again."

She was trying to corral her dog while picking up her morning paper from the end of the driveway. As soon as her back was turned, the Pomeranian saw her chance to escape.

Ginger scampered next door, and I watched as she began sniffing around for a good spot. Just as she found it, I heard the Davises' screen door slam.

"Get out of here, you mutt!" Mr. Davis yelled. "I'm tired of you using my yard for your toilet!"

"Ginger, get over here, right now," Mrs. Googan hollered. "Ginger!"

The dog was ignoring her owner, and though I hated to get involved again, I couldn't stand by and watch Ginger get hurt.

Doug opened the front door with his hair standing on end and was dressed only in boxers and a T-shirt. "Please watch the puppies," I said. "Mrs. Googan needs a hand with her dog."

Though he looked like I had awakened him from a sound sleep, he became alert. "Why don't you stay here and let me corral that dog?" he said. "Remember what happened the last time you chased her? Body parts started turning up everywhere."

"You aren't presentable to go out in public," I said, "but I'll holler if I see a gun, machete or other lethal weapon."

As I dashed across the yard, I saw Mr. Davis heading toward Ginger. He had a walking cane raised above his head, and I knew that if he made contact, the dog would be history.

"Mr. Davis, stop!" I yelled, cringing as the curl of the cane missed Ginger's head by only inches. Ignoring me, he raised it up again, but before he could hit her, I reached down and scooped her into my arms.

"You're lucky, Missy," he hissed. "I could break your arm with this cane and the law couldn't touch me. Defending my property is a constitutional right, and you've been warned about trespassing."

As I stood glaring at the cruel man, I said, "I know what the constitution says, Mr. Davis. But I also know the laws about cruelty to animals."

Mrs. Googan ran over to me. "Oh, thank you, Allie. I don't know what I'd do without Ginger." Taking the dog from my arms, she cuddled her, then took a step back to see what was going to happen next.

My guardian angel was definitely with me because at that very moment, a patrol car drove by and stopped in front of the Davises' house. Carl Floyd rolled down his window and called out, "Hey, Allie. Everything alright?"

I looked at Mr. Davis. "What do *you* say? Is everything going to be alright?"

He gave me a hateful look, then shifted his attention toward the street. "Everything's fine, Officer," he said. "This young lady was just helping get her neighbor's dog back home."

Carl didn't look like he believed him, and I figured it was because Frankie had alerted his co-workers about my trouble with the Davises. But since Ginger was safe and I didn't want to miss my flight, I said, "It's okay, Carl. We've straightened out the situation."

Nodding at us, he waved, then cruised on down the street. I was sure Frankie would hear about this before my plane left the tarmac.

"That mutt's hide was saved this time," Mr. Davis snarled, "but if I catch her in my yard again, she'll be sorry."

Without saying another word to him, I turned around and walked away. Before she took Ginger back inside, Mrs. Googan thanked me again for my help. Doug had put on some jeans and a ball cap and was walking across his yard to meet me.

"I see you got Ginger back," he said.

"That man is one of the meanest people I've ever seen," I told him. "If I hadn't reached her in time, he was going to beat that little dog with his cane. Poor Mrs. Googan didn't know what to do, and it would have devastated her to see her dog hurt, or worse."

"You've got guts, I'll give you that," Doug said.

I saw my dad's pickup coming up the street. "Please don't tell Dad about this. It's all over now, anyway, and I don't want him to worry anymore than he already does."

"Okay, Amazon woman. I won't say a word."

He ducked as I threw a punch at him.

Laughing, he said, "How about a hug before you fly off into the wild blue yonder? And don't worry, I'll take good care of our children while you're gone."

Wrapping my arms around his waist, I gave him a squeeze, then waved good-bye as I walked to the driveway to meet my dad.

By the time we got to the airport and checked in my suitcase, I had only a few minutes to spare before I boarded the plane. After finding my row, I pulled out the novel, then stowed my carryon bag. A window seat in front of the right wing had been reserved for me, so I killed time watching the baggage personnel load suitcases onto the conveyor belt. The sunlight was sparkling like diamonds on the metal wings.

Soon the engines roared to life, and cool air started shooting from the vent above me. In twelve hours, I would be landing in Honolulu. With the time change, it would only be mid-afternoon there. Determined to ignore the butterflies in my stomach because of the upcoming interview, I focused on seeing Traci and going to exciting places with her. The last thing I remember is the plane climbing and the pilot welcoming everyone aboard.

I woke up when a flight attendant asked the lady behind me what she would like to drink. Wiping some drool off my chin, I poofed up my hair and glanced at my watch. I was surprised to see that an hour had passed since we had taken off. Between getting up at 5:00 and dealing with the stressful situation at the Davises', I guess my body needed the rest.

After drinking some root beer and eating the bag of peanuts I was given, I thought I had better check to be sure that I still looked presentable. Reaching into the side pocket of my purse, I fished for my compact and was surprised to find it wrapped in money. When my dad had hugged me good-bye, he must have slipped in the two fifty-dollar bills. He was determined to make sure I didn't get stranded without cash.

After touching up my face with the powder and disposing of my trash, I put the tray table back up and settled in to read my book.

By the time we landed in Salt Lake City, I was starving. The glass of orange juice from home and the snacks on the plane were long gone. It would be an hour before the plane left for Los Angeles, so I scouted through the airport until I found a Subway sandwich shop. I ordered a footlong club sandwich with extra mayo and added a bag of Cheetos and chocolate chip cookie to my tray. I opted for bottled water so I could save a few calories, then I checked out. After locating an empty table in the food court, I sat down to watch people while I ate.

From an early age, my mother had instilled in me that if you couldn't say something nice, don't say anything at all. I suppose that goes for thoughts, too, because more than once I admonished myself for being judgmental. So what if someone's tie didn't go with their shirt or that the woman was a little old to be wearing her skirt so short. *Mind your own business, Allie,* I thought.

Stuffed after eating every bite, I got rid of my trash, then started looking for the ladies room. By the time I freshened up and walked back to my gate, the attendant was calling for boarding to begin.

The flight to Los Angeles was bumpy, and I berated myself for eating so much. When drinks were offered, I took a Sprite, and it helped calm my queasy stomach.

When the plane landed a little late in L.A., I had less than an hour to walk the long concourse to the other side of the airport. At my gate, an enormous 767 was waiting to take us on to Hawaii. Boarding had begun, and as I drew closer to the door of the plane, I could hear ukuleles on the audio system strumming, "Aloha Oe." I smiled when I thought about how much this version differed from Frankie's.

After walking through spacious first class, the seats became smaller and more compact. There were rows of two seats along each side of the plane and three in a row through the center. Mine was on the left side in row eighteen on the aisle.

The flow of traffic was interrupted when a large man with his arm in a sling stopped at the row in front of mine. He was trying to put his heavy bag into the overhead compartment. He wasn't making any headway because previously stowed bags were turned sideways and were taking up most of the space. Used to making every inch count in my closets at home, I set my carryon bag and purse down and offered him my assistance.

While trying to hold his bag in the air with his good arm, he looked at me and said, "Do you have any suggestions? Those other bags are taking up too much room."

"If I can get on the other side of you, I think they can be turned, freeing up some space," I said.

The passengers behind me were getting impatient to pass. He pressed himself against his seat and I squeezed between him and the seat across from his. After I got around him, I reached into the compartment and quarter-turned one bag and made it fit in less space. I tried the same procedure with the second bag and though it was about the same size, it weighed several more pounds than the first one. The bag was tilted at an awkward angle, so I reached in for a better grip and pulled harder on it. It popped into place, but in the process, I lost my balance and toppled into the lap of the man sitting in the aisle seat behind me.

My legs were dangling over the edge of his armrest, pinning his left arm. I tried to lift my legs off of him and get up, but ended up kicking the thigh of the man with the sling.

Surprised and embarrassed, I apologized to the man, then turned to face the person I was sitting on. Looking into brown eyes that reminded me of pools of melted chocolate, I lost my train of thought. Charcoal black hair fell over his forehead, and his lips were parted, showing even, white teeth.

Smiling, he nodded toward the aisle. "When that guy gets situated, I'll help you up, though you're welcome to stay here as long as you like."

"Thanks; I mean no thanks," I sputtered, but his widening smile put me at ease. "I'm sorry about this."

"Well, I have to tell you, it's the most enjoyable thing that's happened to me all day." Bringing his right hand between us and extending it toward mine, he said, "I'm Simon, by the way."

"Hi, I'm Allison Kane." His hand encircled mine like a glove, and I was reluctant to pull it free.

The man with the sling had settled into his seat, and the aisle was clear. While still being cradled in Simon's arms, he lifted me up. I only weigh a hundred and twenty pounds, but in the cramped quarters of the plane, it took real strength for him to do it.

He set me in the aisle. "There you go, Miss Kane. Good as new."

A few passengers, who had been watching the ordeal, started clapping. I could feel the heat in my face, and I knew I must be as red as a beet.

"Thanks for your help," I said. "Now I'd better get to my seat."

Before picking up my carryon bag, that still rested where I had put it, I reached inside and pulled out the novel. I placed the bag in the overhead compartment, then picked up my purse. As I turned toward my seat, I glanced Simon's way and saw him wink at me. Still embarrassed by the ordeal, I just smiled, then sat down and buckled my seatbelt.

By the time the plane had leveled off at thirty thousand feet, the Japanese man sitting beside me had introduced himself. He had been born and raised on Oahu and was returning home after visiting his sister, who now lived in Washington.

"She left the island over twenty years ago," he said, "but I intend to be buried there."

With pride in his voice, he said he owned the *Hawaiian Star*, a bi-weekly newspaper that had over twenty thousand subscribers throughout the occupied Hawaiian Islands. He had started the paper when he was in his thirties with only a hundred customers, and I guessed that he was in his seventies now.

"The *Star* may not be a daily paper, but people like to hear what I have to report," Mr. Masaki said. "I go beyond the simple facts and don't stop until I get to the meat of the matter. My staff examines all the angles, even after the other rags have forgotten about it."

After the attendant brought us our dinners, we continued to chat about teaching kids today and more about the newspaper business. I told him I had always been interested in writing and covered the elementary school news for the *Paradise Progress*. When I was twelve, I convinced Aunt Marilyn, the owner of the paper, into letting me submit stories covering the events at my school. By the time I reached high school, she was paying me a salary to write weekly articles, and she hired another person to help me with the event calendar.

Handing me his business card, Mr. Masaki said, "If you're interested, come by my office in Kalihi. I'd like to show you around. Then you can go back to Oklahoma and tell your aunt how the *Star* compares with your hometown paper. After seeing the place, you might decide you'd like to move to Hawaii and work for me."

I knew that was unlikely, but thanked him and told him I would try to make it down for a tour.

"I'm going to hush now," he said, turning on his laptop, "so you can watch the movie."

I adjusted my earphones and leaned back in my seat as shades were drawn and lights were dimmed.

The movie was a comedy and one I hadn't seen before. Absorbed in the story and laughing until tears rolled down my face, time flew by. When it was over and the lights had come back on, the pilot announced that we were starting our descent and would be at the Honolulu airport within thirty minutes.

I hadn't wanted to miss any of the movie to go to the bathroom, so my bladder was about to explode. The lavatory ahead of me was occupied, so I looked behind and saw that one near the galley was open. Feeling the need to freshen my makeup and brush my hair, I picked up my purse and started down the aisle.

Walking past Simon's empty seat, I was relieved that I didn't have to face him after our earlier encounter. But I also realized that I was a little disappointed. As I neared the bathroom, I could hear the crew laughing, then saw him leaning against one of the counters. He looked at me and waved.

Nodding at him, I hurried inside the compartment, then closed and latched the door.

After using the toilet, I washed my hands and was shocked when, in the mirror's reflection, I saw the straps of my purse dangling on the inside of the door. The bag itself was hanging on the outside of it!

Berating myself for not noticing sooner, I tried to move the latch, but it wouldn't budge. The extra bulk from the leather straps was causing too much strain on the opening.

Determined not to be outwitted by a bathroom door, I pulled on the doorknob while pushing hard on the latch. When it released, I heard a thump as my purse hit the floor. Hoping it hadn't been noticed by too many people, I shoved open the door and heard a loud *"Bang!"*

Someone hollered, "Ouch!" Through the opening, I could see Simon sitting on the floor, holding my purse in one hand and his head in the other.

"Oh, I'm so sorry," I said. "I didn't realize anyone was there."

He looked up at me, and I could see a large, red bump starting to form on his cheek. Handing my purse to me, he said, "I believe this belongs to you."

An attendant showed up carrying a small bag of ice and handed it to him. "This should help control the swelling," she told him.

"Thanks, Marcia," he said.

Turning to me, she said rather coldly, "The captain has turned on the seatbelt sign. Please take your seat."

Feeling like a complete idiot, I knelt next to Simon. "At least let me help you up."

He moved his elbow so that I could get my hand beneath it. Grinning, he said, "You won't drop me, will you?"

I couldn't help smiling back at him. "Not more than once or twice."

Though I wasn't sure if I was helping or hindering, he managed to stand up. He handed the ice pack back to the attendant, then turned to me.

"The plane's about to land," he said. "I'm not sure if Hawaii is ready for you, Miss Kane, but I've enjoyed meeting you. I wish you the best and hope you have a great vacation."

A strange sadness swept over me at the thought of never seeing him again. Brushing the feeling aside, I said, "I'll try not to do too much damage while I'm here. Thanks for being such a good sport."

After I returned to my seat and buckled myself in, Mr. Masaki said, "He seems like a nice young man. I believe he's been in some photos I've taken for the paper, though I don't recall now what the occasion was."

By the time we taxied to the gate and the seatbelt sign went off, everyone was gathering their belongings and crowding the aisles waiting for the door to open. As we started moving, I glanced back one last time, but didn't see Simon. Following Mr. Masaki out the door and up the ramp to the terminal, I focused my attention on trying to find Traci.

When I reached the baggage area, I saw her and her husband, Tommy, waving and hurrying toward me. I rushed to meet them.

"Girl, you look great!" Traci said, hugging me. "You haven't gained an ounce, and your hair is shorter. I'm so glad you're here!"

"I've missed you so much!" I said, "and you look great, too, though I believe you've gained a few pounds."

Proudly touching her stomach, Traci said, "Yes, I've gained ten pounds, but I won't need maternity clothes for another month at least, darn it. I can't wait to be a Mommy!"

Walking up to Tommy, I put my arms around him. "Sorry to ignore you, big guy. It's good to see you, too."

"Same here," he said, returning the hug. "I'm glad you're going to be around for a few days. Traci has been pretty homesick. Maybe you can bring her out of the doldrums."

"It probably has to do with a change in hormones, but I have been kind of gloomy," she said. "I wish Mom was around to share in my excitement about this little guy and help me plan the nursery. But, until we get back to Oklahoma in June, e-mail and phone calls will have to do."

When I pointed out my bag as it came around on the carousel, Tommy pulled it off and released the handle. "Come on, girls. Let's go home."

❁　　❁　　❁

Barely taking a breath between sentences, Traci and I chattered all the way to their high-rise apartment in Aiea. When Tommy pulled into the parking lot, we passed by the garden units and headed to the tower garage. Looking at the building stretching skyward, I told Traci that it was a far cry from her parents' sprawling ranch back in Paradise.

"You'll find that the sprawling on the island goes upward, instead of out," she said. "Land prices are beyond the reach for common folk, and simple frame houses sell for hundreds of thousands of dollars."

After insisting that Tommy take some pictures of us in front of the building, we stopped at their mailbox before getting into the elevator. Traci punched number seventeen, and I teased them, saying that I might get a nosebleed staying up so high.

When we walked into their small apartment, the first thing I saw was the breathtaking view through the glass door. I dropped my carryon and purse next to their couch and walked onto the lanai for a better look. Their apartment faced eastward, and in the distance, I could see the curve of a rainbow against a few dark clouds. To the left of the building was a manicured golf course, speckled with players and carts.

Stepping out alongside me, Traci said, "It's pretty, isn't it?"

"Pretty doesn't begin to describe it!" I said.

"Take a look toward the south," she said. "That's Pearl Harbor. You've got to see the USS *Arizona* Memorial while you're here. I still get misty whenever I go there and see all those names representing the lives that were lost that day."

Just then, Tommy hollered from inside. "You'd better let her get unpacked, Traci. Our reservations for dinner are in less than an hour."

"Reservations? Don't feel like you have to wine and dine me while I'm here. Sandwiches and chips would be fine."

"We couldn't let you spend your first night in Hawaii in a stuffy apartment, so we're taking you to one of our favorite cafés on the beach," she said. "On Saturday nights, they're so busy, you have to make reservations or end up waiting an hour for a table. There is live music, and dress is casual. I knew you'd be tired from traveling, and with the four-hour time change, you'll probably want to get to bed early. The reservations are for 6:00, so we'll be home by nine."

"Sounds like fun," I said. "If you don't mind, I'll take a quick shower and change clothes."

"Right this way."

We walked back inside, and she gave me a quick tour of the two-bedroom apartment. Tommy had already set my bags in the guest bedroom, which contained a double bed and matching dresser.

"I've set out some towels, soap and washcloths for you, and if you need anything else, just let me know," Traci said.

I unpacked my suitcase and hung up a few things, then gathered up some toiletries and headed to the shower. Feeling refreshed once the traveling grime was washed away, I blow-dried my hair and put on fresh makeup. I dressed in a light blue skirt and matching top, then put on a pair of strappy sandals.

When I came into the living room, Tommy had changed shirts and was watching the news on television. Turning down the volume, he said, "How was your trip?"

I told him everything went well and that I'd met some interesting people on the plane, skipping the parts about the embarrassing blunders. While I was telling him about Mr. Masaki, Traci walked into the living room. When we looked at each other, we both burst out laughing.

"I see you still have good taste in fashion," she said. She was dressed in a baby blue skirt with a coordinating top and her sandals were identical to mine. When we were growing up, we had favored the same colors and styles and often dressed alike. Our years apart hadn't changed that.

We left the apartment and walked to the car. While driving to the café, Traci drilled me about the latest happenings in Paradise. The only time Tommy could get a word in edgewise was to point out an attraction along the way.

I couldn't believe I was finally in Hawaii! I could taste the salt air on my lips, and though the humidity was playing havoc with my hair,

I didn't care. It was great to be with my good friends in this heavenly place.

The Red Reef Café was located a short distance from Waikiki and was frequented by more locals than tourists. The specialty was shrimp and oysters served with greens grown in nearby Waimanalo. We stuffed ourselves while enjoying the music from two different bands, but by 8:30, I was trying to stifle my yawns.

"You know, it's after midnight in Paradise, and traveling wears you out," Traci said as we walked to the car. "I told you I thought you'd be ready for bed early."

"I guess I'm a little jet-lagged, but I can sleep at home. While I'm here, I want to do and see everything I can. Those bands were great, and the food was delicious, though I ate enough to last me for the next three days. Thank you for a terrific evening."

"We love it down here," Tommy said. "Though we don't eat out a lot, we treat ourselves to the Red Reef a couple times a month. We're trying to pinch the extra pennies I got with my promotion to get stuff for the baby."

Driving back to their apartment, we discussed the baby, and I tossed in some advice from the experience I had had taking care of my nieces. The couple couldn't agree on any names, though Traci was adamant that, if they had a girl, she wouldn't be called Ima Lou after Tommy's aunt.

As we neared their apartment building, I saw an elderly couple on the sidewalk. Reminded of my grandparents, I said, "Gramma asked about you and told me to give you her love."

"She is so sweet," Traci said. "I probably wouldn't be playing the piano at church if she hadn't encouraged me to practice."

"Speaking of church, what time do I need to get up in the morning?"

"It takes about thirty minutes to get to Kaneohe from here," Traci said. "I like to have materials spread out before my students arrive, so we leave home about 9:00. I'll just fix some sweet rolls or scrambled eggs and toast for breakfast if that's alright with you."

"I'm so full now, I may not want anything," I said.

After the car was parked, we walked around to the back of the building and looked at the swimming pool reserved for tenants. Soft lights shone in the water, and lanterns were hanging on poles scattered around the edge of the patio. A few people were lying on lounge chairs, talking and listening to oldies music playing on a radio.

"I hate to leave you alone while I'm teaching this week, but you can always come out here and work on your tan until I get home each afternoon," Traci said.

"Don't worry about me. I'll help out in your classroom on Monday until my interview, then I might take 'The Bus' to that shopping center we passed."

"Ala Moana is one of the largest centers in the world, and you should be able to kill several hours there," she said.

Walking into the apartment building, I was ready to call it a day. I balked when Traci suggested we get off at the tenth floor and walk the rest of the way to the seventeenth.

"We need to work off some of our dinner," she said. "I wouldn't want you to get fat while you're here."

I was dragging my feet by the time we stepped out of the stairwell into the hallway. Sure that someone would have to carry me into the apartment, I was rejuvenated when Tommy opened the door. Through the windows, the lights of the night were breathtaking! I stood on the lanai for a few minutes letting the warm sea breezes sweep through my hair. Then, pulling myself away from the view, I told them goodnight and got ready for bed.

With the traffic noises coming from H-1, one of the three state highways that run through the island, I figured I would have a hard time sleeping. But as soon as my head hit the pillow, I was out like a light.

CHAPTER 12

When the bright sunlight coming through the window the next morning woke me up, it took me a minute to orient myself. I heard the sound of aluminum pans clanging on the stove in the kitchen and horns honking from the freeway below.

I grabbed my robe from the end of the bed, and walked barefoot into the bathroom to wash my face. The right side of my hair was smashed, so I pulled a brush through it a couple of times, then headed toward the kitchen. I smiled when I saw Traci stirring eggs in the old skillet her grandmother used to cook in.

"You sound just like her, you know," I said.

Traci looked at me standing in the doorway. "Yes, I pride myself in carrying on the family tradition. Grandma always needed the pan on the bottom, and instead of lifting the top ones out, she just pulled out the one she needed, causing them to fall and make a racket."

Traci and I had spent many nights with her Grandma Ruthie, and we would always be awakened the following morning by the crash of pots and pans.

"I hope the traffic didn't keep you awake last night," Traci said. "About 3:00, there was a wreck a half mile down on H-1, and at least four ambulances responded."

"I didn't hear a thing. In fact, I don't think I even turned over from the way my hair looks this morning."

"Yeah, it really looks terrible," she teased. "I don't know how you go out in public everyday with a mop like that."

Though she had always been good-natured about it, my manageable hair tended to be a thorn in Traci's side. Her hair was thin and curly, and it definitely had a mind of its own.

Carrying the pan full of scrambled eggs and a plate stacked with buttered toast to the table, she said, "Would you please grab some of those napkins and that plate full of bacon on the counter? You'll have plenty of time to do something with that mess on your head after breakfast."

"What's the matter with Allie's head?" Tommy asked as he walked to the table. "It looks fine to me."

Since he had only heard the last part of the conversation and didn't know the story behind the comment, Traci said, "Nothing, honey. Sit down and eat before your breakfast gets cold." Smiling at me, she took her place at the table and said grace.

I helped myself to two pieces of toast, a large spoonful of eggs and some bacon. Tommy had two large helpings of eggs, four slices of toast and five pieces of bacon. When I was finished, I felt like a glutton because Traci had eaten less than I had, and she was supposed to be eating for two. I pushed back my plate so I wouldn't be tempted to eat more. Tommy made a bacon sandwich out of the remaining toast and meat.

Carrying some dishes to the kitchen, I said, "I was sure after last night's feast that I wouldn't be hungry, but that was the best breakfast I've eaten in ages."

"It's the sea air," Traci said. "When we first moved here, I gained twelve pounds in six weeks. I had never had trouble with my weight until then, but I had to start swimming and running to get it off."

When the table was cleared and the dishes were in the dishwasher, I excused myself to get ready for church. Traci had told me that, for women in Hawaii, the traditional dress was muumuus and sundresses and that they rarely wore pantyhose. Delighted to be able to go casual, I put on one of the new dresses Dad had paid for. The day was warming up, so I swept my hair into a knot on my head, leaving some tendrils hanging along my neck and ears.

With time to spare, Traci suggested to Tommy that we take the Likelike Highway through the mountain to Kaneohe. "The tall trees and foliage along the highway are gorgeous, and I want her to see the view when we come out on the other side," she told him.

He agreed to take that route, but he said we would need to use H-3 coming home. "I need to stop by the base for a few minutes after church," he said, looking at me through the rearview mirror. "While we're there, I'll give you a short tour."

Enjoying the scenery along the way, it wasn't long until I saw a sign on the side of the road that said the Wilson Tunnel was just ahead. Tommy turned on his headlights and told me that it had been completed in the early 1960s, right after the Pali Tunnels were done. He had to raise his voice as we drove through it because the engine noises were amplified as the sound bounced off the walls.

"Up to that time, people had to drive around the island on the Kamehameha Highway to get from one side to the other," he said. "Drilling tunnels through a mountain is pretty amazing, if you ask me."

As we neared the end of the tunnel, Traci said, "Get ready now."

"What am I supposed to be looking for?" I asked.

"That!"

She didn't have to say any more. The sight of the crystal clear ocean stretching to the horizon at the base of the mountain left me breathless. The sunlight glistened off the shades of aqua, sapphire and royal blue. As the car wound down the mountain, I couldn't take in the beauty fast enough. The curving highway offered several angles from which to view the display as we descended to the outskirts of Kaneohe.

"Isn't that the most beautiful sight you've ever seen?" Traci asked. "I've seen that picture hundreds of times, and I still can't take my eyes off it when we drive over here. To me, it looks like God took a huge canvas and started splashing every rich, magnificent color He could find onto it."

"I agree. I wish I had thought to take some pictures as we came down, but maybe I'll be back over here again this week. Mom and my grandmothers would go wild if they could see this."

We took a side road to reach the small, white church. When we got inside, Traci and Tommy started introducing me to everyone. Each person I met was friendly and treated me like royalty. The furnishings were simple, and no air conditioning was needed because the windward breezes were blowing through the slatted windows.

I followed Traci to her Sunday school room and helped her put out the supplies. When the students came in, I couldn't help comparing them to my kids at home. The shades of their skin were different in some cases, but their desire to be there was written all over their faces.

When church was over, everyone shook my hand and told me they hoped that I would enjoy my stay on the island. Climbing into the car, I said, "I didn't mean to hold you up. Those nice people were determined to wish me well."

"I knew you'd be bombarded with welcomes," Tommy said. "This is one of the kindest, most eager to help congregations on this side of the island."

I relaxed in the back seat and enjoyed every bit of the view to the Kaneohe Bay Military Base. After clearing security to get inside, Tommy pointed out various buildings and gave me a mini history lesson about the base as a whole. He took Traci and me inside to see his office, and he introduced me to a couple of men there.

He said he only needed about ten minutes to gather some things to finish a report that was due the next evening. While he collected what he needed, Traci and I found a shady spot near the entrance to sit and watch people.

"How about going to the beach after lunch?" she said. "I can still squeeze into my bathing suit, and I'm sure you brought a new one along."

"Two, in fact," I said. "Do you know a place we can go that's not covered wall-to-wall with people?"

"I sure do, and it's not too far from the apartment. Tommy will be busy with his report, then watching basketball on television, so we can take our time and gossip without him around."

"Sounds like fun."

Tommy came to get us, and before leaving Kaneohe, we stopped at a fried chicken place for lunch. I insisted on paying for our meals. Before they gave me any trouble about it, I told them about the stash that my dad had put in my purse at the airport.

Traveling home on H-3, I got to see different sites. When we reached the apartment, Traci and I put on our swimsuits and headed toward the beach. True to her word, it offered some privacy, though there were several families and a couple of body surfers testing the waters.

After applying sunscreen onto her fair skin, Traci adjusted her hat and then stretched out on a large beach towel. Being one of the lucky ones to tan instead of burn, I just put a dab of low strength sunscreen on my cheeks, nose and shoulders.

I stretched out on my towel next to Traci. She asked what was new with the Lester Crane story. I relayed to her what Frankie had told me. Then I mentioned meeting Simon and the incident with the man's bag and my purse getting caught in the door on the plane. Sitting up, she took off her sunglasses and wanted to know every detail.

"He sounds like a dream," she said. "Too bad you didn't get a last name. If he lived here, you might have been able to look him up."

"Well, he never offered a last name, and as handsome as he is, he probably has a girlfriend, anyway. Besides, I wouldn't have the nerve to call him."

"You've got to be more assertive with men. They like to be pursued."

I wasn't sure I agreed with her, so I let the matter drop.

Between stories about school and our families, we paddled around in the water. After she beat me in a race back to shore, we flopped down on our towels and started brushing off the sand that was sticking to us.

"This reminds me of a time when we were in kindergarten," she said.

"You mean when you terrorized David Jones."

"Defending your honor is more like it."

When we were five, we were playing in the sandbox at school. While I was kneeling down, working on my sandcastle, David came up behind me and dumped a big cup of sand down my pants. When I stood up, it ran down my legs, and the back of my shorts were droopy. Embarrassed, I started crying, and Traci came over to find out why.

Instead of going to get the teacher, she took matters into her own hands. Though he was several pounds heavier, she pushed David to the ground, then straddled his chest and rubbed a handful of gritty sand into his hair. By the time the teacher saw what was happening and got to them, Traci had collected a bunch of spit in her mouth. She was about to deposit it into David's mouth, unless he told me he was sorry.

The teacher pulled Traci off of him, and both sets of parents had to come in for a conference. But David never bothered me again. From that day forward, Traci and I had been best friends and taken the heat more than once for each other.

Laughing until my cheeks hurt, I said, "I'm ready to go, how about you?"

"Yeah, I've had more than enough sun for one day."

Gathering up our towels and bags, we rinsed off the salty grit and sand at one of the showers on the beach, then headed for home.

When I awoke at 6:00 on Monday morning, I took some extra care while getting ready. My interview was at 10:00, and I wanted to make a good impression on Miss Kahala. Since Traci had overslept and was rushing to get ready, I fixed some cinnamon toast and cut up some papaya and set it on the table.

"Breakfast is ready," I called to them.

As I set a pot of steaming coffee on the table, along with a pitcher of orange juice I had found in the fridge, Tommy walked into the room. "Well, isn't this nice. I normally have to fend for myself on weekdays."

Traci came in and plopped down at the table. "Thanks, Allie, this is great. I'm lucky if I get a few bites of yogurt or maybe some juice down before rushing out the door on school days."

"Well, I was ready to go and saw you needed a hand."

"I haven't had cinnamon toast since I was at my parents' house," Tommy said, reaching for a third slice. "I think you should stay and cook for us all the time."

Wiping the papaya juice off her lips, Traci said, "I vote for that. Besides her domestic qualities, she's going to assist me with my class today. I've always wanted a full time aide."

"You couldn't afford me," I said, smiling. "Besides, you'd just get spoiled and lazy."

Traci scooted back from the table and started gathering up dirty dishes. "I hope we'll get to have you around in June. I believe you're a shoe-in for the job. You're qualified, and I'm confident that you'll be able to charm your way into Miss Kahala's heart."

I carried the empty pitcher and fruit bowl to the kitchen. "I hope I get the job. I love it here."

When the table was cleared, I went to brush my teeth and put on some lipstick. Looking critically at the navy skirt and jacket that I had chosen to wear, I started picking at some lint on the sleeve.

"Come on, Miss Perfect," Traci said from the doorway. "It's 7:15, and the school is ten miles away."

Grabbing my purse, I headed out the door with Traci.

As Traci pulled out of the parking lot onto Moanalua Road, I was astounded at the bumper-to-bumper traffic we encountered. Crawling along for fifteen minutes, we only covered two miles. Once we connected to H-1, the flow of cars began to pick up speed.

"There must be some construction or an accident up ahead," I said. "Surely this isn't a typical drive for you."

"A little different than driving in Paradise, isn't it?" Traci said. "It takes at least forty minutes for me to get to work each morning. The afternoon drive home is better, as long as I leave school by 4:00."

We exited the expressway a few minutes before eight, then wound through residential streets to the school. Pulling into the parking lot, several other teachers were just arriving, and Traci introduced me to them as we walked inside.

"I'd like you to tell the kids a little about yourself if you don't mind," she said as she unlocked her classroom door. "For some of them, English is their second language and may live with parents who don't speak it at home. A few have been taught some unusual lessons about mainland living and are curious about the kids there."

"But you came from there, too," I said. "Has that caused problems for you?"

"I had some struggles the first year overcoming the 'haole syndrome,' but you helped me solve that problem."

"I don't have a clue what 'haole syndrome' is, so how could I have helped you solve it?"

"'Haole' means 'not native Hawaiian,'" she said. "I started holding parent meetings at the beginning of the school year like you do. It gives them a chance to look me over, ask me one-on-one questions and see the room in an informal setting. I've had such good luck with it, some of the other teachers are doing the same thing."

"Glad I could be of help, though I didn't realize that I was."

The first bell rang, and after welcoming her second-graders, Traci introduced me to them. Some of them had never heard of Oklahoma, so I pulled down a map hanging above the blackboard and pointed it out to them. One little boy, who had a very thick Chinese accent, asked me if Indians still lived in tepees there. After assuring everyone that tepees had been replaced by houses, I told them a little about the pilgrimage of the Five Civilized Tribes, the Trail of Tears and about my own Osage background.

While all the students were starting center activities, I slipped out for my interview with Miss Kahala. Before I reached the office, a girl that looked to be the age of one of my third-graders came out of a classroom wiping tears from her cheeks. Walking toward her, I stopped and asked if I could do something to help her.

Wringing her hands, she said, "Multiplication is hard. I study at night, but when I get to school, I forget everything."

I stooped down in front of her so that we were at eye level. "Are you having trouble with all the sets, or just certain ones?"

"I finally learned a lot of them, but we've been on the nines for two weeks, and I'm too stupid to remember the answers," she said, covering her face with her hands.

Taking her hands in mine, I said, "What's your name?"

"Samantha Carlson," she said, sniffling.

"Samantha, you are not stupid. Sometimes multiplication *is* hard." Reaching into my pocket, I pulled out a tissue and handed it to her. "Now I want you to take some deep breaths, then I'm going to tell you a trick to help you remember the nines."

"You are?" Her body relaxed with relief.

"The two digits in the answer always add up to nine, and they follow a pattern. For instance, if you have nine times two, the answer is eighteen, because one plus eight equals nine. If you have nine times three, it's twenty-seven, because two plus seven equals nine. Now what do you think nine times four is?"

She thought for a second, then blurted out, "Thirty-six?"

"You've got it! See, that's not so hard, is it? Now go to the bathroom and wipe your face with a wet paper towel, then go show your teacher you can do it."

"Thanks for your help, Miss...," she said.

"Kane," a voice behind me said.

I turned around to find a tall woman in a red floral muumuu standing behind me.

"Thanks, Miss Kane. You've helped me a lot," Samantha said, smiling.

"I'll sign your hall pass for you, Samantha, then go wipe your face like

Miss Kane suggested," the woman said. "It looks like you won't need to visit the counselor after all."

"Not about this, Miss Kahala," she replied, handing a slip of paper to her. Samantha was grinning ear to ear when she turned around and headed back to her classroom.

"You made that child's day," the principal said, "and her parents, too, I imagine. She has been coming to see the counselor at least twice a week all spring, primarily for stress ailments from math. Her teacher is very competent, but hasn't been able to get past the block that has plagued Samantha."

I glanced at the wall clock above her head and cringed when I saw it was after ten. "I'm sorry to be late for our interview, Miss Kahala. I try to always be on time for appointments."

"Time is relative," she said. "You took the time to help a student in distress, and that's more important than trying to impress me with your promptness. Now, let's take a walk, and while I show you our school, we can get to know each other better."

The unique style and character of the old building impressed me. By the displays I saw on the walls, it was easy to see that the teachers took pride in their surroundings and students' work. When we walked outside, the principal explained that, as enrollment grew, prefabs were added instead of building onto the structure itself.

"Resources are tight, Miss Kane." The woman sat down on a bench that was sitting at the edge of the playground. She indicated that I should sit beside her. "My teachers can stretch a ruler into a yardstick, but building on an island is very expensive. Fortunately, I have some leeway with the two summer school positions, thanks to the government grants."

She took her time explaining about the provisions for salaries and expenses, among other things, then asked if I had any questions. Between her explanation and Traci's, I couldn't think of a thing. Walking back into the coolness of the building, I was surprised that she hadn't asked about my teaching methods, or to see my certificate. I hadn't been given an application to fill out, and when I offered her my resume, she gave it a cursory glance, then said she would give it to her assistant to file.

When we reached Traci's door, she said, "I interviewed twelve people last week and still have fourteen applicants to go. My nephew Richard thinks highly of your family, and Traci is one of the most dedicated teachers that I've ever had work for me. I respect their opinions and take their references regarding you seriously. You'll receive a call from me as soon as I've made my decision."

Hoping more than ever that I would make the cut, I smiled and said, "Thank you for flying me in to talk with you. I hope to get the job."

"Thank you for coming, Allison. It's been a pleasure meeting you."

I could hear Traci's students behind the door lining up for lunch. As I opened it, I was bombarded by young voices saying things like, "Hey, Miss Kane's back," and, "Hi, Miss Kane."

I hope I impressed Miss Kahala the way I have these kids, I thought. But, I wasn't sure I had.

In the afternoon, I changed my mind about going to the Ala Moana Center and opted to help Traci by taking down a bulletin board and grading some papers. After school, we walked to the office, and I waited outside the door while she signed out. I was glancing through some safety pamphlets hanging on a nearby bulletin board when I heard the office door open.

"Traci, does your school have a Drug Awareness program like we do back home?" I asked.

Getting no response, I turned around and nearly fell over when I saw Simon standing there.

He looked as shocked as I was. "Miss Kane, this is a pleasant surprise. What brings you here?"

While I stood there, trying to push an answer out of my mouth, the principal and Traci walked through the door.

Miss Kahala looked at me. "I see you've met my nephew. He came by to wish me 'Happy Birthday' since he's working and will miss my surprise party tonight."

"We've met before, Aunt Nalani, but I'm surprised to find her here," Simon said, his eyes never leaving my face.

"I interviewed her today for one of the summer school positions. Then she spent the afternoon working in her friend's classroom."

Embarrassed by his intense stare, I still hadn't uttered a word.

Giving me a puzzled look, Traci stepped over to him and stuck out her hand. "Hi, I'm Traci Morris. How do you know Allie?" Tact had never been one of Traci's strong points.

He turned his attention from me to her. "It's nice to meet you, Ms. Morris. I met her Saturday on a plane from L.A."

By the look on Traci's face, I could tell she was putting two and two together. Before she could say anything I'd regret, I stepped over and took her arm. "We'd better get going. They have a party to attend."

Behind me, Miss Kahala said, "Wait a minute, girls. Simon, I know you're working, but you'll still have to eat dinner. Why don't you take Allison somewhere nice to eat? She's only going to be here for a few days."

If there had been a rock close by, I would have crawled beneath it! Standing at an angle where only I could see her hands, Traci gave me a "thumbs up."

"I'd be glad to take you out, if you don't already have other plans," he said to me. "Do you?"

A pity date, that's what this is, I thought. To save face, he was giving in to his aunt's suggestion.

Before I could answer him, Traci said, "You don't have any plans, do you, Allie? I need to grade some papers and wash my hair tonight, so it will be boring if you stay at home with me. Go out; have some fun."

I gave her a sickly smile because she knew good and well that I had graded all her papers today and she always washes her hair in the morning.

"Looks like you're stuck with me, then," Simon said. "If you'd like to go, give me directions to your friend's place and I'll pick you up about seven."

Remembering my manners and afraid of offending Miss Kahala if I didn't accept her nephew's invitation, I said, "I'd be happy to have dinner with you. Traci, will you please tell him how to get to your apartment?"

"I need to finish a project before I pick you up," Simon said. "If you don't mind, let's walk to the parking lot, and I can get the directions along the way." He leaned over and kissed his aunt's cheek. "Your party was supposed to be a secret, so don't let Mom know that you found out."

"I wouldn't dream of spoiling the fun. Charlene has probably been cooking all day. She gives the best parties on the island, and I plan on attending a lot more of them. Now run along and have a good time at dinner tonight."

Walking beside him, I admired the way his broad shoulders filled out the silky shirt he wore. He looked like he was about six feet tall.

"How should I dress?" I asked as he opened my car door for me.

"Casual is fine. I'll be on call, so we'll have to save the formal restaurant for another night."

Another night? Be still my heart.

CHAPTER 13

Traci insisted on helping me choose my outfit that evening. Though I hadn't brought a lot of dressy clothes with me, we agreed that the new gold sundress and sandals would be fine. If Simon did ask to take me somewhere more formal later on, I would need to go shopping.

When I walked into the living room, Tommy whistled.

"She cleans up pretty good for an Oklahoma girl, doesn't she?" Traci said.

"You're going to knock him off his feet for sure," Tommy said.

"I hope so," I said. I was so nervous, I thought I might throw up.

Tommy turned his attention back to the basketball game on television. "Would you please pass the bowl of potato chips this way, hon?" he said to Traci. "And if you don't mind, I could use another Pepsi while you're up."

"Yes, my lord," she said, handing him the bowl. As she headed to the refrigerator, the buzzer for the security door sounded. She looked at me. "Right on time. This guy's a keeper." She flipped the switch on the intercom.

"It's Simon. Is Allie about ready?"

Taking her finger off the control, Traci looked at me. "Tommy's right. You're going to knock him for a loop when he sees you. Are you ready for him to come up?"

"As ready as I'll ever be, I guess."

Flipping the switch again, she said, "Simon, I'm going to buzz you in. We're on seventeen in number 1707."

"Be right up."

Within a couple of minutes, I heard the elevator bell at the end of the hall. If I had been a nail biter, I would have had only nubs left. I opened the door just as he was about to raise his hand to knock.

"Good timing," he said.

"And you didn't end up on the floor with a bump on your head. See, I'm improving."

"I wasn't going to bring that up, but I did bring you something else."

I hadn't noticed that one hand was behind his back. When he brought it around, he held a large bouquet of red roses.

I was stunned at the kind gesture. "Thank you so much. They're beautiful!"

Taking the flowers from him, I inhaled the heady perfume as he followed me into the living room. He and Traci exchanged greetings, then I introduced him to Tommy.

"I'll put these in some water, then we can go," I said.

As I trailed Traci into the kitchen to get a vase, the men turned their attention to the three-pointer that had just been scored in the game.

"Those flowers are gorgeous," Traci said as she filled a crystal vase with water.

"Yes, and they smell heavenly. Mom charges over forty dollars a dozen for roses like these in her shop."

"They probably cost more than that here," Traci said. "Do you know what kind of job he has?"

"I don't have a clue."

"You don't have a clue about what?" Simon said behind me. I jumped at the sound of his voice.

"Sorry, I didn't mean to scare you, but if you're ready, we should get going."

"Of course," I said, picking up my clutch bag from the counter.

"It was nice meeting both of you," Simon said. "Since I'm working, I'll have her home early."

"See you guys later. Have fun," Traci said, winking at me.

As we walked down the hallway, Simon stayed close but didn't touch me. Following me into the elevator, he pressed the ground floor button.

When it started moving, I self-consciously brushed away some lint from my skirt and noticed his black shoes were buffed to a high-gloss shine. His navy slacks were wrinkle-free and had a sharp crease down each leg.

"You can relax, now. I don't bite; at least not very hard."

"That's good to know," I said, grinning.

I felt some of the tenseness leave my body as I looked up into his smiling face. He pushed a wisp of hair that had fallen over his forehead back into place, and I saw a jagged scar on the side of his hand. The pink color disrupted the even tan that extended up his arm.

"You look pretty tonight," he said as the elevator doors opened.

"Thank you. So do you," I said, stepping into the foyer. "I mean you look handsome, not pretty." *Good start, Allie.*

He grinned at me. "Sorry that I'm working and can't take you dancing or to a movie after we eat."

"That's okay, I understand. What kind of work do you do?"

He opened the car door for me, and as I climbed inside, a voice drowned out his answer. "Unit 43 responding to domestic disturbance at 83-121 Bertram." Then I heard, "10-4, Unit 43."

Simon rounded the front of the car, and I located the source of the voice. Mounted below the dashboard was a two-way radio with "Hawaii State Bureau of Investigation" engraved along the bottom. A cell phone lying on the console between our seats started to ring.

When Simon crawled into the car, he looked at the readout on the phone. "Sorry, but I'd better get this." He started the engine, and a whoosh of warm air blew into my face, sending my hair in all directions. As I adjusted the vent, I heard him say, "Kahala."

Listening to the voice on the phone, he backed out and started toward the exit. When we reached the street, he turned on the left turn signal, but then he started turning the wheel to the right.

"What time did they find it?" he said into the phone. While he listened to the response, he looked at me and reached over to move a strand of hair lying on my cheek back to its proper place. He seemed oblivious to the personal gesture, but my cheek tingled where he had touched it.

"Okay, Marshall, I'll be there in about fifteen minutes. I need to drop off a friend first."

As he ended the call, he frowned and said, "I guess you've figured out what I do for a living. I'm afraid I'll have to ask for a rain check for dinner.

One of the district detectives needs some help down at Ewa Beach, so I'd better take you home."

I tried to hide my disappointment. "Maybe we could get something to eat when you're finished. I don't mind waiting awhile."

"I don't think I'll have to be there long, so if you don't mind waiting, we'll go out later."

As he was shifting into reverse, a thought popped into my head. "Simon, I have a cousin back home that's a detective, and he lets me ride along with him once in a while." Actually, I was stretching it a little because it had only been one time, and Frankie had vowed to never let me do it again.

He had been giving me a ride home from my parents' house because my car was in the shop getting a window replaced. Before we got there, we came upon a stolen car that the department had been looking for. He told me to stay put while he checked it out.

As he walked up to talk to the driver, I saw a hand holding a gun slide out the window on the passenger's side. I realized that Frankie couldn't see it from his position, and when the guy aimed it at Frankie's head, I jumped out and hollered at him to get down. He ducked as a shot was fired, but the bullet ricocheted off the top of the car and grazed the top of my head. It had only been a flesh wound, and the suspects were apprehended, so I didn't see any reason to bore Simon with all the details.

"Could I go with you?" I asked. "I'll stay out of your way."

I could tell by his expression that he was torn about whether or not to take me. I was hoping that his desire to be with me was as great as mine was to be with him and he would let me tag along.

After a few moments of consideration, he put the car into drive and said, "Okay, let's go."

As he turned out of the parking lot, he hit the siren and put a flashing red light onto the top of the car. Traffic was light, and most cars pulled off the road when they heard us coming. When we hit a two-lane road, Simon used whatever lane was open, then drove on the shoulder when we hit a jammed intersection. We made the fifteen-minute drive in eight.

Pulling into the park, I could see five police cars, an ambulance with lights flashing and a car marked "Coroner" off to the side. A lot of people in swimsuits and shorts were standing on the beach observing the action.

Parking close to the other vehicles, Simon rolled down the windows and said, "There's a nice breeze, so you shouldn't get too hot."

"Don't worry about me. I'll be fine."

He got out and opened the back door of the car. He pulled a badge from the pocket of his jacket lying on the back seat and clipped it onto his shirt. The shield had wings and the word "Detective" on it in capital letters across the top. Next, he pulled out a pistol and attached it to the right side of his belt. Before closing the back door, he said, "Be back as soon as I can."

I nodded, and he started walking toward the group of policemen on the beach.

For a while, I sat in the car and watched, but as the crowd grew, my view was blocked. After thirty minutes, I needed to stretch my legs and find a bathroom. Expecting there to be public facilities like Traci and I had used the previous day, I walked past a clump of palm trees and saw a small building about a hundred yards away. I could see Simon hunched down near the water with his back to me. I figured that if I hurried, I could do my business and get back to the car before he did.

The sand was getting inside my sandals, so I slipped them off and carried them. When I reached the facilities, I bent down to brush the sand off my feet. Suddenly the door flew open, missing my head by mere inches. A young man wearing a flowered bandana on his head rushed out, tumbling over me and knocking me on my rear end. He landed on his stomach in the sand with an "umph."

"Hey, be careful where you're going!" I said, trying to stand up while keeping my dress from rising higher on my thighs.

He looked at me and muttered, "Stupid haole," then started running toward the palm trees. I watched him for a minute as I brushed off my dress, then I turned and walked into the bathroom. It seemed odd that he had been using the ladies' side, but I thought that maybe the men's side was out of order.

I set my purse and sandals on the edge of the sink before going into the stall. When I finished my business, I went back to scrub my hands and noticed in the mirror that there was a smudge of mascara under one eye. As I walked back into the stall to get a piece of tissue, I saw that the toilet was still running. I tried jiggling the handle to make it stop, but it didn't work. The water level was rising higher, so I reached for the shutoff valve near the floor, but the knob on it was rusted and wouldn't budge.

Water was spilling over the bowl, so I pulled some paper towels from the dispenser, then lifted the tank cover. I reached inside to push down the rubber plug that was allowing the water to flow in, but stopped when I saw what was holding the valve open. A small revolver was lying on the bottom of the tank, and the tip of the barrel was stuck beneath the edge of the stopper.

Setting the tank lid onto the toilet seat, I tiptoed on the slick, grungy floor to get my purse. I took out two red grading pens from inside it. While raising up the floater in the tank with one pen, I fished for the gun with the other one. After several attempts, I was able to slip the tip of the pen through the trigger guard and lift it out of the water.

While balancing the dripping pistol on the pen, I picked up my purse and sandals and headed toward the door. With the hand clutching the sandals, I pulled the door open and almost bumped into a teenage girl who was coming in.

"Something has happened in here," I told her. "I need to take this gun to one of those policemen. I'll give you five dollars to stand here and keep everyone out until one of them gets here."

Staring wide-eyed at the revolver, the girl was probably trying to decide if she should trust me or run. But with the cops so close, she must have decided she was safe, so she took me up on the offer. I left her standing guard while I shuffled across the beach carrying the gun.

As I neared the group of officers, one of them stopped me a few feet from the crime tape. He placed his hand on his gun when he saw what I was carrying.

"It's okay, Ricco, she's with me," Simon said, coming up behind the officer.

"Oh, sure thing Lieutenant," he replied. "You can't be too careful, though, when a woman's got a weapon in her hand."

Simon smiled, then lifted the tape and stepped in front of me. "What have you got there, Allie? Been out exploring?"

"I come bearing gifts," I said, handing him the pen holding the dangling revolver.

He listened to my explanation about where I had found it and about the fleeing man in the bandana.

"The coroner told us that the victim was shot with a small caliber weapon," Simon said. "Some of the men have been combing the area by the body for the gun, but they haven't found anything. You'll be saving the taxpayers some overtime pay if this proves to be it."

"So you're not sorry you brought me along, even if I didn't stay put?"

"Even if you hadn't stumbled upon this, I'm glad I brought you along." Turning toward a man who was standing a short distance away, Simon yelled, "Hey, Marshall. Bring one of those evidence bags over here, will you?"

"Be right there," the man answered.

While we waited, Simon asked me a few questions about "Bandana Man." I told him all I could recall, then remembered the teenager at the bathroom door.

"You are going to check the bathroom for fingerprints, aren't you?" I asked. "I figured you would, so I offered to pay a teenager five dollars to keep everyone out."

"For an amateur detective, you think of everything don't you? We'll check it out, but since it's a public facility, there's going to be a lot of prints in there."

"I'm sure there will be, but probably not that many on the tank lid and floater inside."

"Probably not," he said, grinning. Just then, Marshall walked up carrying a plastic bag, and while he held it open, Simon let the gun slide off the pen into it.

"After you tag that, would you ask Mike to join me at the restrooms over there?" he said to him.

"Please," I said.

Marshall looked at me, then at Simon. Taking my suggestion, Simon said, "*Please* have Mike join me at the restrooms. Thank you, Marshall."

"Sure thing, boss," Marshall said. He started walking away, then glanced back with a perplexed expression on his face.

"You're going to make him think I'm turning into a nice guy," Simon said as he handed my red pen back to me.

"A little politeness never hurt anyone. Even for a big, bad detective."

"You're right. Sometimes I forget to thank the people that make my job easier." He took hold of my hand. "Come on, Miss Kane. Let's go pay that five bucks you owe."

It was another hour before Simon was willing to leave the crime scene in the hands of the district detective. By the time we left, my stomach felt like it was eating itself, and I was glad when he stopped at a restaurant close by.

"This isn't where I had planned to take you, but they have good food here and lots of it," he said as he helped me from the car.

He held my hand while we walked across the pea gravel and shell parking lot. Little shivers were travelling up and down my arm. "I wouldn't want to see you trip," he said.

"You don't have to have an excuse to hold my hand," I said, smiling.

"I'll remember that." He didn't release it until we were seated across from each other in a booth.

Over deviled crab and thick steaks, he asked me about Oklahoma and my family. He was particularly interested in Frankie, and though I hadn't intended to say anything about Luke Davis, it spilled out.

"You need to stay away from that guy," Simon said. "When you get back home, ask Frankie to dig deeper into his background. He might find something in his past that will get him off the streets and away from you."

Touched by his concern, I assured him I would. Changing the subject, I said, "I know that both you and Richard are Miss Kahala's nephews. Are you brothers?"

"Yes, Richard is a year younger than me and an accountant. He's married and has two great kids. How do you know him?"

I told him about Michael's high school trip, and he couldn't believe that I was related to him.

"What a small world," he said. "Michael was a great guy, and we loved having him stay with us. Richard studied accounting because of his influence, and he's got a very lucrative job now."

I told him that Michael was the controller at Kane Energy, then changed the subject. "I noticed at the beach that you were the only detective with silver-tipped wings on your badge."

Glancing at his shield, Simon said, "Oahu is divided into eight districts, all under the jurisdiction of the Honolulu Police Department. Each district has a detective, and until a couple of years ago, I worked one of those districts. As felony person crimes continued to rise throughout the islands, the state legislature created four supervisory detective positions in the Hawaii State Bureau of Investigation. The HSBI assists local law enforcement agencies. The governor offered me the position on Oahu. I oversee the investigation of all homicides and some other types of person crimes here. My office is located at the Honolulu P.D. station downtown.

"Has the crime rate gone down since you took over?"

Looking down at his hands, he said, "A little bit."

"What do you call 'a little bit?'"

"About twenty percent. But just think how much faster it would drop if you moved here and helped me. You seem to have a knack for crime-solving."

I knew he was kidding, but it was fun thinking of working side-by-side with him.

"That's quite an accomplishment. I imagine now that you're in control, criminals think twice before committing a crime," I teased.

"Well, I don't know about that," he said, glancing at his watch. "I'm going to have to go to headquarters and do some paperwork on that shooting. But, before I take you home, would you like to go by my parents' house and see Richard? It's only a couple of miles from here, and I imagine that Aunt Nalani's party is still going on."

"I doubt if he'll remember me, but I'd love to see him."

"Let's go, then." Picking up the check for our meals, he paid at the register, then held my hand as we walked back to the car.

"Surprise! I made it to the party after all, and I brought along a special guest," Simon said.

The room grew quiet, and I felt self-conscious when everyone turned to look at us. Three people were seated on a rattan couch against one wall, while several others stood in different spots throughout the room. A tall, robust man with dark hair streaked with gray was trying to get out of a recliner similar to mine at home.

"This blamed thing is stuck again," he said. "Charlene, will you please give me a hand here so I can get up and greet our guest?"

A short, slim woman putting a piece of birthday cake on a saucer said, "Just hold on, Dennis, I'm coming."

She set the serving knife down on the table and moved toward us while wiping icing from her hands with a dishtowel. Simon and I were standing between her and the man having trouble getting the footrest down. As she drew closer, I could see that she had eyes just like Simon's.

"Allison!" a man shouted as he strode across the room. When he reached me, he pulled me into his arms and gave me a big hug. He stepped away and looked me over. "Boy, have you changed! You've turned into a real beauty!"

Though his face had matured and he was more muscular, I knew this had to be Richard. "Thank you, Richard. It's good to see you, too. How are you?"

"Doing great. Trying to keep my big brother out of trouble," he said, grinning.

Dennis had been rescued from the chair and was standing with Charlene near Simon.

"Mom and Dad, this is Allison Kane," Simon said. "Allie, I'd like you to meet my parents, Dennis and Charlene Kahala."

I stuck out my hand, but his dad ignored it and wrapped his strong arms around me. My arms were pinned against my sides as he lifted me off the floor.

"It's nice to meet you, Mr. Kahala," I said into his shoulder.

"Dennis, please set her down so that I can hug her, too," Simon's mother said.

She stood about five feet two, and the couple seemed mismatched. Charlene walked toward me. "Welcome to our home, Allie. It's nice to have you."

"Thank you. It's very nice to be here."

After Simon introduced me to the other relatives there, we sat down and visited for a while. His Aunt Nalani was in her element as she joked and laughed with the crowd. Richard told stories about his antics with Michael as well as some tales regarding Simon. Charlene insisted that we eat a piece of cake, though we told her we had just finished a big dinner. She had put a strawberry-kiwi filling between layers of butter cake, then covered it with light, strawberry-almond icing. The satiny texture melted in my mouth, and I ate every crumb.

It was after 10:00 before the party began breaking up, and as we started to leave, everyone had to hug us goodbye. Richard said that he would e-mail Michael the next morning, and tell him that I had arrived safe and sound.

Simon promised his mother that he would drive carefully, then we walked to his car.

"Mothers are the same everywhere, I guess, worrying about their children no matter how old they are," I said.

"Yeah, it's great, isn't it? But I don't dare tell her much about my job, or she'd sit and worry all the time."

"I imagine she worries whether you tell her about it or not. I know I would."

We drove to Traci's complex and parked by the front door of the tower. After killing the engine, Simon turned to face me.

"You would worry, huh?" The wisp of hair that wouldn't behave had fallen back onto his forehead. With the security light shining through the windshield, I could see him studying me. "You have to care about someone before you worry about them."

Okay, Allie. It's time to fish or cut bait, as Grandad would say. Looking at his fingers playing with mine, I said, "Yes, I guess you do."

He leaned over the console and lifted my chin with his free hand. As I stared into his eyes, I couldn't help wishing that I had the thick, long eyelashes that he had. I could feel a hint of whiskers on his jaw as he gently rubbed it against mine. He kissed my right cheek, then turned my head and kissed the left one. My heart was thumping so loudly, I was sure he could hear it. Looking into my eyes, he moved closer, and I melted when his lips touched mine.

Don't stop, don't stop, I was thinking. Much too soon, he pulled back, and I felt like I was in a fog. I didn't open my eyes until he spoke.

"I'd better get you inside, or your friend Traci will be sending out a search party."

He came around and opened the car door for me, then we walked up the sidewalk with hands clasped and arms swinging.

"Have you got plans for tomorrow?" he asked when we reached the door. "I'll have to go to work for a couple of hours in the morning, but then I should have the rest of the day off. I'd be glad to show you some sites on the island if you'd like me to."

"That sounds like fun. Traci and Tommy have to work all week, but I was hoping to get to see some things while I was here. It would be nice to have some company while I'm doing it."

"Okay, I'll pick you up about 10:00. Wear comfortable shoes, and you might want to bring along some sunscreen. Now you need to call Traci to buzz you in because I need to get down to the station."

As I dialed Traci's apartment number, he moved closer and put his arms around me. While he was kissing me, I heard Traci's voice on the intercom saying, "Yes? Allie, is that you?"

Leaning against the door for support, I said, "Yes, it's me. Will you please buzz me in?"

As Simon moved away, he said, "Tell Traci you won't be home until late tomorrow night."

Late, huh? "Okay. I'll see you in the morning."

I watched him as he got into his car, then I walked inside. With the adrenaline still pumping and the anticipation of getting to be with him all day tomorrow, I didn't expect to get much sleep. When Traci let me in, we sat up for over an hour talking about my evening. I gave her most of the details, but kept the kisses to myself. That was something I wasn't ready to share, not even with my best friend.

CHAPTER 14

Right on time the next morning, Simon pulled up in front of the building. I had been ready for thirty minutes, so I was in the foyer watching for him.

Dressed in a new pink top and shorts, I had pulled my hair into a ponytail and had added a pink hibiscus bloom from a plant Traci kept on her lanai. As I walked down the sidewalk toward his car, the sunshine felt warm on my arms and legs.

Coming around the front of the car, Simon said, "Pretty in pink." He planted a kiss on my forehead before he helped me inside.

"Thanks," I said. "Did you get some work done?"

"I got it started. I was at the station until about 2:00 this morning, then went back at eight. Marshall will be working on the case today, and I don't think he'll call me unless he gets in a bind."

"So what are we doing today? My family instructed me to take lots of pictures while I was here, so I brought along a camera."

"I thought we'd take Kamehameha Highway through the middle of the island, then travel part of the North Shore to the Polynesian Cultural Center. It takes a little longer that way, but it's a beautiful drive. When we get to the Center, they have a lunch buffet, then the various ethnic presentations start at 12:30."

"It sounds wonderful."

Simon proved to be a very good tour guide. Having lived on the island all his life, he knew of hidden places that most tourists never saw. He told me that, before the freeways had been built, most people used Kamehameha, or Kam Highway. It encircles all of the eastern shore as well as most of the northern and southern sections.

When we left Aiea, we traveled north through Wahiawa to Haleiwa. We stopped along one secluded stretch of beach and watched a fisherman mending his nets. He and Simon talked about the sparse amounts of ulua fish that were being caught this year. They each expressed their opinion of why they thought the numbers were down. Before we left, I asked if I could take a picture of him, then he offered to take a picture of Simon and me.

Down the road, we saw some teenagers surfing, so we stopped and joined other spectators on the beach watching them. The boys seemed to enjoy entertaining their audience while riding the twenty-foot-high waves. Three of them slid into shore, then plopped down on a spot of beach near us. We walked over, and Simon struck up a conversation with them about the upcoming world surfing competition. He told them that years ago, he had competed in it and wished them good luck. Before we left, they offered to let him take a spin on one of their boards and to give me a free lesson.

"Those guys have a lot of talent," he said as we walked back to his Jeep. "Though I wouldn't want anyone else teaching you how to surf but me, their offer for a free lesson beats the hundred bucks per hour it usually costs."

We drove up the highway past Waimea Valley, then meandered toward Turtle Bay. Along the way, we saw several vegetable stands, and we passed the Kahuku Sugar Mill. As we entered Laie on the northeast shore, we passed the Hawaii Temple. Simon said that the Church of Jesus Christ of Latter-day Saints constructed it in 1919 and that it was the first Latter-day Saints temple built outside of the mainland United States.

"We can take a tram from the Polynesian Cultural Center the short distance to the Temple's Visitor Center this afternoon if you want to," he said. "We can hear about the history of it then."

After Simon paid our admission to the Center, we entered the front gate, and I felt like I had traveled back in time. Costumed people were everywhere, and if Simon hadn't been there, I wouldn't have known where to start.

"Most of the performers are students from Brigham Young University—Hawaii, and they do a great job sharing old Polynesian customs from their home countries," he said. "But before we start touring the villages, how about lunch? I'm starving!"

"I am, too. My nose is leading me straight ahead. Is that the way to the lunch buffet?"

"Good olfactory senses, young lady. Please follow me." He reached for my hand.

He led me to a massive straw-covered hut that was open on three sides. There were four serving lines, so we got into the shortest one, and soon were loading various meats, vegetables, salads and breads onto our plates.

We found a table for two overlooking a crystal blue stream.

"What would you like to drink?" Simon asked.

"How about iced tea with sugar?"

"Coming right up." I watched him walk toward the area where beverages were served.

During the meal, we discussed his success in the surfing competitions as well as his other athletic accomplishments. Though I had done all right playing high school basketball, he had excelled in all types of sports in school. As I sat admiring the strong muscles in his arms and shoulders, I could tell he still worked out.

"I take advantage of the police department's gym as often as I can," he said. "I never know when I'm going to have to chase down a bad guy."

I gazed at the gorgeous flowers outside our window and told him a little about Paradise Petals. "Mom would have a field day with the plants along that path. Though I'm sure she would be able to name a lot of them, I don't have a clue."

"This afternoon, we'll come back to the stream and watch the canoe pageant," Simon said. "The fragrance of flowers fills the air and enhances the sights and sounds of the presentation. But now it's time for dessert."

"You've got to be kidding," I replied, laughing. "Have you got a hollow leg you haven't told me about? You couldn't possibly hold any more after all that you ate."

"Hey, I only had a waffle, sausage and coffee for breakfast. Besides, I eat when I'm happy, so you can blame yourself if I start getting fat."

I didn't know if he meant that I was the reason for his happiness, but it was nice to think so. "Okay, since you got the drinks, I'll get your dessert for you. What do you like?"

"Anything sweet."

"Well, that narrows it down. Can you be more specific? Cake, pie, cookies, or ice cream?"

"Yes," he said, smiling. "Just surprise me."

"Okay, I'll try. But if I bring back something you don't care for, don't say I didn't warn you."

I could feel his eyes on me as I walked toward the dessert tables, and it was the first nervousness I had felt all day. Being with him felt natural, like we were meant to be. *You had better watch yourself, Allie,* I thought. *If you're not careful, you'll get your heart broken.*

I loaded a dinner plate full of goodies, then walked back to the table with it. *Maybe if I fatten him up, it will keep some of the other girls away,* I thought. Sighing, I decided he could put on another hundred pounds and they would still flock to him.

As I set the plate down in front of him, he said, "You know you're going to have to help me eat this." He scooped up a big bite of peach cobbler and directed it toward my mouth.

"I can't eat any more. Everything on that plate is for you to enjoy."

"Oh no, you don't. I won't take no for an answer. Now open up."

Afraid he would hold it in midair all day if I didn't comply, I leaned toward him and ate the warm cobbler off his fork. It wasn't Nana Kane's, but it was scrumptious nonetheless. The tart peaches were wrapped in a pecan crust, and I could taste a hint of cinnamon.

He polished off the plate of desserts, minus a cookie that he insisted I eat.

"Well, that should hold me until the luau later," he said. "Let's start touring the different villages. There's a lot to see before the show tonight."

We visited the Tonga, Fiji and Samoan villages, and I discovered that I knew very little about the different cultures. While waiting for the New Zealand presentation to begin, Simon explained the significance of the colors displayed on the walls of the hut and on the costumes. When the dancing and jousting began, the performers stuck out their tongues, and the audience was told later that their ancestors had used this tactic to scare away their enemies.

When the presentation was over, we walked to the stream where the canoe pageant would be held. We weaved our way through the crowd and found a perfect spot under one of the large shade trees.

Called the "Rainbows of Paradise," the pageant told about legends of old Polynesia through a variety of songs and dances. Large, double-hulled canoes carried performers dressed in majestic costumes. Brightly colored feathers and flowers adorned the boats, and the music was enchanting. Every performer wore a smile and made the stories come to life.

After the canoe pageant was over, we visited the Hawaiian village. Simon's chest puffed out a little when he said, "Now you'll get to see some of the ways of my ancestors. I'm a quarter Hawaiian and an eighth Filipino."

"Which side of your family is Hawaiian?"

"Dad's mother was full blood Hawaiian, and most of his family still lives on Maui. Mom's family came to Oahu from the Philippines a couple of generations back."

"How did your parents happen to meet?"

"Dad came here to attend the University of Hawaii. Mom was already there studying to be a nurse, and their paths crossed one day in the cafeteria over a plate of meatloaf. According to him, there was only one serving left, and he gallantly offered to let her have it. She told him that she would share it with him, so they sat together, and the romance began."

"Meatloaf, huh? So if more than one serving had been available, they might not have gotten together?"

"Well, according to Mom, they didn't just happen to be standing side-by-side in the serving line. She had had her eye on him for a few days, and she didn't even like meatloaf."

"You know what they say. The way to a man's heart is through his stomach," I said.

"I'm sure when you met him you could tell that Dad loves to eat. After the meatloaf lunch, Mom invited him for dinner at her parents' house, and they've been together ever since."

"I've heard that real estate is very expensive here. Do they own their home?"

"They've lived in the same house since 1969. They were still in college when they got married and could only afford to rent it. About a year after they graduated, the landlord decided to sell it to them. Since they were from Hawaii, they only paid a few thousand dollars for it. It's a three bedroom frame house, but they could easily get five hundred thousand dollars for it today."

"Good grief! You could buy a huge, fancy house in Oklahoma for that amount."

"I don't know about Oklahoma land, but island property is very expensive. Despite that, people move here from the mainland every month. I know another couple who lives in your friends' building, and they had to pay over four hundred thousand dollars for a two-bedroom apartment on the tenth floor. In Hawaii you pay for the view, and it doesn't come cheap."

By late afternoon, we had gone through each of the seven villages, and I learned a lot about each culture. After being entertained by hula dancers and knife jugglers, we rode the tram over to the Hawaii Temple.

At 5:00, the luau was set to start, and after eating such a big lunch, I didn't think I would be able to hold more. But I found that with all the walking, laughing and sightseeing we had done, I was ready for dinner.

We each received a fresh orchid lei when we entered the area, which was near a fifty-foot waterfall. A variety of beverages were available, so I chose a crushed strawberry drink, and Simon got a tall glass of pineapple-mango juice for himself.

There was a wide selection of foods to choose from, including the luau favorite, kalua pig, mahi mahi fish and several types of chicken. Simon talked me into trying the poke, a marinated raw fish. I had to admit that it wasn't bad, though I didn't intend to start adding raw fish to my diet. We were serenaded by a talented trio during the meal and visited with a couple of newlyweds that were seated across from us at the long table.

"You're going to have to roll me out of here if I don't stop stuffing myself," I told Simon as we stood to leave.

"I noticed your shorts are tighter than they were this morning," he said, glancing at my bottom.

"Are they really?" I started pulling my shirt down lower in the back.

"Stop tugging on your shirt, I was just kidding," he said, laughing. "We've walked so much today, I imagine we've probably lost weight, despite the large meals. Besides, it wouldn't hurt you to gain a pound or two."

"Nice save," I said, nudging his arm with mine. "But I don't want to gain any more weight. I'm happy being a size eight."

"Yeah, I think you're just the right size." He draped his arm around my shoulders and pulled me to him. He kissed me, and my head started swimming. I rested my forehead against his. "This is very nice, but we need to be heading to the amphitheater so we can get a good seat for the show."

"Uh huh," I said, forcing my eyes open. "Whatever you say." I would have been content to stand there by the hut for a while longer.

We stepped away from the building and strolled toward the amphitheater hand-in-hand. When we reached the crowded pavilion, we found two seats eight rows back in the center, so we had a perfect view of the show. The audience came alive with excitement as music, lights and color filled the place. Over one hundred brightly-costumed performers held us spellbound for two hours with their singing and dancing. It was one of the best live shows I had ever seen.

After it was over, Simon bought a videotape of the performance for me. Carrying it in my hand as we walked toward the exit, I said, "I'll take this to school and share it with my students. They'll love seeing the fire dancers, and it will be a great multicultural teaching tool."

"It's not as good as the live presentation, but they can get the gist of it," he said. "And when you watch it, you can think about me."

I knew I wasn't going to need a tape of the show to remind me of him and the wonderful time we had spent together. In fact, I was already dreading the end of the week. But determined to keep the mood light and enjoy the time we still had, I said, "Oh, you might cross my mind once in a while."

"I'd better." He took hold of my hand as we walked toward the car.

It was after 10:00 when we headed east from the Center. The highway followed the shoreline, and a cool breeze was blowing off the water. I leaned my head back against the headrest and savored the smell of the pungent, salty air mixed with the fragrance of ilima and ginger blooming along the road. Closing my eyes, I listened to the slap of the waves on the beach and let the song caress me into a dreamy state.

"Not going to sleep, are you?" Simon asked. He reached over and started massaging the back of my neck with his fingers.

"I will be if you keep doing that."

Opening my eyes, I sat up straighter and looked over at him. The lights from the dash outlined his strong jaw. The unruly wisp of hair had fallen over his forehead and I fought the impulse to put it back into place.

Just then, his cell phone started ringing. Pulling his hand away from my neck, he reached into his pocket and took out the phone. Before my eyes, I watched him transform from soft-spoken entertainer to no-nonsense detective. His face muscles tightened as he listened to the voice on the other end.

"Did they get any prints off the revolver?" he asked.

Wishing I could hear the caller's reply, I hoped that the gun I had found would lead them to the killer of the man on the beach.

"I'm supposed to be off tomorrow, but in light of this, I'll come in for a few hours," Simon told the caller. "Make sure I have a copy of all the reports on my desk." Starting to pull the phone away from his ear, he glanced at me and quickly added, "Thanks, Marshall. I appreciate the update."

I suspected he was about to hang up before offering his thanks, then remembered my lesson on manners from the previous night. "See, that didn't hurt a bit, did it?" I said while trying to hide my disappointment that he would have to work the next day.

"No, but I almost forgot until I looked at you. Maybe you should give me a picture of yourself to glue onto my phone until I get into the habit of being more courteous."

I wasn't sure if he was teasing about wanting a picture, so I said, "The roll of film I took today is ready to be developed. I can get double prints made of the ones of us together if you'd like me to."

"I'd appreciate that. There's a one-hour photo place in the Pearlridge Center, right across the street from the apartments where you're staying. That would be convenient for you if you wanted to take it there."

"I need to look for some souvenirs for my family, so I might go there and drop off the film at the same time." I sat quietly for a few moments, hoping that he would tell me what he had found out from Marshall about the case. When I couldn't contain myself any longer, I asked, "So, what did you find out about the fingerprints?"

"I wondered how long you'd be able to wait before asking," he said, smiling. "An I.D. came back on the gun, and it's registered to a man who reported it stolen about a month ago. There were several sets of fingerprints lifted from it: his, the victim's and two others that we still haven't been able to identify."

"The victim's prints were on it?"

"Yes, and it's not as unusual as it may sound. He may have been the one who stole it, or he and someone else could have struggled for it. Any number of things could account for his prints being there."

"But you still don't know who the guy was that I saw running from the restrooms?"

"There's a gang on the island that wears blue and white bandanas, so we're checking the whereabouts of all the members that night. But lots of people wear bandanas, and it could just be coincidence that the guy you saw was wearing one the same color as theirs."

Before I knew it, we were back at Traci's building. As we pulled up to the front door, I asked, "Why do you think the guy I saw was hiding the gun in the toilet?"

Simon turned off the car engine and looked at me. "If he had placed it another half inch from where he did in the tank, there wouldn't have been a malfunction with the rubber stopper. The gun could have stayed hidden there for years without being found."

"Pretty smart of him to hide it in there, wasn't it?"

"Yes, it was," Simon said, taking my hand from my lap. "That's not all that Marshall had to tell me. A detective friend of mine on Maui needs some help with a tough case that is connected to one here. I had been expecting him to call, but was hoping that it wouldn't happen until next week. I'm sorry, but I have to fly over there tomorrow night."

Not as sorry as I am, I thought. "How long will you have to be there?"

"I'll take the latest flight I can, then try my best to be back on Friday evening before your plane leaves. You said you were going shopping in the morning, but what are your plans for the rest of the day?"

"Nothing special, since Traci will be in school. What did you have in mind?"

"Well, you can't leave Hawaii without touring Pearl Harbor and the USS *Arizona* Memorial. I should be finished downtown by noon. If you're interested, we could grab some lunch, then take the tour."

"I'd love to see it," I said. "Every morning since I've been here, I've walked onto Traci's lanai and stood mesmerized at the beauty of the harbor. The view has been a little different each time. One time it was misty and serene, and on another day it was clear and pulsing with energy. Yesterday when I looked down there, a perfect rainbow encircled it. It's like God is standing guard over the area and the scene changes according to His moods."

"That's a comforting thought. Protection for the living while paying homage to the dead."

"It's a date, then," I said. "I'll be ready at noon tomorrow."

"As much as I hate to end this day, I'd better get you inside." He climbed out of the Jeep and came around to help me out. "I'd like to take you and your friends to a nice place for dinner tomorrow night. Do you think they'd like to join us?"

Since I wanted Traci and Tommy to get to know Simon better, and because I felt a little guilty about being gone so much, I was glad for his invitation.

"I'm sure they'd enjoy a night out," I said. "Since she's probably asleep now, I'll leave Traci a note to wake me in the morning before she leaves for school. I can ask them at breakfast and let you know their answer when you pick me up."

"The restaurant I have in mind is semi-formal and has a dinner show," he said. "I'll bring you back by 5:00, then pick up all of you about 6:30."

Assuming I'd be late coming in, Traci had given me her key to the front door. I turned toward Simon and said, "I had a great time today. I learned a lot, ate too much and enjoyed being with an expert tour guide."

Moving closer to me, he placed his palms on the door behind me, leaving only a breath of space between us. When I looked into his eyes, though they were shadowed, there was no mistaking the look in them. He gently kissed me, and I knew that heaven couldn't possibly be better than this.

As he stepped away, I could feel cool air replacing the warmth where his body had been. I longed for more of the sensations I had just experienced, but knew better than to push it too far.

"It's time your tour guide went home," he said. "A man can only take so much temptation, you know."

Hmmm. So he found me tempting. "I'll be ready at noon tomorrow," I said, then turned to open the door.

"Sleep tight."

Yeah, right, I thought, still tingling all over.

CHAPTER 15

"Allie! Wake up, night owl," I heard a voice calling. "You left me a note to get you up before I left for school, though I can't imagine why."

Forcing my eyes open, I saw Traci's face above me and tried to remember why I wanted to get up so early. Suddenly, I remembered Simon's invitation from the night before, and I couldn't wait to share the news with her.

Throwing back the covers, I said, "This is important. Simon wants to treat all of us to dinner and a show tonight. You and Tommy don't have any other plans, do you?"

She stood there with a smile on her face watching me tear through the blankets like a madwoman trying to find my robe. Walking over to the bedpost, she lifted the garment off of it and handed it to me. "Is this what you're looking for?"

"How did it get up there?" I said, taking it from her. I was having a lot of trouble getting my arms into the sleeves.

Watching me struggle to find the armholes, she took it back from me. "Let me help you get this thing on, or we're going to be here all morning." As she held the robe open, I slipped it on. "Now, sit down here and tell me more about Simon's plans."

Flopping down on the bed next to her, the information came pouring out. "He has to go to Maui tonight, but before he goes, he wants to take all of us out to a formal restaurant that has a dinner show. I realized after I came in last night that I don't have anything to wear. Then I got worried that you and Tommy might have other plans and not be able to go. But this may be our last day together and I would like for you to get to know

Simon better. So what do you say, will you come with us tonight?" I was out of breath by the time I finished.

Traci leaned closer to me and looked into my eyes. "I haven't ever seen you so nervous about a date or known of you spending so much time with one man. Is there something else you want to tell me?"

Looking wide-eyed at her, I said, "Like what?"

"I've seen how handsome he is, and you've told me how much fun you've had with him. He's thoughtful and attentive. So, how are you going to feel when you have to go back to Oklahoma on Friday?"

A sinking feeling filled my chest as I stared down at the blanket. I tried to swallow the lump in my throat so that I could tell her that I would be fine. But I realized that it wasn't the truth. It was going to hurt like mad when I had to leave.

Traci put her arms around me. "Just what I was afraid of. You're in love with him."

"That's crazy," I said. "I've only known him for two days. I can't be in love." But the thought of never seeing Simon again was heartbreaking. *Get hold of yourself, Allie,* I thought. *Long distance romances don't work.*

"Come on," Traci said. "Let's go talk to Tommy about tonight."

As we walked into the other room, Traci mentioned some places in Pearlridge where I might find a new dress for the evening. When we told Tommy about Simon's invitation, he was eager to go and brag about Oklahoma reaching the Final Four in basketball. By the time we finished breakfast, I was anxious to get showered and dressed so I could hit the stores as soon as they opened.

At 9:00, with purse in hand, I walked the two blocks to the shopping center and started browsing in the largest department store there. I tried on a pink chiffon sheath dress with a scooped neck. Then I spotted a pale blue, silk dress with a beaded bodice in my size. Both were flattering colors for me, but before settling on one, I decided to look at the other two stores that Traci had suggested. I saw some dressy heels on sale in an assortment of colors and made a mental note to pick up a pair to match my dress selection.

Heading to another store, I passed a souvenir shop and strolled inside to look for gifts for my nieces. They had a variety of toys and dolls as well as T-shirts. I settled on some blowup swimming pool toys and shirts with Hawaiian children in grass skirts printed on them. Near the checkout counter, there was a rack containing key chains. After searching for a while, I found the chains with the Hawaiian names for all my adult cousins, their spouses and my brothers. The spaces for Kristin and my sister-in-law, Nicole, were empty, but I found some reasonably priced coral earrings for each of them.

I handed both of the fifty-dollar bills that my dad had slipped into my purse to the clerk. She handed a twenty and some change back to me. With my parents' and grandparents' gifts yet to buy, I was grateful for Dad's generosity. I had had only a little money left from my shopping spree before the trip, so a new dress and shoes were going to take a bite out of my budget.

Dawdling in front of the window of another clothing store, I saw the reflection of a maroon car pulling out of a parking space in the lot right behind me. It took me a minute to realize that the car was moving slowly toward me. When I turned around, I saw that the male driver, wearing a blue and white bandana on his head, was staring right at me.

I recognized him from Ewa Beach, and I wasn't about to let him get away again. I jumped off the curb and ran the short distance to the driver's side of his car. While holding the doorhandle, I started banging on his window and yelling, "Hey, buddy, I need to talk to you!"

His mouth dropped open, and he looked at me like I was nuts! Other shoppers were starting to notice us, and I guess he didn't appreciate the attention. He threw open the door and knocked me down onto the pavement.

"Stay away from me, lady!" he yelled. "I don't want to have to hurt you!"

As he slammed the door and sped away, I saw the numbers 436 on his license tag. Still sitting on the ground, I pulled a piece of paper and a red pen from my purse and wrote down the numbers. A heavy-set, elderly man wearing a purple and yellow aloha shirt hurried over to help me up.

"Are you okay, Miss?" he asked. "I take it that guy wasn't a friend of yours."

"No, but we've run into each other before," I said. *Literally.* "You didn't happen to see the license plate, did you?"

Taking his hand off my elbow, he said, "As a matter of fact, I did. It was 2HI-436."

After I added the missing half to the sheet of paper, I wrote the word "maroon" beneath it. I'm not the greatest when it comes to identifying cars. Lucky for me, my rescuer was.

"Yes sirree, it was a 1999 Toyota Corolla," he said. "Used to have one myself, until my knees got so bad that I couldn't use the clutch. Hated to sell her. That baby sure got good gas mileage."

After jotting down the model and make of the car beneath the tag number, I slipped the paper and pen back into my purse, then brushed off my shorts. The old man was still strolling down memory lane, telling me about his former car, while I looked around for a payphone. Not seeing one, I interrupted his speech long enough to thank him for his help, then headed back to the department store to look for a phone.

Locating one on the wall in the lingerie department between a rack of plus-sized panties and bras, I looked up the non-emergency number for Honolulu P.D. in the phonebook. After depositing some coins, I dialed the number.

"Honolulu Police Department. How can I help you?"

"May I please speak with Detective Kahala? It's important."

"I'll see if he's in. Hold please."

Standing there staring at a bra with cups big enough to hold two bowling balls, I tapped my foot while waiting for Simon to come on the line.

"Kahala," I heard the familiar voice say.

"I thought I'd better let you know that I saw Bandana Man while I was out shopping."

"Allie? Where are you? Are you in a safe place with other people around?"

"Yes, I'm safe," I said. "I'm using the phone at a store in the shopping center. I wanted to give you the tag number from his car."

"You didn't approach him, did you? I want you to stay clear of him. You're a liability to him, and he might try to hurt you."

I didn't see any reason to tell him that the guy seemed to be contemplating running me down on the sidewalk, or that I had banged on his window. No use crying over spilt milk. Ignoring his question, I said, "Have you got a pencil?"

"Shoot."

"2HI-436. It was a maroon 1999 Toyota Corolla."

"You know your cars, too. Good job, Miss Detective."

"Thanks, but I had some help from a tourist who was there and saw the whole thing."

"What 'whole thing?'"

Oops! I needed to start remembering that he had a built-in detective antenna. "Just a minor skirmish. Nothing to worry about."

"Uh huh. Well, if there was time, I'd drill you for more details. But I want to run this license plate before I come to pick you up in an hour."

An hour? Where had the time gone? I still hadn't bought a dress or shoes for our date.

"That's okay," I said. "I need to get a move on. See you in an hour."

Before leaving the lingerie department, I picked up a pair of pantyhose and sprang for a new slip as well. I walked back to ladies wear and bought the blue silk dress with the beads I had seen earlier. In the shoe department, I bought a pair of heels that matched the dress.

I hurried back to Traci's apartment with all my purchases. After hanging up the dress, I put the bag of souvenirs in my suitcase. I refixed my ponytail, brushed my teeth and had just finished freshening my makeup when I heard the buzzer for the door.

When I pressed the switch on the intercom, I heard a voice say, "Simon says to hurry on down here; my stomach is rumbling."

Laughing, I replied, "Your stomach is always rumbling, but I'll be right there." I took a final look at myself in the mirror near the door, then headed toward the elevator.

"Here, you finish it. It's yummy, but I'm stuffed," I said as I passed the last half of my lobster salad sandwich to Simon. "If I eat any more, I won't be able to fit into my dress tonight."

He swallowed the last bite of his own sandwich, then wiped his mouth with a napkin.

"We'll work it off this afternoon. Besides touring the USS *Arizona* Memorial, there's a stretch of beach I want to take you to. By the time we walk the length of it and back, these calories will be long gone."

After he popped the last of my sandwich into his mouth, he washed it down with some cola and started gathering up the trash. Depositing everything into the receptacle, we walked the short distance to the tour ticket office.

We watched a short film at the Visitor's Center, then rode a boat to the Memorial. While holding hands, we were solemn as we read the names on the huge wall inside. Over two thousand men died during the Japanese air attack on December 7, 1941. Half of them were entombed beneath the waters inside the USS *Arizona*. Drops of oil shone on the surface of the water, still leaking out after all these years. The place had a somber, eerie feeling, and most everyone was reverent in the presence of such sacrifice.

After about an hour, we rode the boat back to the Visitor's Center. We stood with a small group of tourists and listened to a survivor give us his firsthand account of that terrible day. I was near tears when he concluded his story, and my heart ached for those that had lost their lives. They never got a chance to raise their families, see their children and grandchildren graduate from high school or see how great our nation was today. The whole experience made me more grateful for my family and to Tommy and Kevin for their service to our country.

"So what did you think?" Simon asked as we pulled out of the parking lot onto the highway.

"It's an awesome tribute. I especially liked the story from the survivor. There were a lot of people there listening to him."

"Over a million people come to visit the USS *Arizona* Memorial every year," Simon said.

As we circled west around Pearl Harbor, I realized we were on the road that we had taken the night of the investigation. While traveling at a slower pace than we had that night, Simon gave me some history about the small villages and settlements along the way.

We followed the road toward Ewa Beach, then turned onto a narrower, dirt road. Simon stopped the Jeep under some large palm trees and turned off the engine.

"This is one of my favorite beaches," he said. "My family used to come here a lot when I was growing up."

Following his gaze, I could see the pristine sand glistening in the sunlight and a distant sailboat bobbing on the sapphire sea. The clouds above the horizon looked like piles of whipped cream, and I could have stayed for hours staring at the tranquil scene.

"It's stunning," I said.

"Yes, it is. Come on," he said, taking off his shoes. "Let's get our feet wet."

Slipping off my flip-flops, I climbed out and joined him as he came around the front of the Jeep. Walking hand-in-hand with the soft sand billowing around our feet, we headed toward the water. The waves were gently lapping the edge of the shore. When I stepped into the cool, salt water, I closed my eyes and relished the velvety softness beneath my feet. Some seagulls were diving for fish close by, paying no attention to us.

"Richard and I learned how to swim here," Simon said, pushing a horseshoe crab away with his toe. "My sister Amanda had her wedding here three years ago."

"You didn't tell me you had a sister."

"She's the baby in our family and a smart businesswoman. She and her husband, Rob, live on the Big Island."

"What kind of work does she do?" I asked as we strolled along in the ankle-deep water.

"Rob and his three brothers are all pilots and own a helicopter tour company over there. Amanda runs the office and does the bookings. Thanks to her expertise in advertising, the company profits have doubled since they got married."

"Your parents must be proud of their children," I said. "All of you are successful."

"We had a strict upbringing and were taught the value of hard work early on. Our folks are supportive and loving. I hope I can be as good a parent as they are when I have kids."

Thinking of Simon with children of his own gave me an odd feeling. I had no doubt that he would be a good father, but imagining him being married to some unknown woman was unsettling.

"Now tell me more about your family," Simon said. "Coming from a line of oil tycoons, I'm sure you must be spoiled rotten."

"I most certainly am not!" I nudged my elbow into his ribs. "Both my parents are hard workers, too, and they taught my brothers and me to be independent. I worked at my mother's floral shop after school and during summer breaks. My younger brother, Jeff, is still living at home, but is going to college part-time. He also runs the nursery section of Mom's shop from March through October."

"And what about your other brother?"

"Jamie is twenty-nine, married and has two girls. He was always a brain when it came to computers. He attended the University of Oklahoma, and, in three years, got a degree in Computer Science. Now he's the Senior Computer Engineer at Kane Energy. He creates and maintains the software for the company and oversees seven technicians."

"Pretty impressive. But you didn't stay in the family businesses. Any reason why?"

"I always wanted to be a teacher. I had some inspiring mentors, and though I could have pursued any number of careers, I stuck with that goal. Besides, if I hadn't become a teacher, you might not have had the privilege of meeting me," I said, grinning up at him.

We had been walking for almost an hour, though it seemed like much less time. When we reached a shady area filled with hibiscus bushes close to where the car was parked, Simon picked one of the crimson flowers and put it in my hair.

"Not meeting you would have been a great loss for me, Miss Kane. Now, I think it's time I drove you home."

On the way back, I asked, "Did you have any luck with that tag number?"

"Yes, the car is registered to a fifty-five-year-old laundromat owner in Kalihi. Marshall and Dave were going over this afternoon to talk to him. When some of us met this morning, we realized that the man you described sounds a lot like his nephew, Sammy."

"Can't you compare the nephew's prints to the ones on the gun?"

"He isn't in the database. Except for some minor scrapes when he was younger, Sammy hasn't been in any trouble with the law."

"It seems suspicious that he was trying to hide the gun, don't you think?"

"I'm trying to keep an open mind about it. When we find him, I'm hoping he can clear up some things."

"On the plane, I met the owner of the *Hawaiian Star* and he told me his offices were in Kalihi," I said. "Since I'll be on my own tomorrow, I might take him up on his invitation to give me a tour."

We pulled into the parking lot of the apartment complex. "You would probably enjoy that, but don't get any ideas about searching for the laundromat, or for Sammy while you're down there. You need to let my guys take care of finding him."

182

Maybe it had crossed my mind to try to help, but Simon was probably right. *Probably?* I was thinking more like Aunt Edith every day.

"Don't bother getting out," I said. "You'll be back in no time, and I need to get inside and start getting ready. See you around 6:00."

"Okay, see you then."

The blue dress fit perfectly. Pulling my hair into a twist on the top of my head, I secured the hibiscus blossom that Simon had given me earlier into the curls. A few minutes before six, Traci, Tommy and I took the elevator downstairs to wait in the lobby for him. Right on time, Simon pulled up in a late model silver Jaguar, and we headed for the restaurant.

"You're just full of surprises," I said. "Is this beauty yours?"

"Not on a detective's salary. I borrowed it from Richard. It gets good gas mileage, which comes in handy since gas is over three bucks a gallon here. He lets me use it on special occasions, or if I'm wanting to impress someone."

The subject of how many people each of us had dated had never come up in our conversations. Selfishly, I hoped that he hadn't used the car to impress too many women.

Just a few blocks from the building, we drove around Aloha Stadium, then caught Kamehameha Highway running parallel to the shoreline. Talking along the way, we soon reached the Aloha Tower Marketplace, where we were going to have dinner.

Sitting at the edge of Honolulu Harbor, the ten-story Aloha Tower was a welcoming beacon. Simon said that when it was built in 1926, it was the tallest structure in Hawaii. Though much taller office buildings now overshadow it, the classiness is still present.

In an open-air café overlooking the ocean, we were served a gourmet meal. Though I was hesitant, Simon talked me into trying poi. He explained that it was considered to be the "Hawaiian staff of life" and was made from cooked taro root. Traci laughed at the face I made when I took a big bite of it. Afraid of offending Simon, I forced myself to swallow it, though it tasted like paste.

"So, how did you like the poi?" he asked as the waiter cleared the dishes from our table.

Not wanting to put down one of his native foods, I said, "It has an unusual texture and flavor. Do you eat it often?"

"No, I can't stand the stuff," he said, grinning. "It tastes like paste to me."

A band had been playing Hawaiian music throughout our meal, and when we were finished eating, Simon asked me to dance. Though I had enjoyed the good food and conversation, the best part of the evening was when Simon's arms were around me. Swaying to the strains of a ukulele and slack-key guitar with the sunset vivid in the west, I couldn't have been more content.

A little before ten, while we were slow-dancing, Simon said, "I hate to break up the party, but my flight leaves at 11:00. By the time I get you home and then get back to the airport, I'll be cutting it close to make it."

"I hate for the party to break up, too, but I understand," I said.

When the song was finished, everyone clapped for the band. Simon slipped some money into their tip jar before we headed to the car.

My heart was heavy as we wound our way up the hill to the apartments. When we got there, Traci and Tommy got out and went inside, leaving Simon and I to say our good-byes.

It was important to me that he not feel like he had to commit to anything. Looking out the windshield, I said, "I want to thank you for showing me so many great places while I've been here. I've really enjoyed the time we've had together. Tonight was like frosting on the cake."

When he didn't say anything, I looked at him and was surprised to see a puzzled look on his face.

"It sounds like you're planning on getting rid of me," he said. "I don't know how they do it in Oklahoma, but in Hawaii, we've invested too much time to just end this relationship so soon. Unless, that's what you're telling me you want to do."

I wasn't sure I believed what I was hearing, so I waded in a little deeper. "No, I'm not saying that at all. But I don't want you to feel obligated to keep in touch with me. Oklahoma is a long way from here."

"I realize that phone calls won't be as good as being together in person, and I'm not the best when it comes to e-mails," he said. "But until you get back here for summer school, I expect you to keep in touch."

"But I don't know if I'll get the job. Your aunt told me that there are a lot of candidates under consideration. I may never get back here." The thought of that made me feel sick at my stomach.

"Think positively," he said. Pulling a notepad and pen from inside his jacket pocket, he turned on the dome light and started writing on the pad. "This is my e-mail address and cell phone number. I should be back from Maui by 7:00 Friday night, so I'll walk to the main terminal and locate your gate on the monitor when I get there. You're on Continental leaving at 8:30, right?"

"Yes, but I'll need to clear security by then. Should I wait for you outside?"

"Police officers aren't hindered by security. I'll sit with you at the gate before your flight leaves. You can give me your phone number and e-mail address then."

He slipped the paper into my hand, then we got out and walked to the building. After he kissed me good night, I watched him leave and realized the sadness had left me. At least I had a way to contact him, glancing at the paper in my hand.

Entering the elevator, I pressed seventeen and said to myself, "Absence makes the heart grow fonder." But a nagging voice inside my head was saying, *out of sight, out of mind.*

...ting to go outside. I was groggy ... for ... hour ... more minutes of sleep, but ... not ... I didn't want to be awake enough to have to get up.

I followed the dogs to the kitchen and let them into the backyard. When I turned around, I saw a sack of groceries sitting on the table, next ... a stack of mail.

"Bless you, Doug," I said.

There was a note lying on top of the mail that read, "Milk, cream, ... in fridge. K.I.L. dinner in the fridge? Didn't know if you wanted one tonight."

... He had bought an assortment of lunch foods for me and some ... bones for the dogs. Now I couldn't figure out whether or not to stay the night.

After putting away the groceries ... two thin slices of chicken, the ... potatoes and the can of green ... ... I stood staring at the ... ... I was having, so I ... one ... ... on the ... and ate it as I ... the other fried beans. When I was finished, I set the stepping ... next to the cup of coastline ... ... them that I had already put on the table.

I ate all of the food, except for ... ... by ... opening the piece of ... I lost my appetite when I gave up on ... ... only my ... ... a dozen or rich out of my pocket. I have ... ... messages or addresses on them one other than the postman ... ...

As I was about to open it, the phone started ringing. I knew once the ... I picked up the receiver and ... a ... ... at the other end of the line.

"Well, did you make it back ... ... running some beach ...?"

It was good to hear Frankie's voice, and it ... ... the threat of the letter ... less ominous.

"Three different ones proposed ... ... and accept a new day to ... ... which one will get me," I ... ... before your off ... ... was gone?"

"You know me, Mister ... ..." I said.

"But you let everyone get sick while I was away. What's up with ...?"

"Half this town is sick, or has the flu going, the nubler so far, but ... has been fighting the illness with ... morning sickness."

"Morning sickness? So you and ... are you ... expecting a baby?"

CHAPTER 16

After sleeping until 8:00 the next morning, I showered and dressed, then drank a glass of orange juice on the lanai. Traci and Tommy were already gone, but Traci had left a bus schedule on the table for me. She was familiar with the location of the newspaper and had circled the route I should take. The Ala Moana Center was the hub for the line and the perfect place to pick up the rest of the souvenirs I needed.

I called Mr. Masaki, and he seemed delighted to hear from me. He said he would be at the *Hawaiian Star* all morning and he would be glad to show me around. I put on my tennis shoes and stuck the bus schedule inside my purse. After locking the apartment door, I headed for the elevator. Traci had left a note on the schedule telling me there was a bus stop on the street in front of the building, so I went to find it.

After a short wait, I boarded the half-empty bus and settled into the front seat adjacent to the driver. I had a clear view through the large windows, but caught myself stomping an imaginary brake when the bus got too close to cars ahead of us. About a mile from my stop, a maroon Toyota pulled in front of the bus and missed getting rear-ended by mere inches. I recognized the tag number and the man who was driving it.

Watching the car zigzag through traffic ahead of us, I was glad when a red light forced it to stop. I couldn't tell the bus driver to "follow that car," but the *Star* offices were getting nearer. I had decided to stay on the bus, but then the car turned left off the road and into an alley.

My stop was coming up, and I was anxious to get off and see if I could find the Toyota. After exiting the bus, I crossed the busy street and jogged along the sidewalk to the entrance of the alley. Peeking around the building, I saw no sign of the car. Stepping into the alley and staying close to the wall, I started walking toward an open lot ahead. Just before reaching it, I stopped near an open door of one of the businesses. The familiar smell of detergent and fabric softener permeated the air, and I knew that I had found the laundromat.

I could hear a male voice yelling in a foreign language, then a younger, softer response in English. I wanted to get closer to hear more of their conversation, but two rolls of rusty clothesline wire lying near the door were blocking my way. Shoving one of them aside with my foot, I was able to maneuver between them, then peer through the crack in the door. The young man's back was to me, but I heard him say, "Uncle, it was an accident." The rest of his words were drowned out by the sound of crunching gravel behind me.

I turned my head and saw a black sedan stop a few yards away from me. Marshall was sitting behind the steering wheel and another man was on the seat beside him.

Now I'm in trouble, I thought. *Unless I can come up with some useful information, Simon will be upset when he finds out I'm playing detective again.* Ignoring the policemen, I turned and tried to move closer to the crack in the door, but one of my shoelaces was caught in the wire. Tugging hard to free it, I lost my balance and fell face-first into the door, dragging the ball of wire along with me.

The voices inside hushed. By the time I freed my shoe, the young man was staring down at me as I sat in a heap on the ground. Behind me I heard the slam of car doors and Marshall yelling, "Honolulu P.D. Sammy, we need to talk to you."

Sammy bolted across the parking lot, and I struggled to get up. I heard the pounding of feet on the pavement as the detectives tried to catch him. Outdistancing them by several yards, Sammy scaled a tall fence and disappeared from view. Marshall was being helped over by the other detective, but I sensed it was a futile effort.

Brushing myself off, I walked across the parking lot to the fence and introduced myself to the man who had been assisting Marshall. He told me his name was Dave. Marshall came limping toward us from the far edge of the fence.

"Miss Kane," he said, when he reached us. "Simon said you might be in the area today."

I explained how I had spotted the Toyota during the bus ride, then about the yelling in the laundromat. Concerned that I may have contributed to the guy getting away, I said, "Sorry if he escaped because of me."

"You aren't to blame," Marshall said. "Simon has been after me for months to lose some weight. Dave and I staked out this place all night. Then a few minutes ago, we saw a maroon Toyota being driven by someone resembling Sammy drive by. When we caught up with it and found it wasn't him behind the wheel, we hightailed it back here. In the meantime, I guess he sneaked inside."

"Well, at least you know he's close by," I said. "I'll make a deal with you. I won't tell Simon you couldn't climb the fence, and you don't tell him I was a klutz and gave away our positions."

"It's a deal," he said, rubbing his left knee. "Did you happen to pick up anything useful from the conversation you heard?"

"I heard Sammy say, 'it was an accident,' though I can't be sure what he was referring to. The uncle was yelling at him in a foreign language, so that doesn't help."

"I've known Sammy Cho since he was a little tyke because his parents lived next door to my mother," Marshall said. "When he was in high school, he got into a couple of fights trying to defend the honor of one of his friends. The police were called out, but charges were never filed. If he'd come in and talk to us about this shooting, we might be able to clear up some things."

Just then I heard a door across the alley open and saw Mr. Masaki coming out waving at me. "Allison, are you okay? Some of my staff saw the commotion out here through the window, and I thought I'd better check it out. Do you need some help?"

"No, everything's fine, Mr. Masaki," I said. "These officers were just trying to talk to someone."

When he reached us, he stuck out his hand to the detectives. "Sung Masaki, owner of the *Hawaiian Star*."

The two detectives shook his hand, then made a quick exit. I suspected that they didn't want their names connected to this incident, if something showed up in the newspaper.

As we walked into the building, Mr. Masaki quizzed me for facts about what had happened in the alley, but soon gave up when I wouldn't talk about it. He showed me the presses that were in the process of printing the latest edition of the newspaper. We went into the room where the layout of each section was done as well as other pertinent areas. I met some of the people working for him and was impressed by the operation. Though being run on a much larger scale, there weren't a lot of differences between its practices and those of the *Paradise Progress*.

At noon, we shared a delivery pizza at his desk. His feet were propped on one corner of it, and I was sitting in a chair across from him.

Wiping his mouth with a napkin, he said, "The world is changing, Allie. When I started this paper almost forty years ago, we reported the news without many frills. But today, writing must be sharp and entertaining to draw in young readers. There's plenty of exciting news on this island, but most of my staff is middle-aged or older. They're content to let another paper cover it. I need someone like *you* to add some spice to the *Star*, albeit on a part-time basis."

"I appreciate your confidence in me, Mr. Masaki, and I'm flattered that you think I could be an asset here." I tossed my napkin and paper cup into the trash can. "If I do get the teaching job, I'll give you a call, and we can discuss it again."

"Think positively, young lady," he said. "I've known Nalani Kahala for years, and she's a good judge of character. If she likes you half as much as I do, you'll get that job."

"You're the second person lately that has told me to think positively," I said, remembering Simon's words. "I guess I'd better start doing it."

As I was leaving, I thanked him for the tour and lunch.

"Since you may end up working here, you need to have a feel for what we do," he said, winking. "Here's a copy of the latest edition, hot off the presses. It will give you something to read on your flight back to Oklahoma."

Smiling, I took the paper from him and tucked it under my arm.

While waiting in front of the building for the bus that would take me to the Ala Moana Center, I kept an eye out for Sammy. He didn't show up, so I decided to let Marshall and Dave take over the watch.

When I got to the mall, I began exploring the first level. I browsed through many of the shops and boutiques, then started concentrating on what I needed to buy. In one of the stores, a grass skirt caught my eye for Aunt Edith, and I found some cute T-shirts for Patrick, Joey and Riley. Always eager to try something new in the garden, I bought two large packages of Maui sweet onion seeds for Grandad and Uncle Clarence. For

Mom, the aunts and my grandmothers, I bought ilima orchid bulbs. To complete the list, I found some fishing lures guaranteed to catch whales for Dad, Grandpa and my uncles.

I walked up to the second level and was looking in the window of a large shop that sold pottery and china when I thought of three more gifts I needed to buy. Walking down each aisle, nothing was striking my fancy until I noticed a wall filled with all kinds of coffee mugs. On the top two shelves, each state in the union was represented. I chose three mugs and took them to the checkout counter.

The person at the register told me that if I wanted her to, she would personalize each one at no extra charge. I told her what I wanted painted on them, and she said they would be dry and ready to pick up in about forty-five minutes. I checked my watch and told her I'd be back later.

Roaming through the mall, I stopped in a bookstore and found the latest title by my favorite author. I had never had much luck sleeping on planes and figured that reading would help pass the time. After leaving the store, I bought a frozen yogurt cone, then sat down on a bench to eat it while watching people go by. When an hour had passed, I went back to pick up the mugs. As I watched the clerk put each one into its own box, I was pleased with my decision.

The bus was noisier and more crowded than it had been that morning. School was out, and there were a lot of students riding on it. Shortly after I got on, I relinquished my seat to a crippled man with a cane. In gratitude, he offered to hold my packages for me. While holding the bar above my head, I swayed back and forth but managed to keep from toppling onto him. I was glad when Traci's building came into view.

Lugging the sacks from the bus stop to the tower was a challenge. I was out of breath when I entered the building, but got my second wind by the time the elevator reached the seventeenth floor.

"Honey, I'm home," I sang out. My packages clunked against the apartment door as I made my way inside.

"It looks like you bought out the stores," Traci said, taking some sacks from me. "I hope your family appreciates all of this. You'll be lucky to have enough space in your suitcase for everything."

"Come and look at what I found," I said, setting the stuff on my bed. "Not everything goes back home. To thank you for your hospitality, I bought you and Tommy a little something, too."

"You didn't need to do that. We should be paying you. If you hadn't come, we never would have met Simon and had that wonderful night out last night. We hadn't been dancing since our anniversary almost a year ago, and Tommy was tickled to have someone to talk basketball with. Those two guys really hit it off."

"I'm glad you both had a good time," I said, pulling open the bags. "Now tell me, who do you think this is for?"

When I held up the grass skirt, she took it from me and moved in front of the full-length mirror attached to the closet door. Holding the skirt against her waist, she started swaying back and forth.

"This has to be for Aunt Edith," she said. "She's going to be tickled with it."

After we looked at each item, I said, "Now for your present." I pulled her mug from its box and held it out to her. Painted on it in vibrant colors was a picture of the Oklahoma capitol building, the state flag and some mistletoe. Above the pictures it read, "Oklahoma—where the whole world longs to be!" Below the pictures, I had had Traci's name printed on it in gold leaf, then added *Love, Allie* on the bottom of the mug.

"This is making me homesick," she said, tearing up. "You are the sweetest, most thoughtful friend anyone could ever have. Tommy and I are going to miss you so much when you go back home."

"I'm going to miss you, too." Reaching back into the bag, I pulled out the box containing Tommy's mug and handed it to her. "The pictures on his are the same, but the saying across the top is a little different. Being an OU sports fan, I got one that said, 'OU Sooners—the best of the best.'"

"Thanks. I'll set it on the table tonight, and we'll see how long it takes him to notice it. It looks like you have another mug left in the sack. By any chance is it for a tall, handsome Hawaiian that I'm sure will miss you, too?"

I pulled out the last mug. The message on it read, "Oklahoma—God's Country," and I had had Simon's name painted on it, too. It had felt right buying it that afternoon, but I was beginning to have second thoughts. Maybe I shouldn't have put *Love, Allie* on the bottom. I was about to decide I'd just take it home and use it myself.

"Trying to decide if you should give it to him?" Traci asked. "I know that frown, Allison Kane, and you need to follow your heart."

"Okay, he's supposed to come to the airport. By then, I'll decide whether or not to give it to him."

We had a light meal that evening. After we ate, I helped Traci clean and rearrange her kitchen cabinets. She kept a tidy house, but since she abhorred spring-cleaning, she hadn't cleaned out the cabinets since they had moved in. While we worked, I told her about the encounter with Sammy Cho and my visit with Mr. Masaki. By bedtime, the cabinets were dust free, they had new shelf paper inside, and the dishes were washed and put away.

"Just one more reason for you to stay around," Tommy said to me, setting an empty glass into the sink. "My lovely bride needs a little push now and then to tackle the tough jobs, don't you honey?" Draping his arms over Traci's shoulders, she leaned her head against his chest.

"Well, it's more fun when someone is helping you, hint, hint," she said. "When the baby comes, you're going to have to help out more, my love."

"I plan on doing my share of diaper changes and middle-of-the-night feedings. But since that's not happening yet, would you please get me another Pepsi? The news is about to start." He kissed the top of Traci's head, then walked back into the living room.

"Men! You can't live with them, and we don't want to live without them. What's the matter with us?" she said, reaching into the refrigerator and pulling out a can of Pepsi.

"I'm not the one to be asking," I said.

Traci carried a tumbler full of ice and the soda pop into the living room to her husband. Coming back into the kitchen, she said, "Tomorrow is the field trip to the concert in the park. Are you still coming to school with me in the morning?"

"Absolutely. I'll grade papers or do whatever you need me to, then I'll help corral your students at the park. Are other teachers taking their classes?"

"Well, I know the other second-grade teacher is coming, and possibly one of the third-grade classes will come, too. I think one bus will hold all of us. An aide and a couple of mothers are coming, also."

Looking at the clock, I saw that it was almost eleven. "Since I've been sleeping late all week, I'd better get to bed, or I'm going to have trouble getting up. Be sure and wake me by 6:00."

"I will. We need to turn in, too." We walked into the living room. "Come on, big boy," she said to Tommy. "It's time you tucked me in."

"I was just waiting on you, sugarplum," Tommy said, flipping off the television.

After saying goodnight from my doorway, I got ready for bed, then drifted off to sleep to the tune of traffic sounds floating in my window.

The following morning, I was up before 6:00 and stripping the bed of its linens when Traci knocked on my door.

With her hair sticking out every which way, she yawned and said, "You're exerting way too much energy for this early in the morning. Don't worry about that."

"The least I can do is to change the bed before I go home. If you'll give me another set of sheets, I'll have it done in no time."

She walked over to me and took me by the hand. Leading me out of the room, she said, "Forget about that. Let's go fix breakfast."

Tommy had been delighted with the mug and was sipping coffee from it when we came into the room. While Traci made waffles and I fried some bacon, he set the dishes, syrup and juice carton on the table.

We enjoyed our last breakfast together and discussed the plans for the day ahead. Tommy had to attend some meetings on the base, then was taking off mid-afternoon to play golf with some friends. Traci gave me some background on the Royal Hawaiian Band that we were taking the students to see that afternoon.

"It was founded in 1836 by order of King Kamehameha III," she said, "and it's the only full time municipal band in the United States."

"I think it's great that Hawaii has a band that goes to other countries to perform," I said. "It's too bad Oklahoma and other states don't follow that lead."

"In past years, the concert made such an impression on some of my students, they began taking music lessons," Traci said, "Because it is so inspiring, I've decided to make the field trip an annual tradition."

After clearing the table, we all headed in different directions to finish getting ready. I showered and fixed my hair, then put on a little makeup. I slipped into my last clean dress, a pink and cream rosebud print.

When I walked into the living room, Tommy had already left, so I stepped onto the lanai to wait for Traci. Across the freeway, a rainbow was looped over the golf course like ribbon on a present. Two lawn tractors were creating uniformed rows on the fairway, and sprinklers were spreading a heavy mist onto the manicured greens. I have never been a big fan of golf, but the course was a sight to behold.

Hearing Traci come into the living room, I walked back inside.

"You know, after enjoying all the green grass and trees this week, it's going to take some adjusting when I get back home tomorrow," I said. "Paradise is still bare and the brown, dead grass in my yard is depressing."

Taking her keys from her purse, Traci said, "That's one thing I haven't missed about Oklahoma—the deadness of winter. But I do miss the change of the seasons. Autumn was always my favorite. I used to love to come with you to pick pumpkins from your grandad's garden and to watch the leaves change color all over town."

After we left the apartment, we reminisced about other fall activities we used to share. When we were kids, decorating for Halloween and getting costumes was a big deal. Two large churches in town offered safe alternatives to trick-or-treating by having festivals with lots of games and refreshments. They were popular with most of the kids, and my cousins and I always attended one of them. But we couldn't resist leaving early to go trick-or-treating at a few houses.

Grandpa A.J., Grandad and Uncle Clarence loved Halloween as much as the kids did, and they provided hayrides at the Circle K on Halloween night. Everyone taking the rides could count on a menagerie of ghouls and goblins floating in and out of the trees. No one seemed to know who the ghosts were, but the shrieks and moans from them sent shivers up your spine. The horses pulling Grandad's wagon always seemed to need to stop for a break just as the scariest sounds were coming through the trees.

No one at school knew for certain who was under the sheets, and it added to the excitement to try to guess. When I was fourteen, I happened to be at the ranch a few days before Halloween, and I caught Nana cutting some holes in sheets. She made me promise never to tell that it was her, along with Gramma and Aunt Edith, sailing around the trees and making those fiendish sounds.

During football season, Traci and I bundled up together under blankets to watch the high school games. The bleachers in each section at

Paradise Stadium were twenty feet long, and there were always three to four benches full of our family members. Whether the games were at home or away, we were faithful to support the team.

As we walked from her car to the school building, Traci said, "I still miss the hayrides. Do you remember what happened the year we were seniors?"

"Are you talking about the specter in the trees?"

"Oh, yeah. Tommy and I were in Uncle Clarence's wagon, and he drove it under those monstrous catalpa trees in the east pasture. It was pitch black under the branches, and I felt this webby goo drip into my hair. Like everyone else, I was trying to brush it away, and all at once this gray-shaped monster soared through the branches above our heads! I never told anyone, but I wet my pants right there in the hay."

"That was the year that all the stores in town sold out of silly string," I said. "I got some of it in my hair under those same trees, so I guess the goblins bought it all to use on the unsuspecting riders."

"It scared the daylights out of our wagon load of people, I can tell you that," she said as we walked into the office for her to sign in.

"I was sworn to secrecy about the identity of the three ghosts, but I never found out who the fourth one was," I said.

After the students arrived and morning exercises were done, I helped Traci with reading groups. Miss Kahala came down the hall while we were refereeing bathroom breaks and started chatting with us. She mentioned that she planned to hit the lounge at lunch time to see if she could recruit some teachers to decorate the main showcase in the front hallway. After making me sound like Van Gogh, Traci suggested that I might like to help.

"Would you mind, Allison?" Miss Kahala asked. "I'll get a couple of aides to assist you, and I would really appreciate it."

Traci didn't have anything else she needed me to do, so I walked with the principal to see the showcase. She asked what I could do with it, and after I offered some suggestions, she seemed pleased with my ideas. I met the two aides, and together we set to work on the project.

Just before lunch time, Miss Kahala walked up as I was arranging the last of the construction paper daffodils on the floor of the showcase. One of the aides had just hung the last puffy cloud from the ceiling, and the other one was bagging our trash.

"Hanilei, does the sun look straight to you?" I asked the aide holding the trash bag. I had put a large, yellow, paper ball on the back wall, and she had cut out the rays that extended from it. Tennis ball-sized google eyes gave it a friendly face, and its smile was beaming down on the garden. We had written the names of each student in the school on the daffodil petals. The caption, "It's Sun-sational at Prince Kuhio," had been painted above the sun.

"I think it's sun-sational," Miss Kahala said, smiling. "That is the most cheerful showcase we've had in a long time, and I know the students are going to love seeing their names on display. Good work, ladies. I'm sure the school board will be as impressed as I am when they come here for their tour on Monday."

"It was a joint effort," I told her. "Hanilei and Effie are very artistic. You should let them do this more often."

"I'll keep that in mind, Allie, and thank you for sharing your talents with us. Now, Traci's class is probably getting ready for lunch. You'd better go eat a lot, because those second-graders can be a handful on field trips. Please tell her the bus will be here at 1:00 to pick up everyone."

"I'll tell her. And thanks for asking me to help with this," I said, motioning to the display case. "It was fun."

After taking one last look at the finished product, I walked back to Traci's classroom.

"That's a good sign, you know," Traci said as we rode the school bus to the park. "Miss Kahala is picky about what is displayed in the showcase because it's the first thing people see when they come into the building. Since she let you have free reign with it, I'll bet you're in the forefront for one of the summer school jobs."

"I hope so, but I may have been asked just because time was short and the school board was coming."

As the bus fell in behind a line of other buses at the park, I could hear the musicians on the grandstand warming up. Lining up the students outside the bus, Traci told them to stay close to their partner at all times. To make it easier to see if anyone was missing later, we had the pairs count off. It would be a disaster to lose a student, but it could happen; I had experienced it.

Last fall, all the third-graders from Elliott Kane took a field trip to the large central post office in downtown Tulsa. Most of the time, we were all together, but then the postal guide split us into smaller groups to do some hands-on activities. Rufus Pennington got separated from his group, and nobody noticed until his partner brought it to my attention.

While the other teachers and chaperones watched my class, I looked for Rufus. When I found him twenty minutes later, he was standing alone by a conveyor belt watching packages being loaded into trucks. When I reminded him that he was supposed to stay with his partner, he said he was sorry but that he was watching for the package containing the model his grandpa had ordered for him. He thought he might be able to pick it up while he was there instead of waiting for the postman to bring it to his house.

I told him that the odds were remote that he would see his package being loaded. As we turned away to go find our group, one of the handlers at the end of the conveyor belt called out to us.

"Hey, son, did you say your name was Rufus Pennington?" When Rufus nodded, the man held up a small brown box. "Here's your package. It's going on the truck, so it will probably be at your house this afternoon." So much for remote odds.

The concert was about to begin, and the park was full of spectators. Besides other school children, there were mothers pushing babies in strollers, couples with dogs on leashes and college-aged men and women everywhere. Some people were on roller blades, and there were a few uniformed policemen walking around the perimeter.

We seated all the students on the grass under an enormous banyan tree, then the teachers and chaperones found spots close by to keep an eye on them and enjoy the performance.

The concert was magnificent! A variety of Polynesian songs were played as well as some patriotic pieces. The conductor was marvelous and featured several individual musicians. Though everyone applauded at the end of each song, we gave the band a standing ovation when the concert concluded.

"Boys and girls, please give me your attention," Traci said to the students after it was over. "Be sure to walk beside your partner all the way back to the bus and stay with our group. Now, if everyone is ready, please follow me."

A boy standing by me said he needed to go to the bathroom and couldn't wait until we got back to school. There were some public facilities nearby, so I told Traci that I would take him, then we'd join them at the bus.

When we reached the restrooms, he went inside, and I stood at the corner where I could watch for him. There were a lot of people roaming through the park, but I was surprised when Sammy Cho came around the corner on the opposite end of the building. When our eyes met, he stopped in his tracks, then turned around and started back the other way.

Before he got too far, I hollered, "The police just want to talk to you. It would be in your best interest to stop avoiding them."

He turned around and scowled at me. "You know, lady, you keep turning up everywhere I go. You don't even know me, so what's it to you whether or not I talk to them?"

"Maybe we're running into each other for a reason," I said, walking toward him. "You look like you're about my younger brother's age. If he was in trouble, I'd like to think someone would be there to help him."

"Why would the police believe anything I have to say? I didn't shoot that lowlife woman-beater on the beach, but he got what he deserved if you ask me."

The student I had been waiting for came out of the bathroom door and started toward us. Opening my purse, I took out my pen and the paper Simon had given me with his phone number and e-mail address written on it. I tore off the half showing the cell number, then wrote Simon's name above it.

"Here," I said to Sammy, holding the paper out to him. "Give this detective a call, and tell him your side of the story. He'll make sure you're treated fairly. He's gone to Maui now, so if he doesn't answer right away, keep trying."

He took the slip of paper from me. "And why should I do that?"

I took a step closer to him and looked him square in the eye like I would one of my brothers. "Because eventually you're going to get caught, and the longer you run, the more guilty you look. Now it's time to be a man and do what you know is right!"

He looked surprised at my boldness, but didn't say a word. I guess I was lucky he didn't deck me right then and there. Before the idea occurred to him, I took the student's hand and we started walking toward the bus.

CHAPTER 17

Friday evening after dinner, Traci and Tommy took me to the airport. We had to drive around the parking lot for several minutes before a spot opened up. Waiting in line to check in my bag, my heart quickened when I thought I saw Simon rushing toward me. As the man drew closer, I realized it was Richard.

"Well, isn't this a nice surprise," I said, hugging him when he reached me. "But you didn't need to come all the way out here to see me off. My friends will be with me for a while, and Simon said he'd be here to sit with me at the gate. I do appreciate your thoughtfulness, though."

"Yes, that would have been a thoughtful gesture, but that's not the reason I'm here," Richard said. "I'm sorry to have to tell you that Simon isn't going to get back from Maui tonight. Our grandfather had a stroke about noon today, and Simon's been at the hospital with Grandma. Mom and Dad flew there this afternoon, but I had a meeting with our auditors at 2:00 and couldn't get away from work any sooner. I'm heading to the Aloha Airlines terminal from here."

"I'm sorry to hear about your grandfather's health, Richard," I said. "Is there anything I can do?"

"Please keep him in your prayers. He's a tough old bird, and it takes a lot to keep him down. Sorry about the timing, though. I know Simon is disappointed that he's not going to get to see you off."

"I'm disappointed about that, too, but I'm glad he'll get to be with your family. It's important to stick together at a time like this."

He reached into his shirt pocket, pulled out two of his business cards and handed them to me. "Simon said you were supposed to give him your phone number and e-mail address tonight. If you'll write the information on one of those cards, I'll be sure he gets it. Keep my other card so you'll have my phone number."

I had been scooting my bag along with my foot toward the ticket counter as we had been talking. I was up next, so I quickly jotted down my home and cell numbers as well as my e-mail address, then handed the card back to him.

"Thanks. He would have had my hide if I had forgotten to get this for him." He slipped the card back into his pocket. "I hate to rush off, but my flight leaves soon. I hope you have a safe trip home. Please tell Michael that I'll take him deep-sea fishing if he'll come over for a vacation. I've been after him about working so hard, but I have to admit that I'm as bad as he is about not taking time off from work."

"I'll give him your message and try to do some arm-twisting from my end," I said. "It would do him good to relax on a boat."

Waving, Richard jogged off toward the Wiki-Wiki shuttle that would take him to the Aloha Airlines terminal.

As they walked me to the security gate, I told Traci and Tommy the sad news about Simon's grandfather. When they weren't allowed to go any further, Traci hugged me and said, "I know you were looking forward to seeing Simon before you left. I'm sure he'll give you a call as soon as he can."

I was determined not to feel sorry for myself. "It's okay. He has more important things to look after right now."

I said good-bye to my friends, then went through security. After buying a root beer from a vending machine, I found a seat near my gate and began reading my new book. In no time at all, passengers were called to start boarding.

The flight over the ocean was full of turbulence. We were late getting to Los Angeles, and I had to run to make the connecting flight. In my haste, I broke the heel off one of my shoes and ended up hobbling to the gate. In Dallas, freezing rain was falling, and the plane was in the process of being de-iced for the second time when I called my parents. Dad was supposed to come and pick me up when I arrived in Tulsa, and I wanted to let him know the plane was going to be two hours late.

When Mom answered the phone, she told me that, while I had been gone, the flu had struck some members of the family, including them, so Kristin had offered to come and get me. After hanging up, I started feeling guilty that I had been having fun while people I loved were ill. Combined with exhaustion and all that had happened in the last twelve hours, I was fighting back tears when the plane took off.

As we descended into the Tulsa International Airport, the fog was thick, and I couldn't see the snow on the ground until we touched down. Tall drifts rested against the terminal building, and as we taxied to the gate, the pilot said it was a frigid thirty-six degrees outside. The temperature in Hawaii had been fifty degrees warmer, and I was dressed in summer clothes.

Following the crowd from the plane to the baggage area, I spotted Kristin sitting on a bench close to the Continental carousel. She smiled and waved as I lumbered toward her, dragging my carryon bag behind me.

"Here, let me have your stuff, and you put this on," she said, handing my heavy coat to me. "There are gloves in the pocket, and you're going to need them when you walk outside."

If I hadn't been so tired, I probably would have said something like, "Yes, Mother." But it felt good to let someone else be in charge, so I just thanked her and put on the garments.

While we waited for my suitcase to come around, Kristin asked, "Other than the delay in Dallas, how was your flight?"

"Not the best. If I look half as bad as I feel, I look atrocious."

"You'll feel better once you get some sleep," she said, hoisting my bag from the carousel. "This way, my dear."

I tried to dodge the slush as I followed her across the road. The wind cut through me like a knife, and sharp pellets of sleet were stinging my face and legs. My bare toes were numb by the time I was seated inside her car.

After putting my luggage into the trunk, Kristin got in and reached for an afghan lying on the back seat. "The heater should be warm in a minute, but you can put this over your legs, too, if you want."

I took off my sandals and wrapped my feet and legs in Gramma's handiwork. With the heavy coat and afghan, I looked like a giant cocoon. But I didn't care how I looked; I just needed warmth.

"This crummy weather moved in late last night," Kristin said, starting the car and turning on the windshield wipers. "We had been having some nice temperatures and sunshine until then."

As we moved down the terminal drive onto the expressway, the streets were wet but didn't seem to be slick.

"At least we're not skating home," I said. "The soil temperature must be above freezing."

"This morning the weatherman said that if we hadn't had those sunny days prior to the snow, we could have ended up with eight inches on the ground. It all melted except for an inch or two and the road crews have been working all morning to clear that away. Now tell me about your trip."

I gave her details about places I went, some things I saw and people I met while in Hawaii. I didn't mention anything about the body on the beach, or *helping* with the investigation. By the time we entered the city limits of Paradise, I realized I hadn't let Kristin get a word in edgewise.

"Sounds like a dream vacation," she said. "But I want to hear more about this new man in your life. I can tell he's entertaining and that he spent a lot of money on you, but what is he like as a person?"

Looking out the window, a smile crept onto my face, and I felt warm inside thinking about Simon. "He has black hair and dark eyes with the longest eyelashes I've ever seen. He's considerate, hardworking and—" I paused when I realized how much I missed him.

"And?" she asked.

"And too far away. I can't imagine how you must feel with Kevin in Iraq."

"Uh oh. This sounds serious. You're going to stay in touch with him, aren't you?"

"We exchanged e-mail addresses, and he has my phone number. But I'm going to let him make the first move."

Kristin turned onto my street, and as we passed by the Davises' house, it appeared gloomy and desolate. There was no sign of the wrecker, and several days worth of papers were lying in the driveway. I hoped that Luke's interest in me had waned while I was gone.

When we pulled into my driveway, Kristin tooted the horn, then got out to open the trunk. "Doug wanted me to let him know when we got here. I know he missed you, and though he didn't say so, I think he'll be glad to relinquish the puppies to you for a while. I brought them to my house for a couple of days, but they were his responsibility the rest of the time."

Pulling my carryon bag and purse off the backseat, I heard Doug's front door slam. I saw the puppies bounding toward us, with him close behind.

"Come here, you sweet little darlings," I said, setting down the bags. I scooped the puppies into my arms. They were licking my hands, then my neck and face, and squirming with excitement. I didn't realize until then how much I had missed them.

Doug loped up beside me and put one arm around my shoulders. "Boy, am I glad you're home! We sure missed her, didn't we guys?" He patted their heads but didn't offer to take them from me. "I'll get your stuff and unlock the door."

We all walked up the sidewalk, and I was glad to see that the daffodils were peeking through the soil. Despite the cold day, they offered hope that spring was just around the corner.

When we were inside the house, I set the dogs down, and they headed for their empty food dishes. Taking off my coat and gloves, it felt good to be home. Everything looked the same except for a pile of mail sitting on the kitchen table.

"Thanks for taking care of things while I was gone," I said. "I'm out of milk, or I'd offer you both some hot chocolate."

"Don't worry about it. We're going to get out of here and let you take a nap, right Doug?" Kristin said.

"You get some rest," he said. "I'll go to the store and pick up some milk, bread and a few other things and drop them by. The dogs were outside for an hour before you got home, so they should be fine for a while." After bending down to give the dachshunds a final pat, he and Kristin left.

I filled up the dog bowls with food and fresh water, then went to the bathroom to take a hot shower. After drying my hair, I pulled on some sweats and climbed into bed. The puppies were curled up together in their basket fast asleep. Within a few seconds, so was I.

The clock on my nightstand read 5:45 p.m. when the puppies woke me wanting to go outside. I was groggy after less than three hours of sleep, but knew if I didn't want to be awake all night, I'd better get up.

I followed the dogs to the kitchen and let them into the backyard. When I turned around, I saw a sack of groceries sitting on the table next to the stack of mail.

"Bless you, Doug," I said.

There was a note lying on top of the mail that read, "*Milk, orange juice and a KFC dinner in the fridge. Bread and other goodies are in the sack. Love, D.*" He had bought an assortment of snack foods for me and some rawhide bones for the dogs. Now I wouldn't have to venture out into the cold night.

After putting away the groceries, I put all three pieces of chicken, the mashed potatoes and the cup of gravy on a plate and stuck it in the microwave. I was starving, so I smeared butter on the biscuit and ate it cold while the other food heated. When the bell sounded, I set the steaming plate next to the cup of coleslaw and glass of milk that I had already put on the table.

I ate all of the food, except for a drumstick, while opening the pieces of mail. I lost my appetite when a plain, white envelope with only my name scrawled across it fell out of a grocery ad. There was no stamp or address on it. Someone other than the postman had put it in my mailbox.

As I was about to open it, the phone rang. Dropping it back onto the table, I picked up the receiver and heard a male voice on the other end of the line.

"Well, did you make it back home without marrying some beach bum?"

It was good to hear Frankie's voice, and it made the threat of the letter seem less ominous.

"Three different ones proposed, but I told them I'd need a few days to decide which one will get me," I said, teasing. "Did you behave yourself while I was gone?"

"You know me. Mister Straight and Narrow."

"But you let everyone get sick while I was away. What's up with that?"

"Half this town is sick, or has been. I've dodged the bullet, so far, but Kailyn has been fighting the flu as well as morning sickness."

"Morning sickness? So you and Kailyn are expecting a baby?"

"Due in October," he said, proudly. "Can you imagine me being a daddy? We found out yesterday when I took her to the doctor for the flu. You're the only family member who knows, besides her parents, whom we called last night. We had planned to announce it at the family dinner tomorrow, but since so many are sick, the dinner is being postponed."

The dogs were scratching at the door, so I walked over to let them in.

"I'll keep your secret, so you can announce it yourself. Congratulations, by the way."

I watched the pups prance to their water dishes and saw Rowdy lay something next to his before drinking. Walking over to him, I nearly dropped the phone when I saw what it was.

"Frankie, you're not going to believe this, but Rowdy just set a man's big toe on my kitchen floor."

"You've got to be kidding me! We collected all the toes and other body parts from the Davises' flowerbed."

"This is another right one. It looks like Rowdy chewed on it, but it's still intact."

"Do you know where he's been? Never mind. Keep the dogs away from it and I'll be right over."

He disconnected before I got the chance to tell him about the strange letter, but the bloody appendage took precedence now. Shooing the dogs away from it, I got an empty laundry basket off the top of the washer and turned it upside down over the toe.

While waiting for Frankie to arrive, I decided to go ahead and open the letter. I slit the top of the envelope with the letter opener that I kept in the kitchen. In order to preserve any prints that might be on the inside, I used a pair tweezers to pull out the folded sheet. Laying it on the table, I clamped the tweezers on the top, then slid the tip of the letter opener along the edge to open it.

The words on the page were simple and to the point. *I miss U and I have decided to give you another chance.* A small heart had been drawn at the end of the sentence, but there was no signature. I figured it had to be from Luke Davis.

I heard two cars pull into my driveway and stop. When I looked out the front window, I saw Frankie and Walter Lane, the county forensics specialist, walking across my yard. This felt like deja vu.

As they stepped through the door, Walter said, "We've got to stop meeting like this, Miss Kane."

Rowdy and Precious were sniffing at his shoes, so I bent down and picked them up.

"You seem like a nice person, Walter, but I'm tired of seeing you under these circumstances, too," I said, smiling. "And please call me Allie."

"Are these the dachshund detectives?" he asked, rubbing each of their heads. They both licked his hand like he was their long lost friend. "It's possible that the body buried in your neighbor's yard wouldn't have been found for a while, if it hadn't been for them."

"Is the toe under that laundry basket?" Frankie asked.

"Keeping it safe from further mutilation," I said.

I led the way to the kitchen. Frankie and I watched as Walter picked up the basket and set it out of the way. He pulled a penlight from his pocket, then got down on his knees to examine the toe.

"This is definitely a post-mortem wound," he said. He pulled a pair of latex gloves and two clear plastic zipper bags from his pocket. "There's very little decomposition, so I'd say you're looking for someone who's been dead for only two or three days. It looks like soil around the nail, but I'll test it at the lab to be sure."

Picking up the toe, he placed it in one of the bags, then zipped it up. A speck of blood remained on the tile.

"Do you think the toe was still attached to the body when the dogs found it?" Frankie asked him.

"Judging by the ragged strips of skin above the joint, I'd say one of the dogs chewed it off."

Great! I'm the owner of cadaver eating dogs. I looked at Rowdy, assuming he was the culprit, and thought to myself, *Neighbors beware!*

Frankie nudged my elbow, and I realized Walter was talking to me. "I'm sorry, Walter, what did you say?"

"Since I've got gloves on, if you'll hand me one of those paper towels and some of that antibacterial handsoap by the sink, I'll clean up this spot for you. You never know what diseases may be present."

I got the items that he asked for from the cabinet and handed them to him. He wiped the contaminated area, then put the soiled paper towel and gloves into the other plastic bag.

Looking at me, Frankie said, "Do you have any idea where your dogs may have gotten it?"

"None whatsoever. When I let them out earlier, I saw that Doug had put more chicken wire around the fence while I was gone. I'll go out with you and we can try to find where they might have dug out."

Holding up the toe, Walter said to Frankie, "There's nothing more I can do here. I'm going to take this to the lab and start processing it. I should have a report tomorrow by mid-morning, if you want to give me a call."

"I appreciate that, Walter. I'll walk out with you and get the flashlight from my trunk so I can check for holes around the fence out back."

"Take care, Allie," Walter said. "You have a great pair of dogs. And don't be too hard on the female; she's just doing what instinct led her to do."

"You mean Precious chewed off the toe?" It was hard to believe that the timid beauty in my arms could do such a thing. "Rowdy is the more rambunctious one, and he had it in his mouth when he came inside. What makes you think she did it?"

"When she was licking my hand earlier, I noticed she was missing a couple of her front teeth, but Rowdy still had all of his," he said. "Puppy teeth come out easily, and I saw one caught in the side of the toe. Remember, still waters run deep. That little girl may be more of an instigator of trouble than you give her credit for."

I told Walter good night, then watched as Frankie followed him outside. I put on my coat and went to the pantry to get my flashlight. Flipping it on, I was glad to find that the batteries still worked.

When Frankie came back inside, I switched on the back porch light, then we went into the backyard. Starting with the fence dividing Mrs. Googan's yard from ours, we found that Doug had reinforced the whole section with chicken wire. The only loose dirt around the bottom was from the holes he had filled in. We followed the fence around the back and along the other side and couldn't find a hole big enough for the dogs to get out. The only section left to check was next to the door that led into the garage.

The branches from a cedar tree planted outside the fence covered the eight-foot section facing the street. Doug and I share the yard chores, and when he does the trimming, he is meticulous. I, on the other hand, hate using the weed cutter, so when it's my turn to trim, I tend to do just enough to get by. The last time we did the yard, before the frost last fall, I had neglected to trim this section, so the brittle weeds were over a foot tall.

Shining his light on the ground, Frankie said, "Looks like Doug needs to hire a new person to trim back here. The one who left this is falling down on the job."

Standing behind him in the darkness, I stuck out my tongue.

He crouched down by the wall of the garage and, using his flashlight, started separating the dense vegetation along the fence. A large clump of grass near one of the posts fell into the yard, exposing a hole about six inches wide and several inches deep.

"I'd say this is where they've been getting out," Frankie said, pulling on some loose hair that was stuck to the bottom of the wires. He stood back up and looked at me. "And for the record, I know you stuck your tongue out at me."

"Well, you deserved it!" I said, sounding like a spoiled five-year-old. "I hate trimming! I'd rather mow twice than to trim once. At least we've found the way the pups have been getting out, but we still don't know where they went."

"As young as they are, I doubt if it was too far away, or they probably couldn't have found their way back," he said. "I called you at 6:30. How long were they outside?"

Thinking back, I remembered the clock had read 5:45 when the puppies woke me from my nap. "About forty-five minutes."

"It probably took at least thirty minutes for Precious to chew off the toe," he said. "If you figure in five to ten minutes to dig it out, assuming the soil Walter saw around the nail was from a shallow grave, that leaves about three minutes to get there and three minutes to get back home with it."

Looking at him in the dim light, I thought of a place that fit that distance to a tee.

"Come back inside. I need to show you something," I said. I turned around and started walking toward the back porch.

After Frankie read the letter, he asked me what I thought "give you another chance" meant. I told him about the times that Luke had asked me out. Even though I had turned him down flat, I thought he meant he was giving me a chance to change my mind.

Frankie didn't like the fact that he had written to me, or that he had been close enough to invite me out. He wanted to take the letter with him to get it tested for fingerprints. He said that Luke's prints had been taken the night Lester Crane was dug up and, if there were any on the letter, he wanted them compared.

"I'm going to the station to get to work on this," he said. "You get some rest, then I want to hear about your trip later."

"Oh, wait, I have a present for you."

My suitcase and carryon were still sitting by the couch. I walked over and opened the suitcase and pulled out the bag containing all the key chains with the Hawaiian names on them. I sorted through them until I found his and Kailyn's.

"I know it's not much, Palanaki, but here's a little something for you and Kailine."

"Palanaki? I've been called a lot of things, but it's the first time for that." He held the key chain closer to get a better look. "Thanks, Allie. That was nice of you to think of us."

"I intended to hand them out tomorrow at Gramma's, but since the dinner is being postponed, I'll wait until next week, I guess."

"Since Kailyn's sick, Nana brought us some lunch today. While we were visiting, she said that she and Gramma are starting early in the morning making chicken soup and loaves of bread to take to all our families. Jamie, Michael and I were supposed to deliver the meals, but since this matter came up tonight, I'll need to work. I don't suppose I could twist your arm to take my place and help them tomorrow, could I?"

"Sure I will. I'll call Kristin and see if she wants to help me."

"You're a good girl, regardless of what everyone says about you." He dodged the swing I threw at his shoulder, then walked toward the front door.

"Oh, wait a minute," I said. Picking up the cold drumstick still sitting on my plate, I grabbed a paper towel from the dispenser, then walked over to him. "This is a peace offering for sticking my tongue out earlier."

Taking the chicken leg from me, he took a bite. "You're forgiven. Now, go get some rest."

It was almost 9:00 when I called Nana and told her that I would be taking Frankie's place delivering food the next day. She said they would be cooking at Gramma's, and I offered to come early to help with the preparation. She told me that Aunt Cynthia might need a hand rolling piecrust for the peach cobblers. Thinking about her cobbler made my mouth water.

Last July, Nana and Gramma traveled fifty miles to an orchard in Porter and bought ten bushels of the sweetest, juiciest peaches I have ever tasted. At the Sunday dinner that week, each family picked out a few peaches to take home with them. Nana and Gramma spent all of Monday and Tuesday canning the rest. Some of those jars of fruit would be used for the cobblers.

Promising to tell Nana about my trip when I saw her, I hung up and checked the doors. The dogs had gone out when Frankie and I were outside and they were already asleep in their basket. I turned out all the lights, then walked to the bedroom to get ready for bed.

Snuggling deep under the comforter, I said a prayer for Simon's family as well as my own. As soon as "Amen" passed my lips, I was sound asleep.

CHAPTER 18

When Aunt Cynthia let me in at Gramma's house the next morning, the fragrance of boiling chicken soup, cinnamon peaches and fresh bread filled the air. I had eaten a bowl of Cheerios before I left the house, but I knew right away that my stomach wasn't going to be satisfied with that.

As I walked toward the kitchen, someone was talking, but I couldn't place the voice. When I reached the doorway, I was surprised to find DeLana Miller sitting at the table next to Michael. Riley was across from them watching DeLana measure flour and dump it into a large mixing bowl.

"This brings back old memories," DeLana said. "When I was ten, I spent the summer with my Grandma Miller, and she taught me how to make bread. My mother always hated to bake, so I took on the job at home after that."

"She's a great cook, too," Michael said, taking DeLana's hand. "She made lasagna for Riley and me the other night, and I had three big servings."

"And I'll bet that wasn't all you ate," I said, stepping into the room.

"Well, if it isn't the wayfaring stranger," Michael said, scooting back from the table. "Did you decide to come back from the land of enchantment to labor for the sick people?"

"Yes, and also to honor you with my presence," I said, hugging him.

"Hooray, Allie's back!" Riley yelled as she came running toward me.

After giving her a big hug, I went to the counter and hugged Gramma and Nana. Walking back toward the table, I said, "It's good to see you, too,

DeLana, though I'm a little surprised. You have to be careful when you visit this family. We'll put you to work."

"Both of your grandmothers tried to get me to just sit and visit, but I wanted to help," she said.

"And she's doing a fine job, isn't she, Suzanna?" Gramma said.

"She sure is," Nana said. "The last four loaves of bread wouldn't be baking in the oven right now if I hadn't had her help. Cynthia's been busy with the peach filling, while DeLana's been measuring flour for the crusts. I've got a bowl full to roll, if you're ready to jump in, Allie."

"Coming," I said, setting my purse in a chair out of the way.

I walked to the sink to wash my hands, while Nana unrolled Gramma's thick plastic cover. She placed it on the end of the table. At home, Nana uses a large, wooden cutting board that she has had since Dad was a little boy. Gramma has a similar board, but she put it away last year when she won the plastic cover and a rolling pin at a Tupperware party. Different-sized circles are imprinted on the plastic, and Gramma says that now she doesn't have to guess if the crust is big enough or not.

We worked side-by-side for over an hour before taking a break. Jamie came in just as the last crusty loaves of bread were coming out of the oven. Under Nana's supervision, he and Michael started slicing and wrapping the first four. Only the larger families would get full loaves, so she had them label the partial packages with the smaller families' names.

It was almost noon before all the cobblers were baked and the large pots of chicken soup were ready. While Nana spooned hot cobbler and Gramma ladled steaming soup into dozens of whipped topping containers, the rest of us formed an assembly line to seal, wrap, label and box up the meals. Whenever Kane Energy buys new computers and software, Jamie brings home the empty boxes and puts them in his attic. With a family as large as ours, someone often needs boxes, and today we were using a lot of them.

While we worked, I told everyone about my trip and answered their questions. Gramma asked me if I had met any interesting men while I was gone, and I told them a little about Simon. Michael said he had received an e-mail from Richard, and I told him that he wanted him to come and go deep-sea fishing with him.

"I may take him up on that invitation before long," Michael said. "I haven't taken a decent vacation in over three years. We had a blast when he was here and Grandad and Uncle Clarence took us fishing for crappie at the lake. It's a totally different style than deep-sea fishing, but he loved the fight those crappie gave him."

"After being in the boat under the hot sun fishing all day, you and Richard were burnt to a crisp," Gramma said. "Your granddad and Uncle Clarence wore hats and long sleeves, so they made it alright. You fought me over it, but I finally convinced you boys to let me put some aloe gel on your arms and faces that night. Because I did, neither of you blistered, and you felt better the next day."

Walking up behind her, Michael put his hands on Gramma's shoulders and kissed the top of her head. "If it hadn't been for you, Richard and I wouldn't have slept that night. We were too proud to say it, but we were miserable before you put that stuff on us. I remember feeling like a giant hot tamale. Thanks, Gramma, for being there for me so many times in my life."

"Oh, hush now, it was nothing." She dabbed at her eyes with the hem of her apron, then turned around and looked up at him. She frowned, then touched his cheek with her hand. "Michael, you're hot, and I don't think it's from the heat in the kitchen. Bend down here so that I can feel your forehead." He leaned down, and she touched her cheek to his head. "I'd say you have a fever of at least a hundred and two. When did you start feeling bad?"

"Oh, I woke up with a little headache this morning, but after I took some aspirin, I felt better."

"But now you're feeling bad again, aren't you?" she said. She steered him to a chair at the table.

He rubbed a hand over his face. "Yes, I guess I am. I didn't realize it until you brought it up."

Just then the doorbell rang, and the front door opened. Kristin stuck her head in and yelled, "Yoohoo. Anybody home? It's Doug and me."

"We're all in the kitchen, you two," Gramma hollered. "Come on back."

By the time they got there, Gramma had a thermometer stuck under Michael's tongue. After they greeted everyone, Kristin looked at Michael and said, "You don't look good."

"I don't feel good, either."

Gramma pulled the thermometer from his mouth. "One hundred and two, just like I said. You need to drink some orange juice, then get upstairs to bed."

"But DeLana and I were going to help deliver this food," he said. "Then I'll need to take her home."

"I'm sure that Allie and Kristin would let me go with them," DeLana said, touching Michael's cheek. "You need to do what your grandma says. I'll check on you when we get back."

"Sure, DeLana, you can come with us," I said. I was dying to get her alone to find out more details about her relationship with Michael. "Riley, if you want to, you can come, also."

"The men will be coming in from church soon, and I think your grand-dad is planning on Riley's company to help deliver food to the pastor's house and Sister May's family," Gramma said. "One reason we made so much food is because we got word yesterday that several members of their families are sick. Brother Jim was supposed to preach for the pastor this morning."

"I told Grandad last night that I'd help him," Riley said. "I didn't go with him to Sunday school this morning, because I needed to help here."

"Doug and I will team up and take food to all the Kanes," Jamie said. "Allie, why don't you, Kristin and DeLana deliver to the Winters side?"

Everyone nodded in agreement.

"It sounds like everything is covered, so I guess I'll stay here and rest," Michael said. "Maybe a little nap will perk me up."

I knew that if he was getting the flu that was going around, it would take more than a nap for him to get well. Gramma poured some orange juice for him, then followed him up the stairs to get him more aspirin.

Before we started loading the cars, my two grandfathers, Uncle Clarence and Aunt Edith came in from church. They reported that two families that lived down the road weren't at church because of illness. Grandpa and Uncle Clarence said they would take food to them. While Nana and Kristin started filling more containers, I asked Riley to go out and bring in the souvenir sacks from my car.

When she got back inside, I gave everyone his or her gift and received lots of hugs and thanks in return. Aunt Edith was thrilled with her grass skirt and promised to model it for us when everyone got back for lunch. Kristin and DeLana helped me put the remaining gifts in the correct food boxes, and then we started loading the cars. Nana promised to keep the food hot for us so that we could eat as soon as we got back.

❀   ❀   ❀

"I take it that you and Michael are dating now," I said to DeLana as we drove away from the house. "The last time I saw you two together, papers were scattered on the cafeteria floor and he had invited you to go horseback riding at the Circle K the next day. You need to bring me up to speed."

A smile pulled at the corners of DeLana's mouth. "We went riding that day, then I joined him and Riley at church on Sunday morning. All three of us went to the Cinema Six on Tuesday night to see a new Disney movie, then I cooked for them on Thursday. I think they're both pretty special."

"I'll fill you in on a little secret," I said. "He must think you're special, too, because he has never brought a date to a family gathering."

"Really? We haven't discussed it, but I assumed as handsome and charming as he is that he's dated lots of women," DeLana said.

"Only two, isn't it Kristin?" I asked. "Peggy and Shelly?"

"Those are the only women I know about," Kristin said. "He took each of them to dinner and a movie a couple of times, but that was as far as it got."

"Hmmm. That's interesting," DeLana said, then she changed the subject.

At 1:15, we pulled back into Gramma's driveway. We parked behind Jamie and Doug, and as the three of us were getting out of the car, Grandad and Riley pulled in. Grandpa and Uncle Clarence had been the first to get back, and they had started stacking the empty boxes on the back porch. After adding ours to the stack, we walked into the house. I reported that the Winters clan members were on the mend and much happier after our deliveries.

"They couldn't have been happier than Mom and Dad," Jamie said. "And Nana, Aunt Celeste said to give you this." He walked over and put his arms around her and kissed her on the cheek. "She said she'll give you a call later this evening." Aunt Celeste is my dad's younger sister and Frankie's mother.

"Thanks, sweetheart," Nana said. "I haven't seen her all week."

"Aunt Emily wasn't sick, but she had been up most of the night nursing Uncle Roger and Patrick," Kristin reported. "Allie, Riley and I spread everything on the table and put out bowls and paper plates, so there wouldn't be many dishes used. The twins were feeling better, and they said they'd clean up after the family ate."

We all sat down at the table and started eating the delicious chicken soup. Not a crumb of hot bread was left in the basket when we were done. The meal was topped off with Nana's warm peach cobbler à la mode.

Just as we finished eating, Mom called to thank me for the ilimi orchid bulbs that I had sent over with Jamie. I was relieved to hear that she was feeling better.

"As soon as we were done eating, your dad brought in his tackle box from the garage," Mom told me. "He has everything strung out on the kitchen table, so I know he's feeling better, too. The last time I was in there, he was sorting his lures, and it looked like he was trying to decide where to put the ones you brought him. Keeping him in the house for three days while he was sick wasn't easy. I suspect he'll try to sneak off to the Circle K this afternoon to fish."

"I'm glad my little gift is boosting his spirits," I said. "When I came in to get the phone, Grandad and Uncle Clarence were discussing what time they would meet in the morning to plant the onion seeds I brought them."

Grandpa A.J. tapped me on the shoulder and whispered, "I'd like to talk to your daddy, before you hang up."

Nodding at him, I relayed the message to Mom, then handed the receiver to him.

As I walked down the hallway to go help with the dishes, I heard him say, "James, do you feel like drowning some worms this afternoon? I'm aching to try out these lures your daughter brought me."

I was smiling when I walked back into the kitchen.

"Ain't this a pip, you all?" Aunt Edith said as she modeled her grass skirt for us in the living room. "Daisy will be green with envy, and I can't wait to show it off at the beauty shop in the morning." She swayed as she circled the coffee table. "Gladys will probably want to borrow it. Thanks, Allie."

"I'm glad you like it, Aunt Edith. The moment I saw it, I thought of you."

"If you get that summer school job, I might need to come to Hawaii and spend a week or two with you, if you wouldn't mind," she said. "I'd like to do some shopping at that big mall where you found this skirt. They probably have all kinds of nifty things to pep up my wardrobe. And besides that, Hawaii would be a good place for me to work on my tan, too."

I smiled at her. "Aunt Edith, if I get the job, you're welcome to come with me."

I hope that when I'm seventy-eight years old, I still care enough about my looks to want to work on my tan, I thought.

Aside from Grandpa, Grandad and Uncle Clarence, who had all slipped out to go fishing right after we ate, everyone lounged at Gramma's until after 3:00.

Michael had awakened once and was feeling worse than he had been earlier. Gramma insisted he stay put for the night so that she could take care of him. Since Riley and her birds had been here since Friday morning, I decided to offer to take them home with me.

I walked upstairs. "Michael, Grandad is planning on getting an early start in the garden in the morning. If Riley goes home with me, I can take her to school."

"I would appreciate it, Allie," he said groggily. "I was going to ask if she could stay with you on Monday night because I'm supposed to fly to Dallas for a Tuesday morning meeting. Do you mind keeping her and the birds a couple of nights?"

"Of course, I don't mind. The puppies and I will love their company. She'll be the first to get to try out the new furniture in my guestroom."

Wishing him well, I went to help Riley gather up her stuff. Kristin was going to give DeLana a ride back to Michael's so that she could get her car. As everyone parted, Nana helped me carry things to my car while Jamie loaded the birdcages into the backseat. I turned around to give her a final hug, then thought of something I wanted to ask her.

"Nana, a long time ago you asked me not to reveal who plays the ghosts in the graveyard on Halloween, and I haven't. But Traci and I were discussing the hayride the year when there was a fourth ghost in the catalpa tree.

Even though we were grown, it scared the daylights out of us. Since it was so long ago, would you tell me who it was?"

She glanced across the yard and was about to say something, when Jamie walked up behind me. He cackled in a way that brought back memories of that night, then leaned close to my ear and said, "Boo!"

I whirled around and saw a mischievous smile on his face. "It was you? But you were going to school at OU and didn't come home every weekend."

"That's true. But if you'll think back, I surprised the family at church the Sunday after Halloween, then drove back to Norman after dinner. I made a great ghost, didn't I?"

"People in town still talk about it," Nana said. "We might need to bring back Ghost Number Four this Halloween, Jamie. It would add some new excitement to the hayrides."

"You might be right," he said. He looked at his watch. "I'd better head home. Nicole has been alone with the girls all afternoon, and I'm sure she needs a break. I'll sec you two later."

"See you," I said to him. I thanked Nana again for the wonderful lunch, then climbed into the car with my houseguests, and we headed toward home.

Riley talked up a storm about the things she had done over spring break. As we drove past the Davises', she paused. "That place looks spooky. Does anybody live there?"

"Yes, the man you saw talking to me at the car wash and his father do. But it doesn't look like they've been home in a while." Mail was sticking out of the mailbox, and the rubber band must have broken when the paperboy threw the Sunday paper; sheets of newspaper were strewn all over the yard.

I pulled into the garage, and we unloaded the car. Once inside, I put a thick towel on the dresser in the guestroom for the birdcages to sit on. Riley said that if they were sleeping close to her, they wouldn't squawk in the night.

While she was getting the birds settled, I checked the messages on my answering machine. The first one was from Frankie, telling me that he had some news about the toe. The second message was from Simon.

"Sorry I missed you," he said. "I just got back from Maui this morning after staying up with Grandpa at the hospital all night. I'm going to lie down for a while, but wouldn't mind being awakened by a beautiful woman's voice. I miss you, so please give me a call when you get this message."

He missed me! I listened to his message again and decided to call him back right then. As I hurried to my purse to get the paper he had written his phone number on, it hit me. I had torn it off and given it to Sammy Cho in the park! Mentally kicking myself for not writing it down on something else first, I started searching for Richard's business card.

Disappointed when no one answered at Richard's house, I left a voice-mail telling him that Simon had called, but that I didn't have his number. I asked him to please contact Simon and ask him to call me again.

It was only noon in Hawaii and Richard and his family could be gone all day, so I tried directory assistance, but was told that Simon's number was unlisted. Taking one last shot, I called the operator back and asked for the Honolulu Police Department's number.

"Good morning, Honolulu P.D. How may I help you?" a voice on the line asked.

"Hi, I'm Allison Kane, a friend of Simon Kahala's. I'm trying to return a call to him, but don't have his number. Would you please give it to me?"

She sounded skeptical when she said, "You're a friend, but you don't have his phone number?"

"Well, I did have his number, but I don't now," I said. *Yeah, likely story,* I bet she was thinking.

"We don't give out the officers' personal information, Miss. Would you like to leave a message for him?"

I should have known better. No telling what kind of nut cases would call and harass the officers if they had their personal numbers. Having no other choice, I left a message, unsure of when he would get it.

Knowing there was nothing else I could do but wait, I unpacked my suitcase and started some laundry. I set up the bird perch in the living room, and Riley played with the puppies. While doing my clothes, I had to watch out for Flip. He kept diving at the shiny metal measuring cups I have hanging on a rack by the stove.

Later that evening, Riley and I ate a light supper. I found a deck of cards, and we played several hands of "Go Fish" and "Slap Jack." When it was time for her to take a bath and get ready for bed, I gave Frankie a call.

"What's the news on the toe?" I asked.

"The judge won't issue a random warrant for us to start digging in yards around your house. We've got to come up with evidence pinpointing a more specific area. There's no DNA match in the database, so we have a toe on ice with no body."

"Bummer. I'd bet money that it has something to do with the Davises."

"Probably, but don't you dare go digging in their yard again! I'll figure out something, don't worry."

I told him Riley was spending a couple of nights with me and that I needed to go get her into bed. After the birds were secured in their cages and I had tucked her in, I sat down in my recliner and started thinking about the missing, toeless body. I jumped when the phone next to me started ringing.

Grabbing it on the second ring, I heard a man say, "I understand you gave away my phone number."

Loving the sound of Simon's voice, I said, "I take it you got my message from Richard, or was it from work?"

"I've talked to Richard, Sammy Cho and the dispatcher who took your message within the last hour. Before I get onto you for not minding me about staying clear of Sammy, thank you for trying so hard to get back to me. When I woke up from my nap and you hadn't called, I began thinking you were having second thoughts about us."

"Lots of thoughts, but all of them good. How's your grandfather?"

"Holding his own. Different family members have been taking shifts, so someone is always with him. The doctors think he'll make a full recovery, but it will take time."

While Frankie's information was still fresh on my mind, I told Simon about everything, including Luke's letter.

"Body parts just seem to find their way to you, don't they?" he said. "But the more pressing issue now seems to be that Davis character. Watch your back; he may show up again."

I promised him I would be careful, then asked about his conversation with Sammy. I was pleased that he had taken my advice and contacted Simon. Though he hadn't agreed to come into the station yet, Sammy had told him his side of the story over the phone.

The man on the beach was Dwayne Conway and the boyfriend of Sammy's eighteen-year-old sister, LuAnn. Details were sketchy, but

Sammy said he had obtained the gun from some friend of a friend for self-defense purposes. There had been a lot of muggings in the area where he lived, and he didn't plan to be a victim.

LuAnn was at Sammy's house one day and, while he was busy in the garage, she took his gun. Apparently, she had taken all the two-timing and beatings from Dwayne that she intended to take. When she went to his house, he was there with another woman, so she pulled the gun on him. He laughed at her, then took the gun away from her and beat her half to death with it.

Sammy said that LuAnn called him to come and get her. After he took her to the hospital, he started looking for Dwayne. On a tip from one of Dwayne's former friends, Sammy found him at Ewa Beach in a car with another girl. Sammy told him it was time someone taught him some respect for women.

After taking a few punches, Dwayne pulled the gun. The two men scuffled for it, then it went off, killing him. Though Dwayne's finger was on the trigger when the gun discharged, Sammy was afraid that he would be blamed for the shooting. That was why he hid the gun in the toilet.

"Do you believe his story?" I asked Simon.

"Dwayne Conway was mean and had a reputation for beating women. It's possible that it could have happened like Sammy said. We're trying to find the girl that was with Dwayne in the car at the beach to see if she can back up his story."

We talked until after eleven about lots of things, then said good night. He told me to let him know if I heard anything about the teaching job, and I said I would. It wasn't until after I hung up that I realized I still didn't have his phone number.

CHAPTER 19

The sky was a brilliant blue when Riley and I backed out of the garage Monday morning. Aside from a few muddy spots here and there, all signs of the snow were gone. The daffodils along the sidewalk were getting taller, and the Bradford pear trees in both my yard and Doug's had tiny white buds all over them.

When we got to school, Kristin was pulling into the parking lot at the same time, so we walked inside with her. Riley joined some of her friends at one of the cafeteria tables to wait for the first bell, and Kristin and I went into the office to sign in.

"I got a long e-mail from Kevin last night," Kristin said. "They received our Care packages yesterday, and everyone was elated with the things in them. He said they acted like kids opening presents at Christmas."

"I'm glad they liked everything," I said as we walked into the workroom. "I'll share the news with my class this morning."

Kristin ran a copy of the e-mail for me. "One of the soldiers had been despondent for several weeks after seeing a child lose the lower part of his arm in a roadside bombing," she said. "Kevin said that some of the guys got him interested in one of the video games, and he started perking up. They haven't had enough fun things to do in their downtime to keep their minds off the war, but the things we sent should help."

I headed to my classroom to get ready for the students, while Kristin went in to tell Mrs. Graves about the good news from Kevin. When I walked into my room, it was a different world from the one I had been in the week before, but it felt good to be back in familiar surroundings.

When the bell rang and the students started coming in, I could tell they were as happy to be back as I was. Several of them were anxious to tell me all about the things they had done during their time off. I had brought the video of the Polynesian Cultural Center show to share with them and decided to give them time to share their own adventures, as well.

The morning flew by. After recess, I started reading *The Indian in the Cupboard* by Lynne Reid Banks to them. From past experience, I knew they would be hooked from the first page, so I had allotted some extra time for the book. After the restroom break, we pushed back the desks and sat in a circle on the floor.

"I'd like each of you to tell about something special you did while on spring break," I said. "But before you do that, Mrs. Sinclair's husband sent her an e-mail telling her that his unit received our packages. I want to read some of the soldiers' comments to you."

I hit the highlights of the letter, and the students were thrilled that their project was a success. The smiles on their faces grew wider the further I read. "Thanks for making my day," "I needed these Slim Jims," and "the lotion smells heavenly," were only a few of the messages from the troops. When I finished with, "The Iraqi children love the stuffed animals," everyone started clapping.

After I put away the letter, the children took turns telling about their own adventures. When they were done, I pulled out some pictures from my trip and passed them around. I told them some things about the USS *Arizona* Memorial, and they wanted to know why the ship is still beneath the water. One student asked why our soldiers didn't know that the Japanese were coming the day it was bombed. I answered each question the best I could, then suggested they get on the Internet or go to the library and research more about it.

"I'll set aside some time on Friday for you to give your reports," I told them. "Now, I have a video I'd like to show you."

I had reserved a VCR that morning and sent Rufus and another boy to the library to wheel it down to the room. While they were gone, we moved the furniture back into place. As soon as the boys got back, I started the tape.

As the music played, their feet tapped to the rhythm. I told them different things about the performers and dancers as the show progressed. After the tape was finished, I talked about the villages that I had toured and the canoe pageant.

"It sounds like you had a great time, Miss Kane," Heather said. "You aren't going to move there, are you? I would miss you."

"Don't worry, Heather. Hawaii is great for a vacation, but I couldn't afford to move there."

Too bad, I thought as the image of Simon filled my head. Pushing it aside, I focused on the remaining afternoon lessons.

After leaving school, Riley and I stopped at the grocery store. I hadn't done much shopping since returning from my trip, and I needed to stock up on some things. After spending almost an hour browsing the aisles and filling the basket, we headed to the checkout stand.

While I was writing my check, an uneasy feeling came over me. I stopped writing and looked around, but saw nothing out of the ordinary. Shrugging the feeling away, I handed the check to the girl at the register.

Riley and I were pushing the cart to the car when an old, beige Taurus with a crushed rear fender stopped a few yards in front of us. The driver was wearing a baseball cap pulled low over his eyes, and he had a scraggly beard. He was drumming his fingers on the steering wheel and didn't seem to be in any hurry to move out of our way.

The uneasiness I had felt earlier returned when the man pushed back his cap. I stopped in my tracks when I saw that it was Luke Davis.

"Let's go back inside, Riley," I said as I started turning the basket around. "I forgot to get something." I didn't want to have to deal with Luke while Riley was with me.

She gave me a puzzled look, but didn't question me. By the time we got back into the store, the car had moved on. While she watched the basket, I stepped a short distance away and called Frankie on my cell phone.

"Frank Janson," he said, when he picked up the phone.

"I just saw Luke in the Food Mart parking lot," I said. "He was driving a beige Ford Taurus with a crumpled fender."

"We got word a couple of hours ago that his wrecker was found just inside the Oklahoma/Missouri border. A young woman on the side of the highway flagged down an Oklahoma Highway Patrolman. She told him that the man driving the wrecker ran her off the road, then hijacked her car. Fortunately, he just took the car and didn't hurt her."

"Thank the Lord for that," I said.

"You and Riley stay where you are, and I'll send a cruiser over to follow you home."

When I got off the phone, Riley asked, "What did you forget to buy?"

Remembering the excuse I had given her outside, I said, "How about some chocolate ice cream for dessert tonight?"

"Alright! I love chocolate!"

After buying the ice cream, we put all the bags into my car. As I backed out of the space, a policeman fell in behind us. Riley didn't seem to notice our escort, and I didn't mention it.

When we arrived home, we carried in the sacks, then I locked the door behind us. The dogs were barking to be let out of their crate.

"Okay, I'm coming," I told them.

"Can I take them out back to play?" Riley asked.

I was hesitant to let her go out alone, but since it was still daylight, I didn't think a few minutes outside would hurt.

"There are some doggie treats in the pantry for the pups and some cookies in that bag you just brought in," I said. "Take a snack out with you if you want to."

After putting the groceries away, I noticed that the red light on the answering machine was blinking. There were two messages. On the first one, I could hear someone breathing, but nothing was said. *Probably a wrong number*, I thought. The voice on the second message made my heart quicken.

"Allie, this is Nalani Kahala calling. I told you I'd let you know as soon as I made my decision about the job. Please give me a call when you can."

My hands were sweating as I wrote down her phone number. I knew that she had several more candidates to interview, so I hadn't expected to hear from her so soon. Could one of them have been so outstanding that she didn't need to deliberate any longer? *There's only one way to find out*, I thought as I dialed the phone.

"Prince Kuhio Elementary," a cheery voice said.

"Hi, this is Allison Kane. Is Miss Kahala available? I'm returning her call."

"She went to the first-grade wing for a minute," the secretary said. "If you'll hold on, I'll go get her."

"Thanks, I'll hold."

It seemed like forever before the secretary came back on the line. "Miss Kahala will be here soon. It seems that one of the first-graders got into an ant pile while playing at recess, and she's assessing the situation. While we're waiting for her, Miss Kane, I want to tell you what a wonderful job you did on the showcase."

"Thanks, but I can't take all the credit. Hanilei and Effie worked as hard as I did on it."

"Oh, here's Miss Kahala," she said. "It was nice talking with you."

"Thanks, it was nice visiting with you, too."

After a couple of clicks, the principal's voice came on the line. "Allison, it's good to hear from you. I was hoping you'd call before I got tied up on the school board tour."

"I was a little late getting home today because I had some shopping to do after school," I said. "I'm glad I caught you."

"You seem like a fine person, and I'm glad that I met you," she said. "Over the last few weeks, I've interviewed some excellent candidates for the open positions. Some have taught for many years, while others were first or second-year teachers."

I was starting to get a sinking feeling in the pit of my stomach. *The competition for the job was too great*, I thought. *I didn't stand a chance.* I snapped to attention when she said my name.

"Allison, are you still there?"

"Yes, ma'am, I'm here."

"From our first meeting, your professionalism and credentials, as well as your personal references, impressed me," she continued. "Those things are important, but when I saw your compassion in helping Samantha Carlson that day in the hallway, I knew you were the teacher I wanted on my staff. I hope you'll accept the third-grade position, if you're still interested, of course."

Stunned by what I had just heard, I was speechless. It took me a moment to realize what she had said. Clearing my throat, I said, "Yes, I'm very interested in the job!"

"Wonderful! Though we discussed many of the details during your interview, I would like to send all the information to you. After you've had a chance to review it, if you have any questions, please call me. Your e-mail address wasn't on your application, so if you'll give it to me, I'll have my secretary forward everything to you."

After giving her my address, I said, "Thanks again for this opportunity. I look forward to working with you and your students."

"I believe you'll enjoy working at Prince Kuhio, and before you know it, they will be *your* students. Have a good evening."

After I hung up, I stood up and shouted, "Yeah! I got the job. I'm going back to Hawaii!"

I was dancing toward the kitchen when Riley and the pups came in.

"You're sure excited," she said. "Did something happen while we were outside?"

I lifted her up and twirled her around. "I got the summer job, Riley! Isn't that great?"

After I set her back down on the floor, she had a bewildered expression on her face. "I don't understand why you're so excited about teaching school in the summer," she said. "You do it all year long, and I thought you loved summer vacation."

"I do love it, but this year, it will be extra special," I said, thinking of Simon. "I'll get to spend a whole month in Hawaii with my friend Traci and some other people I met. Spring break wasn't long enough to do everything I wanted to do."

Riley walked into the living room and flopped down on the couch. "I think Paradise is special. You can go swimming and get a tan, just like in Hawaii. And Hawaii doesn't have Grandad's garden and the Circle K, where you can ride horses and go on picnics. Won't you miss the family?"

I sat down beside her on the couch and draped my arm around her shoulders. "Of course I will. But everyone is so busy in the summertime, they'll hardly know I'm gone. Just think how busy you're going to be. You'll be going to Vacation Bible School, then church camp for a week. T-ball games will still be going on in June, besides the swimming and horseback riding you mentioned. And don't worry, I'll be back in time for the town Fourth of July picnic and fireworks display."

Looking up at me, Riley said, "Well, I'll miss you a lot, but since I'll be having so much fun, I guess it's only fair that you have fun, too."

"I'm glad you agree," I said, kissing the top of her head. "Now, you'd better go let the birds out of their cages, and I'll fix us something to eat."

Hopping up from the couch, Riley skipped down the hall, calling to the birds in the guestroom. *It must be nice to get over problems that easily,* I thought.

While I was fixing supper, storm clouds rolled in. Streaks of lightning filled the sky, and the dogs took refuge between my feet and the cabinet when thunder rocked the house. After dodging Flip's multiple attacks on the measuring cups while I cooked, I was worn out when we sat down to eat.

As soon as Riley finished saying grace, torrential rain started beating down. Rivulets of water were spiraling down the sliding glass door, blurring what little daylight remained.

"It sounds like the sky exploded," Riley said. "It's a good thing the dogs were outside awhile ago, because they're not going to want to go back out in this."

It was a battle getting the pups outside when it rained. If I forced them out alone, they stayed on the porch whimpering. When I went into the yard with them, they tiptoed through the grass like they abhorred touching it. Also, when I was out there, they took their time finding a spot to do their business. It was like they were saying, "We'll show you. If we have to come out in this mess, you can deal with it, too."

While we ate, I glanced over and saw that Flip had settled next to Fluff on their perch and was paying us no mind. They were both playing with mirrors and trinkets hanging from twine that I had tied to the perch yesterday.

"I'm glad that Flip has found something else to do," I said. "He must have gotten bored with dive-bombing my head."

"It's a game for him. When Daddy's in the kitchen, he does the same thing to him. I think Flip finds it challenging when an obstacle, like someone's head, is in the way of the object he wants. Sometimes Daddy puts him into his cage because he gets tired of dodging him while he cooks."

After we cleared the table, Riley sat down to do some homework while I loaded the dishwasher. We finished about the same time, and she asked to take a bubble bath. While she was playing in the tub, I turned on my laptop and sent an e-mail message to Traci, telling her that I got the job. The message from the school secretary was in my inbox, so I printed it, along with the four-page attachment, then sat down in my recliner to read the information.

When Riley emerged from the bathroom, she was yawning and ready to go to bed. After tucking her in, I went back to the living room and turned on the television to watch my favorite Monday night sitcom. During the first half of the show, the lights flashed a couple of times. Because there are so many large trees in the neighborhood, it isn't uncommon to lose electricity during storms.

While a commercial was on, I walked to the pantry to get my flashlight in case the lights went off for good. When I flipped it on, the light was a bit dim, so I decided to put in new batteries. I was rummaging through the kitchen drawer where I kept them, when the dogs started growling.

"What's the matter with you two?" They were standing at the glass door looking into the darkness. I walked over and flipped on the porch light, but couldn't see anything out of the ordinary. The rain was now a steady patter on the porch. I walked back to my recliner and sat down. "Come over here and lie down. The storm's not going to get you."

They trotted over and stood next to my chair, but continued whimpering and looking toward the door.

By the time the show ended, the pups were standing at the door barking. I grabbed my umbrella from the hall closet, then picked up the flashlight and stuck it under my arm.

"Okay. Let's go see what's got you so stirred up."

The wind had picked up and was throwing rain against the glass. When I slid the glass door open, the dogs raced out. By the time I got the umbrella open, the kitchen floor was wet, and my hair and face were drenched. Pushing the door closed, I held the umbrella with one hand, while turning on the flashlight with the other. I panned the light across the yard and located the dogs, then I started down the porch steps toward them.

A loud crash by the garage startled me and I slipped on the last step, twisting my ankle. The wind tore the umbrella from my hand and I dropped the flashlight as I fell in a heap on the ground.

I laid there on my side and fought back tears as sharp pains shot up my leg. I could hear the dogs barking and snarling near the fence, so I reached for the flashlight, then struggled to my knees. I stayed in the crouched position for a few moments, then stood up, being careful to keep as much weight as I could off the injured ankle.

Pushing my dripping hair out of my eyes, I tried to see what was upsetting the dogs. I started limping toward the back of the garage. They were growling at something around the corner, out of my line of sight. I gripped the heavy flashlight harder, and as I turned the corner, Luke Davis stepped in front of me.

"Well, well, if it isn't my nosy neighbor," he said. "I've been watching you and that little girl all evening through the windows; just biding my time before coming to pay you a visit. Now I guess my wait is over."

A shiver went through me when I thought of him watching us. The cockiness he had shown during our previous encounters was gone. Tonight he looked hard and dangerous. Not the kind of man you would want to meet in your backyard on a dark and stormy night. The cap on his head was soaked, and water was dripping from the hair sticking out from beneath it. As he moved closer to me, I could see evil in his eyes.

"What do you want?" I asked, trying to keep the fear out of my voice.

He reached inside his jacket and pulled out my trowel. "I wanted to return this to you," he said, dangling it in front of my face. "It wasn't big enough for the job I had to do the other evening." The dogs were nipping at his ankles, but he seemed oblivious to them.

"The job the other evening?" I slowly started backing toward the house.

"Yeah, I had to have a shovel to dig a hole that big. But I was smarter than old man Sanders. I wrapped the body in some trash bags before burying it. No dogs will ever...*Yeow!*" Looking down, he kicked at the pups. "That's the last time you'll bite anybody, you mangy mutts!"

He lunged toward Precious, barely missing her with the blade of the trowel. She scrambled between my feet, trying to seek refuge. Luke reached down and grabbed her by the collar, then raised the tool into the air above her head.

"No!" I shouted, then I hit him as hard as I could on the side of the head with the flashlight.

He slumped to the ground, and I pulled Precious from his grasp. As Luke lay there moaning, I yelled at Rowdy to come. Holding the dogs in my arms, I stumbled toward the house.

My leg and ankle felt like they were on fire as I hobbled onto the porch. I jerked the door open and stepped inside. Before I realized what was happening, my feet slipped on the wet tile and they slid out from under me. The dogs leapt out of my arms and the flashlight flew out of my hand as I crashed to the floor.

While lying on my back a few feet from the open door, I panted to force air back into my lungs. Luke was screaming like a wild animal and getting closer to the steps. Rolling over, I scooted my body until I reached the edge of the doorframe. I pushed the door with all my might. It slammed shut as he reached the porch.

I pulled myself into a sitting position, using one of the kitchen chairs for leverage. Luke stumbled and fell on the slick porch. Just as I touched the lock on the handle, he wrenched the door out of my grasp.

"Oh, no you don't!" he yelled. "I've been waiting too long to get my hands on you!"

Wet grass and mud clung to his clothes, and water was dripping from his beard. His cap had come off, and his thin hair was flattened to his head. His crooked, tobacco-stained teeth looked grotesque in the glow of the kitchen light.

He looked down at me sitting on the floor, and a lecherous grin began forming on his face. Squatting beside me, I saw that he still had the trowel in his hand.

The metal was cold as he rubbed the tip of the blade along my neck.

"Look at me," he said. When I didn't comply, he put the implement under my chin and forced my head up.

As he stared at me, I tried to stay calm. I knew that I had to do whatever was necessary to keep Riley safe, regardless of what happened to me. If I could get my hands on the flashlight or the scissors in the utility drawer, I'd have a chance. But until I could do that, I decided to try to get him to talk.

"You said you were smarter than Mr. Sanders. What did you mean by that?"

"I guess it won't hurt to tell you, since I'm taking you with me anyway," he said.

Not without a fight, I thought.

"A few days ago, my old man started hitting me again with that blasted cane of his, like he's done for years. Even though he was mean as sin to my mom and me, I've taken care of him since he got out of prison. I've worked hard to feed and clothe us and keep a roof over our heads. But he never appreciated nothin'!"

The look on Luke's face was a mixture of pain and despair. I couldn't imagine how he must have felt growing up with an abusive father. If I hadn't been so scared, I might have felt sorry for him.

He stared down at his muddy boots. "Like usual, he was drinking and cussin' me. Then he hit me across the face with that cane. Well, he won't ever do it again, that's for sure!"

I was certain that I knew the answer, but I asked, "What did you do?"

Luke looked back at me. "When he started hitting me, I grabbed the cane and gave him a taste of his own medicine." He stood up and looked out the glass door into the darkness. "I didn't mean to hit him so hard. When I heard his neck crack, I knew I had killed him."

As he continued staring into the night, I started scooting toward the kitchen cabinets. He didn't seem to notice what I was doing.

"I thought about the guy that had been buried under the azalea bushes," he said. "Who would think to look twice in the same place?"

"It sounds like it was self-defense," I said, trying to stand up.

As he watched me, he didn't make a move to stop me. In fact, he reached for my arm and said, "Let me give you a hand."

"No, thanks. I can manage."

"Suit yourself."

With the help of the chair I had been leaning against, I pulled myself up. I tested the ankle, then I limped to the counter.

"Mind if I get a drink of water?" I asked.

"Go ahead. I could use one, too."

He wandered around the kitchen, opening and closing the cabinet doors. The cord looped through the trowel handle was hanging on his index finger, leaving the metal part dangling in the air.

I reached into the cabinet and took out a glass while opening the utility drawer with my other hand. When I touched the cold, metal blades of the scissors, I felt like I might have a chance.

I slid the scissors out of the drawer. Holding them in front of me, I filled the glass with hot water. I moved the hand holding the sheers to my side, then I turned around. Holding the glass of water out to him, I said, "Here you go."

As he reached for the glass, I threw the hot water in his face. He yelped and grabbed his eyes.

I pushed the point of the scissors against his crotch. "There's no way you're going to take me out of here alive. Now, sit down in that chair, before I get careless and neuter you." I didn't think I would have the guts to hurt him, but he didn't know that.

"Okay, okay. Just watch what you're doing."

On his tiptoes, he backed toward the chair like a bowlegged cowboy. Fear had replaced the confident look in his eyes as he slowly lowered himself onto the seat.

"Now put your hands above your head so I can see them." I said.

With the trowel still looped around his finger, he inched his hands upward. All at once, he grabbed the handle of it.

With a twisted look of hate on his face, he lunged at me. I jumped away as the blade sliced through the air, barely missing me.

The scissors fell out of my hand and slid across the floor. Barring a miracle, I was a goner!

Out of nowhere, I heard the loud flutter of wings. Flip soared into the room and rammed his beak into the trowel. It banged Luke in the head, and the force knocked him backward into the edge of the table. As he tried to regain his balance, Flip dive-bombed the trowel again, sending Luke spinning face-first to the floor.

Blood was streaming from his nose. He tried to sit up. He was howling in pain as he cupped his hands around his nose.

He managed to brace himself against the chair he had been sitting in. Flip swooped in and hit the tool again. It slammed into Luke's chin, knocking him sideways. He collapsed to the floor with a thud!

I sank to the floor when I saw that he was knocked out cold. The puppies darted into the room and pounced on him. Precious started chewing on one ear, while Rowdy gnawed on the other one. I could hear sirens in the distance as I pulled the dogs off of him.

"Is he dead?" Riley asked from the doorway. She looked like she was about to cry.

I looked at her standing there and wondered how much she had seen and heard. "No, just unconscious," I said, walking toward her.

"Well, he deserved everything he got!" she said. "Thank goodness Flip was here to help you!"

I smiled and put my arm around her shoulders. "Yes, Flip helped get me out of a sticky situation. But I'm sorry you had to see all this."

"I woke up and heard somebody shouting. I peeked into the kitchen and saw that mean man, then went to your bedroom and called 911."

I heard someone jiggling the front doorknob, then the door flew open.

Doug rushed in holding a baseball bat in his hands. He started looking around the room.

"Frankie called me and said that some guy broke into your house. Where is he? Are you and Riley alright?"

He was pacing and looking around corners, when I pointed to the kitchen floor.

"We're fine, and our neighbor is in there," I said.

While Doug stood guard over Luke with the bat, Frankie and three other police cars pulled up. After they came inside, I explained what had happened. While I was telling the story, Luke roused up. One of the officers patted him down, handcuffed him and then led him out of the house.

My ankle was throbbing, so I limped to my recliner and sat down. Riley got a glass of water for me, and Doug started examining my injury.

Frankie sat down on the couch across from me. "Some interesting information surfaced about your neighbor. When I ran the prints from the letter in the database, they came back belonging to a Larry Dodd. Larry's former boss was a man named Luke Davis, who owned a small wrecker service in Missouri."

"Out in the yard, I heard Luke's father call him Larry, but I didn't think anything about it," I said. "So I guess the father's name is Dodd, also?"

"Hubert Dodd. He has a record for domestic violence and served some time in the state penitentiary in Missouri for beating his wife and children way back when."

"If Larry's prints were in the database, I assume he has a record, too," I said.

"Some juvenile offenses. He was caught joy-riding in a neighbor's car when he was seventeen, and he got into a few bar brawls. But, he seemed to be clean until recently."

Lots of questions were buzzing around inside my head, and I wasn't sure what to ask first. "So have you contacted the real Luke Davis to let him know about his stolen wrecker?"

"It looks like the charges against Larry Dodd may go way beyond stalking and theft. I contacted the authorities in the town in Missouri where the Dodds had lived. When we started comparing notes, they told me that the real Luke Davis's neighbors called last week complaining about a foul odor coming from his yard. When the authorities checked out the complaint, they found him buried behind his garage. He died from a sharp blow to the head."

"So you think Luke, I mean Larry killed him?"

"It sure looks like it," Frankie said. "We hope to know more after questioning him."

Now it was time for me to help him clear up another matter. "Luke told me that his father often hit him with his cane. But the other night when he tried to attack him, Luke took it away from him and hit him with it. The blow killed his father, and he said he buried him beneath the azalea bushes in their yard."

Frankie shook his head. "He's been a busy man, I can say that for him. If his father is buried there, we probably have the owner of our mystery toe."

"I suspect you're right."

After examining my ankle, Doug told me that he thought it was sprained but not broken. He offered to take me to the emergency room to get it X-rayed, but I declined his offer. It wasn't hurting as badly as it had been before. When I stood up, I was able to walk without limping as much.

"I'll have it elevated in bed all night, and I'll be careful at school tomorrow," I assured him.

As Frankie turned to leave, he said, "I think you should call your mother to come over and spend the night with you."

"I agree," Doug said, "or better yet, why don't I spend the night on your couch?"

"The bad guy's in jail now," I said. "We'll be fine."

Before they left, the guys pitched in to clean up the water and mud from the kitchen floor. After they were gone, Riley and I talked for a while, and she seemed to be okay. She did accept my invitation to sleep in my bed, though. Once I had her tucked in, I took a shower and got myself ready for bed.

Wrapped in the quilt Nana had made for me, I took out my laptop and carried it to the kitchen table. Since I had no way to call him, I decided to e-mail Simon.

First I asked about his grandfather, then told him that I had accepted the summer school job. Now that the danger was past, I also wanted to tell him about tonight's incident. I tried not to make it sound too serious, but writing it down made me realize just how dangerous the situation had been. I was near tears by the time I pressed "Send."

Closing the laptop, I patted the puppies' heads, then went to make sure all the doors were locked. As I was about to turn off the living room lamp, the phone rang. I looked at the cuckoo clock and saw that it was almost midnight. I figured that Frankie must have forgotten to ask me something.

"Hello," I said.

"I think it's time I made a trip to Oklahoma."

A NOTE FROM THE AUTHOR

Thank you for spending your time with Allie, Simon, Aunt Edith and the rest of the family and friends. I hope you enjoyed their adventures and will tell your friends about *Trouble in Paradise*.

Please plan to join the cast of characters again as they face new escapades when Allie returns to Hawaii to teach summer school. Watch for the next book in the series, *Revenge in Paradise*, coming soon.

I'd like to hear from you. You may contact me through my website at www.terryerobins.com, or by writing to P. O. Box 335, Chelsea, OK 74016.

BIBLIOGRAPHY

Wallace, Bill. *A Dog Called Kitty.* New York: Holiday, 1980.

Viorst, Judith. *Alexander and the Terrible, Horrible, No Good, Very Bad Day.* New York: Atheneun Books, 1972

Banks, Lynne Reid. *The Indian in the Cupboard.* New York. Avon, 1980.

Senior Living Magazine. Glendale, CA

Television Shows and Films:

CSI: Crime Scene Investigation. CBS, New York. 2005

The Apprentice. NBC, New York. 2005

Wheel of Fortune, NBC, New York. 2005

Dateline, NBC, New York. 2005

60 Minutes, CBS, New York. 2005

Braveheart, starring Mel Gibson/produced by Alan Ladd, Jr. 1995

Homeward Bound: The Incredible Journey. VHS Video by Buena Vista.

Songs:

The Beach Boys. "Surfin' Safari." Capitol, 1962.

Brumley, Albert E. "I'll Fly Away." Copyright 1932, renewed 1960 by Albert E. Brumley & Sons, Inc.

Hunter, William. "I Feel Like Traveling On." Copyright unknown.

Hewitt, Elize E. and Wilson, Emily D. "When We All Get to Heaven." Copyright unknown.

Queen Liliuokalani. "Aloha Oe." Copyright 1878. English lyrics arranged by Charles E. King. Copyright 1923.

Tᴀᴛᴇ Pᴜʙʟɪsʜɪɴɢ *& Enterprises*

Tate Publishing is commited to excellence in the publishing industry. Our staff of highly trained professionals, including editors, graphic designers, and marketing personnel, work together to produce the very finest books available. The company reflects the philosophy established by the founders, based on Psalms 68:11,

"ᴛʜᴇ Lᴏʀᴅ ɢᴀᴠᴇ ᴛʜᴇ ᴡᴏʀᴅ ᴀɴᴅ ɢʀᴇᴀᴛ ᴡᴀs ᴛʜᴇ ᴄᴏᴍᴘᴀɴʏ
ᴏꜰ ᴛʜᴏsᴇ ᴡʜᴏ ᴘᴜʙʟɪsʜᴇᴅ ɪᴛ."

If you would like further information, please call
1.888.361.9473
or visit our website
www.tatepublishing.com

Tᴀᴛᴇ Pᴜʙʟɪsʜɪɴɢ *& Enterprises*, ʟʟᴄ
127 E. Trade Center Terrace
Mustang, Oklahoma 73064 USA